Washtenaw Library for the
Blind & Physically Disabled
@ AADL

If you are only able to read large print, you may qualify for WLBPD @ AADL services, including receiving audio and large print books by mail at no charge.

For more information:

Email • wlbpd@aadl.org
Phone • (734) 327-4224
Website • wlbpd.aadl.org

LAW FOR HIRE:
Defending Cody

*Also by Bill Brooks
in Large Print:*

Buscadero
The Stone Garden: The Epic Life of
 Billy the Kid
Bonnie and Clyde: A Love Story
Law for Hire: Protecting Hickok
Law for Hire: Saving Masterson

—

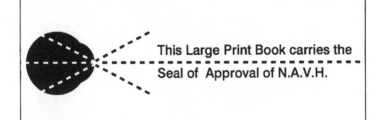

LAW FOR HIRE:
Defending Cody

BILL BROOKS

Thorndike Press • Waterville, Maine

This is a work of fiction. Names, characters, places, and incidents are products of the author's imagination or are used fictitiously and are not to be construed as real. Any resemblance to actual events, locales, organizations, or persons, living or dead, is entirely coincidental.

Published in 2006 by arrangement with HarperCollins Publishers.

Thorndike Press® Large Print Western.

The tree indicium is a trademark of Thorndike Press.

The text of this Large Print edition is unabridged.
Other aspects of the book may vary from the original edition.

Set in 16 pt. Plantin by Ramona Watson.

Printed in the United States on permanent paper.

Library of Congress Cataloging-in-Publication Data

Brooks, Bill, 1943–
 Law for hire. Defending Cody / by Bill Brooks. — Large print ed.
 p. cm. — (Thorndike Press large print westerns)
 ISBN 0-7862-8463-3 (lg. print : hc : alk. paper)
 1. Buffalo Bill, 1846–1917 — Fiction. 2. Abbott, E. C. (Edward Charles), 1860–1939 — Fiction. 3. Bodyguards — Fiction. 4. Large type books. I. Title: Defending Cody. II. Title. III. Thorndike Press large print Western series.
PS3552.R65863L38 2006
813'.54—dc22 2005036800

For Greg & Manon,
who live out there and
pursue the ghost horse still.

As the Founder/CEO of NAVH, the only national health agency solely devoted to those who, although not totally blind, have an eye disease which could lead to serious visual impairment, I am pleased to recognize Thorndike Press★ as one of the leading publishers in the large print field.

Founded in 1954 in San Francisco to prepare large print textbooks for partially seeing children, NAVH became the pioneer and standard setting agency in the preparation of large type.

Today, those publishers who meet our standards carry the prestigious "Seal of Approval" indicating high quality large print. We are delighted that Thorndike Press is one of the publishers whose titles meet these standards. We are also pleased to recognize the significant contribution Thorndike Press is making in this important and growing field.

Lorraine H. Marchi, L.H.D.
Founder/CEO
NAVH

★ Thorndike Press encompasses the following imprints: Thorndike, Wheeler, Walker and Large Print Press.

Prologue

Drunk as weasels, Billy Cody and Texas Jack fell into a mud wallow.

They lay there looking up at the stars.

"We'll be up there someday, you and me," Billy said.

"With Georgie and Wild Bill and all the rest of them old boys."

"We'll die like they did and become one of them stars."

A mongrel dog ran up and began licking their faces.

Billy said, "Shoo!"

"We go home drunk and muddy," Jack said, "the girls will skin us . . ."

They thought of their wives: Louisa and Josephine.

"Ain't it funny we both married foreign women," Billy said.

"I like to think of it as exotic."

"Me too."

Henry Egg, a constable with a belly that hung over his belt and a sidearm riding high on his hip, came and stood over them and said, "You boys better crawl out of

that mud hole before a wagon comes along and runs over you."

"You know who this is?" Jack said with drunken indignation to the lawman.

"Why, by God, it looks like none other than the beautiful Buffalo Bill," Henry said. "And wouldn't it be a shame for everybody to read in tomorrow's newspaper how the famous scout and Indian slayer was run over and killed by a goddamn lumber wagon whilst lying drunk in the middle of the street."

Billy rose to one elbow and looked at the fellow.

"You've no respect for your betters," he said.

"Why, Bill, I knew your daddy and he'd be rightfully ashamed he was to see you thus."

"Oh, it's you, Henry," Billy said. "I didn't recognize you in this poor light."

The deputy scratched behind his ear, said, "I wonder, is this what they mean when they say fallen heroes?"

Suddenly Billy felt badly for his public behavior of drunkenness.

"Come on, Jack," he said as he rose out of the mud wallow, taking Jack by the wrist and pulling him to his feet. Henry Egg watched the two of them staggering down

the street like the last two of their breed, slouching off toward an unknown destination and uncertain future.

They slept on Billy's front porch rather than go into the house and rouse the women, knowing as they did the temperamental capacity of their wives — one being of French blood, the other Italian.

"It'd be better if we was to just sleep here on the porch," Billy suggested. Jack did not argue but promptly fell asleep in one of the high-back rockers.

Before they knew it, morning light crawled over the porch slow as a snake. The warmth of the autumn sun touched Billy's cheek and Jack's boots about the same time. Billy opened his eyes to see the severe face of Louisa staring down at him.

"You stink like a saloon," she said.

"It ain't no wonder. Me and Jack about drank the Yellow Dog dry last evening. But it could always be worse, you know."

"I don't see how."

"I could be lying out in them toolies dead instead of just here on the porch hungover."

"I might prefer the former rather than see you thus — covered in mud, bleary-eyed, and stinking."

9

"Oh, you know how to hurt a man's pride . . ."

He saw her look over to Jack and shake her head before going back inside.

The silence, once inside around the breakfast table, was mean enough Billy could have shot it. He could hear the others breathing through their noses, hear their teeth grinding food. And each time he looked up, he saw Louisa's cold stare. He thought at such moments how preferable it was to be out fighting Indians or flirting with actresses than sitting there in his very own home with wife and daughters acting churlish toward him.

Jack's wife had been much more magnanimous about Jack's disheveled condition. Josephine was young and pretty and still stained by new love such that she was capable of overlooking Jack's indiscretions — at least for now, Billy thought. *But wait till later on after you've been married a few years . . . You'll see, Jack, old son, how tolerant wives remain of you.* He thought of that old Bible passage about a man being honored everywhere but in his own home. *Ain't I still a most famous and honored man everywhere but here in my own house?*

★ ★ ★

Later, after hot baths and fresh clothes, Billy and Jack went riding out a good distance from the large house with its wives and children and hunted rabbits with a pair of needle-guns Billy kept for just such sport. The trick was to shoot the hares on the run and not catch them squatting by some sage, warming themselves in the sun.

"There's no sport in shooting a creature that is napping," Billy said to Jack.

But Jack couldn't get the hang of it, shooting a rabbit that ran and dodged the way that rabbits did. A man had to be an uncanny shot to hit a running rabbit.

"I'd need a scattergun to hit them dang things."

"Like this," Billy said, and showed him, knocking down the first three rabbits they flushed; Jack thought Billy's shooting was akin to magic.

But in his heart, it made Billy sad to be shooting rabbits on such a pretty day. For rabbit shooting hardly held the thrill to it that riding into a thundering herd of buffalo and firing down on them did. But the buffalo were all gone from the prairies now. Nor did shooting rabbits hold a candle to riding scout for the army in pursuit of the warrior Sioux. But the Sioux

were mostly all gone too. And shooting rabbits sure didn't compare to consorting with the likes of Georgie Custer and Wild Bill — both now as gone as the buffalo and wild Indians. Someday the land would be so tamed a man wouldn't even need to arm himself, except for the poor sport of shooting rabbits. Billy didn't care much for the thought of such a day coming. But he knew the West was going away fast and that there had to be some other diversion for him, and the only one thing he thought he'd still be good at was being a showman. The West was about gone, except in the memory of men who'd been there and lived it.

About noon they paused along a sparkling stream so they could water their mounts and Jack said, "It looks like our ponies are drinking diamonds." And when Billy looked, he could see the sun-shattered water dripping from the horses' muzzles. Billy admired Jack for his poetic ways.

They rested while their horses drank and cropped a circle of grass. Billy looked off toward the aspens with their gold leaves fluttering in the branches while Texas Jack took a short siesta. The trunks of the

aspens looked like scarred bones and the sky above was blue as a china plate. It was a pretty place all the way around and he hoped someday there wouldn't be houses built all over it and railroad tracks and fences and towns to mar its beauty. He took a short siesta too, and awoke with his head full of new ideas. Texas Jack climbed out from under his sombrero and said, "That was refreshing."

"I was thinking," Billy said, "about putting together a new combination show."

Texas Jack suddenly looked sheepish.

"I didn't know how or when to tell you, Billy, but me and Josephine has been talking about putting together a show of our own . . ."

It was disappointing news to Billy's ears — especially after all that had happened over the last few months with Georgie Custer getting slaughtered and Wild Bill shot dead by a drunk. It felt like some sort of extra hole through his heart he couldn't put a bung in.

But Billy's pride was such that he made out like it was wonderful news what Jack had just told him, and he smiled until all his teeth showed and slapped Jack on the back in congratulatory fashion, saying, "I

can't blame you for wanting to make a great name for yourself, old son."

Texas Jack's cheeks grew crimson with embarrassment.

"It was more Jo's idea than mine. You know I ain't never been one to make a big show of myself, don't you, Bill?"

"Can't blame a woman for wanting to succeed, old son. Jo's a pretty gal with lots of talent and ambition. You'd do well to keep your wagon hitched to her."

"I know it," Texas Jack said. "I'd jump over the moon for her."

A flock of geese honked their way out of the sun and flew south along the course of the Platte River like it was a water road they were following.

"If we had the right guns we could knock some of them fat geese down," Billy said.

Jack knew Billy was disappointed that he and Josephine would be striking out on their own; he could tell by the sound of Billy's voice — the way it sort of cracked with melancholy as he was talking and watching those geese fly away.

"I'm sorry, Bill . . ."

Billy walked over and adjusted the cinch of his saddle, saying over his shoulder, "Oh, don't worry none about it, I reckon I

can still put together a good combination, even if I don't have you and Jo in it." But Jack knew that Billy was thinking about how Wild Bill would be missing too, and how it would never be the same again as when all three of them had gone East together to play the theaters.

They rode back to the house in the mid-afternoon, the light weaker now than it had been, and the shadows lying long across the land. The sun in that season had lost the fierceness it had when Custer and his boys got trapped down in that Powder River country. And surely it must have been hot as hell that August day Wild Bill went into a saloon and never came out again but feet first.

Soon enough the sun would lose all its strength and snow would come to that country and turn the rivers black and every speck of land would become quiet as death as it slept under winter's white blanket.

Billy rode ahead, stately, like a man leading a parade, the needle-gun balanced across the pommel of his silver-studded saddle, and Texas Jack knew the man had a history to him few other men had.

They say dying comes in threes and Jack

wondered if Billy Cody might be next on fate's list to be taken. Georgie and Wild Bill had both been about the same age as Billy was now — men in their thirties and of good vigor when struck down within six weeks of each other. Men in their prime, like Billy was in his.

Jack sure hoped not. Once Billy Cody was gone, it would signal the end of something great. He spurred his horse ahead to catch up to Bill's and said, "We don't none of us know what the future holds, do we?"

At first Billy did not reply and Jack thought maybe he hadn't heard the question, and they rode along for several minutes with just the creaking of their saddles to interrupt the silence.

Then another larger flock of geese flew high overhead and Billy looked up at them with eyes that seemed to Texas Jack to be more sorrowful than he ever remembered them looking. And when the geese had disappeared in the ocean of blue sky, Billy said, "We've no more control over our fate than those geese do, Jack. We're just another of God's unprepared creatures doing what's natural in us to do . . ."

That night Billy lay abed next to Louisa. Unable to sleep he slipped from the covers

16

and went to the window and looked out at the moonlit yard. He had thought he'd heard a noise, somebody walking around, their boots crunching on the dry grass.

It still darkened his mood, the fact Jack and Josephine were breaking off to go on their own. He adored them both and their loss would be great, both as friends and performers. Still, it felt to him a bit like betrayal. The bad dreams he'd been having lately didn't help his mood. Then too there was Louisa and her many manifest moods. She bedeviled him with her concerns about all manner of things, money and children and his being gone a great deal of the time. Seemed like ever since their son Kit died that spring, things had not been good between he and Louisa. He called her Lulu when he was pleased with her and Louisa when he was not.

He left the room and walked down the hall and looked in on his sleeping daughters — Irma, Orra, and Arta. They were like angels resting in their white beds with the moonlight flush in their golden hair.

He went down the stairs thinking he would have something to drink to relieve his unease. Found a bottle in the cabinet and poured two fingers of whiskey in a glass and took it out onto the porch.

Oh, he felt somehow cursed of spirit. Clouds drifted before the moon, then drifted away. The land lay quiet until coyotes set to yip off in the distance, creating a good kind of ruckus, then fell silent again. Wind blew gently up from the south, carrying with it the smell of the river, that ancient scent of something that had existed as long as time itself and would never pass from the land.

He sat in one of the rockers and sipped his whiskey and thought about the combination he'd put together for the tour. Captain Jack Crawford, the cowboy poet, might be a good man to have onboard. Maybe Crawford could play the part of Wild Bill. Ned Buntline was probably available to help him write a play or two. He could write an act about the killing of Yellow Hand . . . call it *First Scalp for Custer.*

He thought of the irony, how he'd killed the old Indian quite by goddamn accident. The dudes back East would pay to see it. Maybe he could get Buck Taylor to play Yellow Hand; Buck was himself a swarthy fellow . . .

"Hey," he thought he heard somebody say.

It gave him a start that caused him nearly to spill the whiskey out of his glass.

18

He didn't see anyone.

Instinct told him to rise, go in the house and get a gun . . .

But then he saw them and eased himself down again.

"Oh, it's just you two."

Georgie Custer and Wild Bill stood there in the moonstruck yard looking at him.

"Shit, I thought you boys was gone under . . ."

In unison they said: "It was no fault of our own, darlin' Bill . . ."

And across the moon he thought he saw a herd of buffalo racing and it caused his throat to go dry. He downed the liquor in one gulp and, when he looked again, the boys had gone and he wondered where. Then he could hear the thunderous applause as he brought the whole shebang (he'd call it *A Scout's Farewell*) East again to a roaring success.

The whiskey and memories of how it used to be caught fire in him and he went inside and up the stairs and awakened Louisa, much to her dismay, saying, "I'm feeling like a man again, like my old self. I'm feeling glorious and unfettered, like I got wings I could fly all the way to that old moon with."

She was, of course, aghast at such wild

behavior and started to tell him so.

But she would not be able to deter the famous Buffalo Bill Cody from pursuing his destiny, or the woman who was still his wife and whom he still loved a little and desired much in that fateful moment.

"I'm going to put together a new stage show and take it East," he said, slipping out of his nightshirt.

She saw before her a lean naked man with pieces of moonlight glinting in his eyes. It was a vision she'd seen often enough before, but he still looked a lot like a stranger to her in many ways.

"Oh, Holy Jesus," she said when she saw he was aroused.

"Move over," he said.

"I'll sleep in the girls' room," she said.

"Not tonight, Lulu," he said.

And later when she asked when he'd be leaving again, he replied simply: "Shortly enough, not to worry. I won't be in your hair too very much longer. I've just got to raise a little capital, is all."

"How are you going to do that?"

"Same as I done it before — I'll head up a hunting party for some swells. I've still got good contacts back East. I'll wire Ned to put out the word."

"Ned Buntline, that old reprobate?"

"I've known worse."

"Well, I sure haven't."

"Oh, Lulu, don't distress me so. In a little while you won't have me underfoot; you'll have the house and the girls to yourself. Why, I'm practically doing you a favor."

She hadn't the resolve to tell him what was in her heart.

And he hadn't the heart to tell her what was in his.

And neither contemplated there could be murder in their future.

Chapter 1

The door ringer sounded like loose change in a cowboy's pocket and when Teddy Blue opened the front door of his mother's house, George Bangs stood there under a rain-spotted bowler.

"Come in before you drown," Teddy said and George stepped into the foyer and shucked off his overcoat and hung it on the hall tree and did the same with his hat.

"I guess you didn't come just to drink a whiskey with me," Teddy said, remembering how the detective was a teetotaler.

"No, sir, I didn't. I've some news for you on your brother's death, and this . . ." George handed him a letter. It was post-marked: *Las Vegas, N. M. territory.*

"What about my brother?" Teddy said, leading Bangs into the large living room, where flames licked away at several chunks of oak in the fireplace.

George went and stood before the fire and warmed his hands.

"As I told you before, we've located the man who killed your brother. In fact, he

confessed to the killing," George said.

Teddy was pouring himself two fingers of bourbon into a crystal tumbler. His father had good tastes in liquor, his mother in glassware.

"Go on with it, George . . ."

Teddy felt the liquor burn in a pleasant way before it caught fire in his chest, then settled down to a nice warmth.

"The man's name is Carnahan, Ludlow Carnahan."

"He in jail now?"

"No, Teddy. He's dead now."

"What am I missing here, George?"

"The man gave a deathbed confession."

"How'd you learn of it?" Teddy poured two more fingers of bourbon.

"Allan still has his sources inside the police department."

"Pretty convenient, don't you think?"

"What is, Teddy?"

"That the man they're blaming Horace's murder on is himself now dead. Who was this man, exactly? What more do you know about him?"

"I'm still looking into," Bangs said. "But as I promised you before, we'll put all of our resources behind it. You're one of us, Teddy."

"I'm not a Pinkerton, George. Hell, you

know I didn't do a good job with that Hickok situation."

"You did fine with it. You saved his life twice. It was his decision to go it alone up into that country and get himself killed. We can't save people from themselves."

"I need to find out more about this Carnahan," Teddy said, swallowing the last of the bourbon. "I need to know why this man shot Horace and who he was. I need to know everything about him so my brother can rest in peace. He stole a lot from my family, George."

"I know he did. We'll have all the answers soon enough, trust me."

Teddy watched the cold rain sliding down the windows and reflected on just how he'd come to this point in his still young life. Three years earlier he'd been a student in law school, if not a very enthusiastic one. He'd had a family — a brother and father, as well as a mother. But now his brother was dead from assassination, and his father was dead as well — from grief. His family had been shattered by this Carnahan that George had just spoken of. An unknown assassin with unknown reasons.

George Bangs, right-hand assistant to Allan Pinkerton, a soft-spoken but per-

suasive man, had recruited Teddy into becoming an operative in return for a promise to apply every last resource of the Pinkertons to find Horace's killer. His first assignment had been to protect Wild Bill Hickok. And just like that he'd gone from a rather naïve law student to guarding the West's most famed shootist. It seemed too impossible to be considered mere fate, but what else could he call it? He wondered, standing there looking at the rain, how much more his life would yet change, knew that if George had any say in the matter, it might change mightily and in ways he never counted on.

"They say that work is the best thing a man can do to keep his mind off his troubles," George Bangs said.

"I don't know, George. Everything seems so unfinished, as far as Horace's death is concerned."

"We could use a man down in Missouri," George said. "Governor wants us to send some operatives down there to help him catch this bank robber and his gang — Jesse James. They are raising quite a bit of hell down there."

"Bank robber? That's unique," Teddy said.

"It's a wonder nobody's thought of it be-

fore," the detective said. "But this fellow has practically turned bank robbing into a specialty. His gang has been robbing banks all over Missouri and some of the surrounding states as well. You interested?"

It was then that Teddy remembered the telegram Bangs had given him, the one from his old friend, John Sears. He'd slipped it in his pocket when the detective mentioned the situation with his brother's killer. He took it out now and turned so that the muted light from the window would fall upon the page.

To the attention of Teddy Blue, Pinkertons, Chicago . . . Well, old son, I'm up against it hard now. Am here in the calaboose in this hell-forsaken place waiting to go on trial and sure to a hanging if they find me guilty. I got word through the grapevine you'd hired on with the Pinkertons and I figured was there any way to reach you it'd be through them. I'm hoping I'm right and I ain't dead by time this reaches you, if it ever does. It's a lot of story to go into and my pencil is about wore down to the nub. Best save it all for when you get out here, if you get out here. You're about the

only friend I got that's still yet alive that I know of. The rest has been scattered to the wind, them that ain't under the sod. You know how cowboys are when it comes to staying in one place too long. I understand if you can't help, but I'd sure appreciate it if you could. And if you hear they hung me, well, I'll leave word with the hanging people to send you the news.

Yr. Pard, John Sears, Esq.

Teddy felt something hard ripple down through him. John Sears had been like family to him, had befriended him when he first quit law school and drifted west and hired on with a cow outfit in Texas. John had taught him the ways of being a cowboy, to rope and shoot and fight when he needed to. Had taught him to drink and cuss and know the pleasures of women in the cowtowns. John seemed to him as much a brother in some ways, as did Horace. He quickly read the letter again, saw that it was dated two weeks earlier. John could already be dead. But there was every chance he might still be alive and if he was . . .

"I've got to catch a train," Teddy said.
"Where to?"

27

Teddy handed George the letter while he rushed upstairs to pack a valise. George followed, folded the letter after he read it.

"Maybe I can help."

"How so?"

"I can send a wire ahead saying that we're sending an operative, that your friend is one of ours, something, anything just to prevent them hanging him if they haven't already."

"Why would you do that, George? I know you're too damn honest and a straight shooter to do something that could possibly jeopardize your position."

"Because whether you accept it or not, you're still one of us, Teddy. You're still a Pinkerton in my book."

"But old John isn't one of yours . . ."

"Doesn't matter. He's your friend."

"Okay, if that's what it takes, okay. I'd appreciate it and I know old John would, as well."

"Then maybe when you've finished up your business out there, you'll go to Missouri?"

"Nobody would ever mistake you for rube, would they, George?"

"I'd hope not. Send me a telegram when you get there, let me know what I can do." They shook hands. George was a good man.

★ ★ ★

Teddy was on the evening flier, a bottle of whiskey in his pocket, a valise with a change of clothes, the Birdseye Colt strapped under his coat in a shoulder holster and a head full of worries.

He had wanted desperately to learn more about Horace's killer before leaving Chicago, but point in fact, his staying in Chicago and what he might learn would not bring Horace back. He trusted George to follow through; George understood the importance. John Sears, on the other hand, might yet be saved. You just didn't turn your back on your friends, especially ones who were like blood.

He watched the city lights shrink into the darkness as the train pulled out of the station. He reached into his pocket for the bottle and his fingers touched the badge and he brought it forth. The tips of his fingers rubbed over the raised lettering: PINKERTON NATIONAL DETECTIVE AGENT. The brass felt cold and smooth like the barrel of a revolver, like a bullet, like the skin of a dead man. Maybe it would prove to be the key to John's jail cell, or maybe it would prove to be only a worthless piece of metal, a target for some drunken shootist, as it almost had been before.

He slipped the badge back into his pocket and took out the bottle of whiskey. He drank to the steady rhythm and rocking of the car.

He closed his eyes and thought of John sitting in some lonesome jail, possibly waiting for the morning they'd come and put a rope around his neck and drop him from a tree limb, foregoing the need to do anything as elaborate as building a gallows.

He thought too about Kathleen Bonney, the woman he'd met in Cheyenne and fallen in love with and the illness that had her in its grip. He thought that once he got things settled with John he would ride down to Silver City and pay her a visit. He wondered how she was making out — whether her consumption had gotten worse.

The train rocked along and he drank and after a time sleep took him, and when it did, time or whiskey didn't matter there in the darkness under his hat.

Chapter 2

Billy wired and told 'em all to come quick.

Big hunt, plenty of swells, easy pickings. You boys need new boots, pistolas, whiskey?

White Eye Anderson got a wire, so did Yankee Judd.

They came in from the gold fields, their knees wet from kneeling in the cold creeks and saw the telegrams as a divine intervention.

"Anything has to be easier than panning gold," White Eye said. "Burying Wild Bill was easier."

"I never buried nobody," Yankee said, "so I couldn't say if burying fellers is easier or not."

"Trust me, it is."

So they packed their gear and hopped the Deadwood–Cheyenne stage, then the train from Cheyenne to Denver, and from there they rode the Union Pacific east to North Platte, where Billy was waiting for them in a fresh snow.

"Glad to see you boys are still alive and

have not met your death up in that desperate gulch like Wild Bill met his," Billy said.

"I helped bury him," White Eye said. "He was the prettiest corpse I ever seen."

"Fine, fine," Billy said. "We oughter get out of this snow or we'll freeze and become corpses ourselves."

Billy put them up in one of the hotels that had a bar and iron beds.

"Got Buck Taylor coming too, and Ned Buntline's rounding up the swells — they'll be here in a week or less."

"Who you getting to do the cooking?" Yankee said. "I'm particular about my grub."

"Thought I'd ask Jane."

"Calamity, or Jane Nebraska?"

"Jane Nebraska," Billy said.

"Whew, that is good news then," White Eye said.

"Last I heard of Calamity, she was screwing miners for drinks," Yankee said. "A good woman gone bad . . ." Yankee looked forlorn, for he'd once been in love with Calamity Jane when they both first came to the West, having met in Kansas. Early on in their courtship he considered proposing marriage to her. A life on the prairies with kids, a soddy maybe, a few

head of cattle seemed a pleasing idea to him. Then Jane disappeared one day and did not return for three months and when she did return and Yankee asked her where'd she been, expressed his concern she'd been scalped by Indians or worse, Jane laughed in that horsey way of hers and said she was just a free-spirit woman set on this earth to enjoy life's pleasures. Yankee did not think he could marry such a woman and he went north and left Jane to frequent the saloons of Dodge, where she eventually met and fell in love with Wild Bill, who would ignore her at every opportunity.

"I'll need you boys to purchase what is on this list," Billy said, handing them a piece of paper he'd scribbled down needed supplies on. "Buck will find the horseflesh we need once he gets here. There ain't a more knowledgeable man in all the country when it comes to horse-flesh."

White Eye looked over the list: tents, Sibley stoves, canned goods, blankets, sugar, coffee, bacon, cartridges of various calibers, knives, pots, pans, and several cases of champagne.

"We'll need to rent a few wagons, as well," Billy added. "Just use my name

wherever you go and tell 'em to put it on my credit."

Then he was off again.

Yankee and White Eye saw him riding up the street from their hotel window, riding through the still-falling snow that was as deep as his horse's knees.

"Look at him," Yankee said. "He looks like he's riding out to kill Indians."

"Billy sure likes to strut his stuff," White Eye said.

"Let's go find us an eatery," Yankee said. "I could stand some regular grub, couldn't you?"

"I could eat the ears off a donkey," White Eye said, and off they went to a café just up the street where they ate large plates of potatoes and beef and washed it down with beer while they waited for their slices of vinegar pie to arrive. They ate the pie with gusto and kept washing everything down with beer until the snow stopped.

Billy rode through the snow on his high-stepping horse, Buckskin Joe. Rode all the way to the cabin on Stinking Creek where Jane Nebraska lived with her crazy father. Silas Nebraska hadn't always been crazy. He had been an army surgeon during the war, had cut off shattered arms and legs of

screaming boys and seen every kind of deprivation that lead and steel could do to the human body. And after four years of seeing and dealing with such, he went from a sane, thoughtful, introspective man to one that was plum crazy. The shot of war had shot his mind along with the bodies of those young lads who adorned his surgeon's table.

He moved from a fine Virginian colonial home to a run-down cabin in the toolies of Nebraska and changed his name from Silas Fox to Silas Nebraska because he didn't want anyone to know who he was or what he had been. He married a widow ten years his senior, who bore him a daughter and promptly died. Silas named the infant Jane. He didn't know why he named her that, other than Jane sounded like a simple name, one he could remember easily. He took up cattle breeding, but his cattle all froze the first hard winter. Then he took up farming, but a plague of grasshoppers wiped him out. All this made him a little crazier than he already was. He felt akin to Job, like God had personally picked him out to test him. But old God might have saved his strength, the way Silas saw it — for he'd pretty much given up on the goodness of God a long time ago.

Recognizing her father's difficulties early on, including his shortcomings as a provider, Jane learned to hunt squirrels and beavers and prairie chickens at quite a young age. As she grew older, she got good enough to track antelope and deer. She learned to cook by dint of necessity and the help of a kindly neighbor woman, who ended up getting lost one winter and who was not found until spring, curled up by a big rock less than two hundred yards from her back door; this event was just one more sign to Silas that kindness and goodness earned you no points in God's book.

Wild Bill had introduced Jane and her crazy father to Billy a few years previous when the two men were putting together their first hunting party for the Grand Duke Alexis of Russia.

"I was attacked by a bear and mauled bad," Wild Bill had related to Cody. "I stumbled across their cabin on the Stinking Creek and the old man sewed me up good and sang songs backwards and read books upside down. I didn't care he was crazy, he was a good medico who probably saved my life."

Jane was a raw-boned tall girl with hair the color of an autumn sunset. The first time Billy met her he asked Wild Bill on

the sly if the two of them had ever shared any intimacies. Wild Bill's reputation as a ladies' man was well known.

Wild Bill scratched his jaw and said, "I guess that wouldn't be a thing I'd talk about if I had." But more than once on the hunt, Billy had seen Wild Bill saunter over to Jane's tent and pay her a visit as Billy and the others sat around entertaining Alexy.

" 'Lo the cabin," Billy called when he rode up.

There was a trickle of black smoke rising from the chimney. Steam rose off Stinking Creek just beyond a stand of willows, where it ran dark as indigo along the snowy banks. Billy saw a hog hanging up-side down by its back legs from a tripod, its belly split open from chest to nuts, its flesh nearly as white as the snow, except where the hog had been bled out and the snow beneath it had been turned pink. A kettle of boiling water hung over a fire.

The cabin door opened finally and the old man stood there with a long army musket in his grip, squinting against the glare of the sun-struck snow.

"It's me, Billy Cody," Billy called.

Then Jane appeared and she placed her

hands on the musket's barrel so he'd lower it down and not accidentally or otherwise shoot someone.

"Glory be," Silas said.

Billy had brought gifts, of course, and took them now from his saddlebags: a tin of horehound candy and a bottle of Simmons' Liver Regulator for Silas, and for Jane a lovely red parasol.

Well, they sat and talked awhile, then Billy got down to business, saying how he wanted to hire Jane to cook for his new hunting party, to which she quickly agreed.

"Is that scamp Wild Bill going to be in the party?" Silas asked.

"No, Wild Bill got killed," Billy said. "A drunk shot him cold."

"Well, it's good . . . I mean, that he won't be there. I don't trust him with my child."

"You'll not have to worry about him, Mr. Nebraska."

"You'll see she ain't molested by no-account galoots?"

"Yes, sir, I will."

"Good, good. Now let me have a spoonful of this liver regulator. I haven't been feeling myself lately."

Jane walked Bill outside to his horse.

"He gets a little worse in the head every year," she said.

"I'll send a man to check on him every few days while we're gone if it will make you feel better," Billy said.

"It will."

Billy started to mount by putting one foot in the stirrup. He felt Jane's hand on his backside.

"I surely am looking forward to some new scenery, Billy," she said.

He looked at her without removing either his foot from the stirrup or her hand from his hindquarters.

"I mean, a girl needs to get the attention of a feller every now and then," she said with a wink.

Billy eased himself on up into the fine Mexican silver saddle that had been a gift from Tecumseh Sherman.

"Now, Jane, you know how a bunch of men out alone in the West can get without their wives or gal friends present to keep an eye on them."

"I know, Billy. But a plain girl like me sure don't mind the attention when it's paid to her, you can understand that, can't you?"

"I'll do my best to keep my bargain with your pa. But I reckon you're a grown woman of legal age and can do what you want . . ."

She looked up at him with her moss green eyes.

"I'd not be opposed to handsome feller like you paying me some never mind, Billy . . ."

Billy had trouble clearing his throat. It was a mighty tempting offer, to be sure, but he could see real quick how any action on his part might blow the whole shebang out of the water. First, there was Lulu to contend with. If she even thought he had amorous designs on another woman she'd turn into a hellion, probably divorce him and ruin him financially. Then too there was Jane's papa. He was crazy enough to shoot them both. No, best he just stick to the plan and avoid any distractions of the feminine variety.

"Well . . . er, Jane. It's mighty flattering you'd find a feller my age to your liking, with you so young and lovely . . . I don't quite know what to say, but I'll cogitate on it . . ."

She smiled. She had big teeth, but straight.

Billy turned his horse away from the cabin and back in the direction of North Platte. The sun was starting to set low in the sky and he knew he'd probably not ar-

rive back home until after dark. He could always stay the night at the cabin, of course, but that might lead to trouble. No, he better just push on home and keep his mind on the business at hand.

He had ridden about halfway in that country seeing nothing but the glittering snow and copses of trees black and bare, and occasionally a crow or a whooping crane went flying overhead. Crows always raised a racket, whereas cranes flew silent, except for the *whoomph* of their large wings. He paused by a small spring and dismounted and let Buckskin Joe drink his fill. He realized in that moment the utter silence that surrounded him. He felt shrunk down to nothing being out there alone in that vast country.

Why, it's like I'm the only living soul in the world, he thought.

Silent as death, he thought.

The only sounds were of his breathing and the crunch of his boots in the snow when he walked around to keep his feet from getting overly cold.

He saw something protruding from the snow and bent to pick it up and when he did the air cracked like it was being split in two and a piece of bark flew out of a nearby cottonwood tree. He knew the sound of a

41

rifle shot when he heard one and instinct made him fall flat down into the snow.

He lay there several long seconds, then scurried to pull his rifle from its scabbard — it was that fancy Winchester repeater Custer had given him — and he swung it around to cover the ground in every direction. His heart was thumping in his ears.

Could be a stray Indian, he told himself.

Could be somebody out hunting and just missed badly.

"Hey!" he called out. "What you shooting at?"

He waited for an answering call, but nothing came.

"Hey!" he shouted again.

Silence.

He saw how low the sun was beginning to sink. Come dark, he'd be a shadow moving over the snow. He didn't like the thought, but figured he didn't have any choice. He stood up, then dropped to his knees, figuring to draw fire from whoever might be out there.

Nothing.

"Well, whoever it is is gone now," he said to the horse with a voice not all that convincing.

He figured he was only an hour from North Platte, but it seemed like a hell of a

lot longer than that by the time he finally saw the first lights of the town twinkling in the distance.

He slipped into bed next to Louisa after he had himself three, four quick shots of whiskey. It helped relieve him some of the shivers and jitters. He wasn't sure how much of his shivers and jitters was from the cold and how much was from nearly getting his melon shattered by a bullet.

Had to be a accident, he told himself as he snuggled up to his substantial wife.

She did not move but he could tell that she wasn't sleeping.

"You asleep?" he asked.

She was as silent as the snow.

"I rode all day to Stinking Creek and back," he said.

She did not move.

"I went to hire Jane Nebraska to cook for the hunting party, just in case you was wondering where I've been."

She sighed.

"You know I ain't got nothing for her, right?"

The house creaked, the boards shrinking with the cold.

"I mean, maybe I ain't the best husband in the world, but you know I'd never be unfaithful to you, right?"

"Go to sleep," she said.

"Well, at least that's something," he said.

"Go to sleep . . ."

"I almost got shot today, in case you care."

She didn't say anything at first. Then, without turning to face him or offer any sort of comfort, she said, "It is probably a sign."

"A sign of what?"

"That you should settle down and forget about hunting parties and Wild West combinations and being a showman and all the rest . . ."

"A sign from the Almighty, you mean?"

"It is very possible. You scoff at such things, you always have, but someday your vanity will come home to roost . . ."

He had no will to argue with her. The long ride had exhausted him. Instead, he fell asleep and dreamt of running buffalo and a beautiful woman who turned into a shadow of someone following him. He ran, but he could not outrun the shadow. He awoke with his nightshirt soaked in sweat.

Threes, he thought. *Death comes in threes. First it was Georgie, then Wild Bill. I'm next. All of us killed in the same year, the same season of our regret.*

He crawled out of bed, his limbs

shaking, and went to the window and looked out at the snow that lay like a blanket of silver in the yard. He stood for a long time looking, then he saw three shadows together, and he knew what the shadows meant.

He closed his eyes, hoping they would go away, but when he opened them again, the shadows were still there.

He went to the bed and shook Louisa awake.

"What, what!" she said in a voice near hysteria.

"Come and look," he said.

He led her by the hand to the window.

"They're out there," he said.

She looked.

"Who's out there?"

"You see them, don't you?"

"Who?"

Swallowing down his fear he looked again.

"Jesus God, I saw them, Louisa . . ."

"The liquor has stole your brains. I knew that it would someday."

Grumpily she went back to the bed and crawled under the covers.

He stood there trembling.

I ain't afraid of death, he told himself. *I ain't afraid* . . . But in truth, he knew he

was too young to die, too unwilling to leave behind his three little daughters to the cruel world.

It was a bad sign seeing them ghosts. It was twice he'd seen them now in the last two nights running. He knew the next time he'd see them it would be in another world. How close had that bullet come today to making him a ghost? It was a warning, Louisa was right. Something was trying to warn him before it was too late.

He thought all the rest of the night on it and by morning had made a decision.

Chapter 3

Saturdays they held dances in the plaza. John Sears could hear the music from his cell, could hear the guitars and trumpets. He could hear the laughter of the senoritas too. The old jailer, Ramon, brought him a tray of grub — beans, a little pork, a few tortillas.

"I bet you'd like to be out there dancing instead of having to wet-nurse me, eh?" he said to Ramon.

Ramon shrugged his shoulders.

"I'll go later."

"Listen," John said. "I decided you can have my spurs after they . . . you know."

"You want something to smoke after you eat?"

"That would be decent of you."

"I'll get you some tobacco and paper and matches."

"They're good spurs," John said. "I bought them in Texas. You ever been to Texas?"

Ramon shook his head.

"I never been nowhere but here."

John took the tray and sat on his bunk and ate while Ramon watched him for a few moments before turning and going out the door that led to the front of the jail.

John could hear the clapping of the women dancers, the boot heels of the men clicking on the plaza stones. It caused him to lose some of his appetite. He finished eating and lay back and closed his eyes and threw his arm over them and tried to think about something other than where he was or how he'd ended up here.

Teddy Blue stepped off the evening train — a chuffing black locomotive and three passenger cars. There weren't many others getting off, but several getting on for the trip back down to Albuquerque.

He saw the plaza and the dancers under the lights they'd hung in the low branches of cottonwood trees. The music from the bandstand rose and fell like a rush of wind. It was a cool evening. The sky was blue black, shot through with stars.

Las Vegas looked like some of the villages he and John had visited down in Mexico.

Teddy asked a man squatting on his heels listening to the music and drinking from a small clay olla where the jail was.

48

The man looked up at him, pieces of light caught in his dark eyes. He showed a few yellow teeth when he spoke.

"It is over there, my friend." The man pointed with a stubby brown finger across the plaza toward a small adobe building. "Next to the undertaker's." The man turned his attention back to the dancers.

Teddy crossed the plaza and pushed at the wooden door. A thin man in heavy cotton clothes looked away from the window. He had a big pistol riding high on his hip and was hatless.

"I've come to see John Sears," Teddy said, taking the badge from his coat pocket and showing it to the man.

"I'm with the Pinkertons. I'm also John's lawyer."

"I was thinking about going over to the dance," the man said.

"Don't let me stop you."

"Oh, you think maybe I'll go over there and then you'll let your friend out of the jail, is that it?"

"I'm not here to break anybody out."

"Open your coat."

Teddy did as he was asked. The man looked at the Birdseye Colt hanging from the shoulder holster. Teddy released it and handed it butt-first to the man.

"Shake them legs, mister."

"Why?"

"See if anything falls out, like another gun or something."

After he was satisfied Teddy wasn't armed any further, Ramon led him back to the cells.

John was lying there with one arm flung over his face.

"I'm surprised you're not out dancing," Teddy said.

John lowered his arm, sat up.

"You made it, old son."

"I came soon as I got your letter."

They stood eyeing each other, then John stuck his hand through the bars and Teddy shook it and said, "I sure hate to see you this way."

"You and me both."

Satisfied the two men weren't going to try to break the jail, Ramon turned and headed for the door, then paused when he got to it and said to Teddy, "It locks from the other side. It's the only way out, in case you were wondering," then went out and closed the door and slid the bolt shut.

"My boss sent a telegram on your behalf," Teddy said.

"Won't do any good."

"Might."

"Hell, I reckon not this time around."

"You want to tell me about it, why you're in here?"

"I guess I owe you that much."

Teddy reached into his pocket and took out the makings for a shuck and handed them through to John, who deftly rolled himself a smoke, then struck one of the matches off the bars. He cupped the flame in his hand out of old habit because of the way the wind blew steady on the prairies.

John took a deep draw and then exhaled the smoke and said, "That tastes damn good. You remember that time we had them whores in that big tank of water last time we were together?"

Teddy nodded, waited.

"I shot a woman, is the reason I'm in here," John said forlornly. "It wasn't something I was planning."

Teddy listened until John finished telling him the story.

"I know it don't look good," John said. "How could it?"

"They give you a fair trial?"

"Fair enough, I reckon."

"I guess I could try and talk to the judge."

"You'd be wasting your time."

"When did they set the date, John?"

"This Saturday. Morning's when they

said. I reckon I'd just soon it be then as anytime. Morning's a good time, don't you think?"

"I don't know."

"Maybe if you'd gotten here in time for the trial you might have been able to do something, but I doubt it."

"Saturday's just two days off, John."

"I'm trying not to think too hard on it."

"I meant it doesn't give me much time."

"You'd be a damn fool if you're thinking what I think you're thinking."

"I know it."

"Let it go, old son. No point in you —"

"I can't let them hang you."

"The local law is a bad hombre, Teddy. He kills men because he likes to."

"I figure he must be pretty tough to have you caged up."

John tried handing him the makings back but Teddy told him to keep them.

"I never took up the habit, but I knew you had it so I came prepared the best I could."

"I don't want you to do nothing," John said. "I guess I deserve what they're going to give me."

"Where's your boots?"

"They took them."

"Why?"

"Figured if I broke out, I couldn't get too far barefoot."

"I guess they never heard of anybody stealing a horse."

John laughed.

"I guess they never did."

Teddy went to the door and knocked and Ramon opened it from the other side after sliding back the bolt.

"I'll take my gun back now," Teddy said. Ramon took it off the desk and handed it to him.

"I guess I'll go over to that dance," Teddy said.

Ramon eyed him suspiciously.

"Where's your boss at?" Teddy asked, sliding the Colt into the shoulder rig, then dropping his coat over it.

Ramon looked at the clock on the wall above the gun rack.

"Probably eating his supper."

"He have a regular place?"

"El Toro Cantina is mostly where he eats." Ramon walked to the front door, opened it and pointed with his nose. "The bull café is what it means, in case you didn't know."

Teddy couldn't tell if Ramon was simply trying to be helpful or secretly making fun of him.

53

"Take good care of my friend," Teddy said. "I'll be back tomorrow," then went on down the walk toward the cantina.

Hoodoo Brown liked to play whist while he ate his supper and was doing so when the tall young man walked up to his table. Hoodoo's companions looked up when Hoodoo did.

Teddy introduced himself, mentioned the telegram George Bangs had promised to send on John's behalf.

"You're the Pinkerton," Hoodoo said. "He's the Pinkerton, boys," Hoodoo said to his friends.

"Pinkerton?" said a curly-haired fellow whose sombrero hung down his back from a stampede string.

"We never sleep, ain't that what you Pinkertons say?" Hoodoo said. "What do you want?"

"Nothing," Teddy said.

Hoodoo Brown looked at him. Looked at him hard. Hoodoo took a bite of chicken drumstick that had been lying on his plate, set it down again, chewed what was in his mouth. Chewed slow and curious.

"He's a goner, your friend," Hoodoo said after he swallowed the chicken meat.

54

"Tried and convicted. You come a long way for nothing."

"Just some things a man has to do," Teddy said, and turned and walked out.

The night air was chill and festive with the music and the lights in the trees. Teddy looked over toward the jail, how it stood in deep shadows, except for the one lone light glowing from the front window. It wasn't any damn place for a man like John Sears to be, to spend his last days in.

It was late. Most businesses were closed, including the livery.

He found a saloon; a place called El Capitan. There were several vaqueros sitting out front listening to the music from the plaza. They spoke Spanish with one another and passed a bottle of greasy-looking liquor back and forth.

He went inside and up to the bar and ordered bourbon and frijoles and tamales, then found a table to eat them.

He noticed a dark-eyed little man sitting in the corner: black frock coat, hat, moustaches, milk white skin. The man played solitaire with a dog-eared deck of cards. Teddy ate the food and was grateful for the privilege. The dark man coughed several times, spat into a handkerchief, went back

to his game, sipping whiskey in between laying out his hand.

Teddy swiped up the last of the chilies with a tortilla, ordered a beer to wash it down. In the morning he'd wire George Bangs, then he'd go see about buying a pair of fast horses. John would need a pistol and a new pair of boots. He'd have to stop by the jail and ask him what size he wore.

He finished his beer and went back out again. The music drew him to the plaza. The dancers whirled and laughed and flirted. He thought of Kathleen Bonney, wishing she was here with him now so that they could dance. And he thought of his brother, Horace, who would never again dance or hear music, happy or otherwise.

It made him sad, all this happy music, these happy people. He asked one of the musicians when they took a break from playing where a man might rent a room and was told a fellow might rent himself a room at the Las Vegas Hotel. It stood on the corner of the block, not far from the jail.

Four dollars rented a modest room on the second floor. Good enough for a night's rest, a chance to plan the thing he had in mind. He kept thinking the whole

time about the woman John had shot and the reason.

It seemed an unlikely act by a man of John's reputation. But then jealousy fueled by whiskey made lots of men do things they normally wouldn't.

He could hear the muted sounds of the music through the walls, could feel the sag of the cheap bedsprings underneath him.

It was hard to sleep.

Chapter 4

Word of death traveled by wire: The white man's wire in the white man's world in the white man's language. The white man had given him a white name and had cut his hair in the white man's style and given him white man's clothes to wear. And the white man had taught him what the white man knew and this he learned with a great hunger. For such knowledge made him superior, made him a better enemy to his enemy.

He was seventeen and had lived five years now in the white man's world when the word of Yellow Hand's death traveled the wire. A reporter, a scatter-haired, bespectacled man with a funny accent, even by white men's standards, came to the school and sought him out and got permission to talk to him.

"You know how to read English?" the reporter, who said he was a correspondent with the *New York Herald*, said.

At first he didn't say anything and the reporter looked befuddled and said, "You

are the son of Yellow Hand, ain't you, kid?"

The reporter seemed surprised when he answered him in the white man's tongue.

"Yes, I am, how did you learn about me?"

"Oh, hell, we got our ways, kid. That's what the newspaper business is all about, finding out things on people."

The reporter handed him a newspaper clipping and waited for him to read it.

What the reporter may not have known was Yellow Hand had become lost to him years before this day when the headmaster summoned him to his office where the reporter sat stinking of liquor and both he and the headmaster with their pasty white skin looked old and sick in their clothes.

"Bob, I'm very sorry for the news to have to come to you this way . . ." the headmaster said.

Bob read the article.

And though it had been five years since he'd last seen his father, he had never forgotten the man with the eyes that could see far. Nor, for different reasons, had he forgotten the mother who took him and went off and married the evangelist who brought him east to this place, to this school where he was made to wear shoes and wear a

necktie. And once they had put him in this school they went off together to speak what the old fool had said was the WORD. The white people were full of words and little else.

"Well, you're his boy, right?" the reporter said again, taking a stub of a pencil and a small writing tablet from his pocket.

O, the white men were full of words and questions and opinions.

"Is there anything I can do, Bob?" the headmaster asked . . .

and . . .

"Your mother and father won't return until the spring and we've no way of reaching them — they've gone to Brazil, as you know . . ."

Bob.

That is the name they gave him. *Bob Parsnip.* The old fool's name was Jonas Parsnip. Bob's mother was once called *Woman Who Sleeps by Water,* but the old fool had her change it to Margaret and now she was just as white in her ways as he was. Both believers in a man who was nailed to a tree, died, and it was said had come back to life again. What foolish shit.

The headmaster had the eyes of a sad dog.

"Bob, will you be all right?"

"Yes, sir."

"It just proves, I suppose, that war is a senseless thing . . ."

He wondered what a man who ran a school for Indian kids knew about war.

The reporter said, "I'd like to ask you a few questions about your father. How do you feel about the famous Buffalo Bill Cody being the one who killed him in revenge of Custer?" And so on and so forth; questions he did not answer, for only a fool would carry on a conversation with another fool.

And when he did not answer the reporter's many questions, he scribbled some things in his little book anyway, then left muttering something about "Indians being close-mouthed little savages . . ." leaving the newspaper article for Bob to contemplate.

That night Bob dreamed of his father. In the dream he could see his father riding his pony upon a ridge, the sky blood red with evening sun. He could see stars falling. He could see the stars turning into soldiers that rained from the sky and were scattered across the hills and in the dry washes and in the wet rivers.

He could see a Wasichu with golden hair sitting dead, stripped of his tunic, his bare chest leaking blood from several wounds.

61

And blood dripping as well from his ears where squaws wandering onto the fields of the dead punctured their eardrums so they couldn't hear the great Creator calling them to the happy hunting ground. The Wasichu opened one eye and looked at him in the dream, then closed it again. Bob could hear throbbing tom-toms and see shadows dancing in firelight and hear brass bugles that sounded like the shrieks of women. He could see horses running with fiery manes across the grasslands.

He awoke, his nightshirt damp with sweat, and saw the frosted panes of glass in the dormitory glowing pale from a hunter's moon. He dressed in his white man's clothes and put on his white man's coat and white man's hat and went out from the dormitory, where others like him slept in iron beds in neat straight rows.

Down the back stairwell he went, silent as an . . . Indian, and slipped out the back door and across the triangle of lawns to the headmaster's house. The wind trailed after him. Once inside he easily followed the trail of snores to the bedroom where the head-master slept. Moonlight fell across the bed; the old man slept on his side. Bob went quickly and strangled him.

A quick search of the house gained him a

small amount of money from the wallet found in the headmaster's trousers. Another search found him a pistol heavy as a brick inside a desk drawer. They were the only things he would take from the Wasichu — the only things that the Wasichu seemed to worship.

When he placed the pistol in his pocket, his fingers touched the newspaper clipping and the paper felt like fire, and the name written on it — the one who it said had killed his father, burned like fire on the tips of his fingers: *Buffalo Bill.* What had the reporter called him? *Legendary. Indian Slayer. Scout Supreme? King of the Border Men?*

All he knew was, it was too many names for a white man.

The reporter had said other things as well, his fool mouth running like water in a fast stream.

Oh, you know Colonel Cody is planning a whole series of stage shows demonstrating how he killed your father . . . He's gathering a whole cast of actors and they're going to travel all over the East and put on reenactments of the event. You know what reenactments mean, Bob?

North Platte, Nebraska, is where the

newspaper clipping said: *". . . Colonel Cody keeps a ranch from which he guides hunting parties . . ."*

Bob found a butcher's knife in the kitchen lying alone atop the table, its long sharp blade agleam with moonlight, and thought briefly of scalping the headmaster. But the old man had nothing but a few sprigs of thin hair growing from his knobby old head. Besides, he wasn't sure how a man should be scalped. They'd taken most of the Indian out of him.

But not all.

And into that cold, handsome silvery night full of the hunter's moon he went in search of this Cody, this Indian Slayer. If this Wasichu was such a powerful warrior, then he had it in him to slay one more Indian, or himself be slain.

Bob had come to know enough of the white man's world to go in the direction of the trains whose steel tracks lay just to the north of the school. He had often listened to their whistles, those long haunting sounds that were like that of squaws crying in grief for ones who were dead.

Trains went everywhere the white man wanted to go — to the places where other white men were. He would go to Nebraska and find this Buffalo Bill, this Indian

Slayer, and bring on him revenge. Then he would go home again to his own people — his true people and not the ones who kept him like a dog, or the ones who stole him.

He raced across the town, keeping to the shadows as he jumped fences and heard the ruckus of dogs barking. He felt his young heart sing for the very first time since he'd ridden his pony out onto the prairies with his father.

He waited there in the bull rushes beside the steel rails until a slow-moving freight heading west rumbled by and climbed aboard, rolling himself into one of the boxcars, eager in his heart to become an Indian again.

The train's whistle blew low and sweet into the long darkness.

Chapter 5

Morning sun crept along the streets, climbed the east walls of the adobe buildings, flowed over the plaza like empty gold, the plaza empty now of dancers.

Teddy awakened to the sound of church bells. He pulled on his trousers, then his boots, stood and stretched out the kinks in his back from the bad mattress. He secured the shoulder rig, then donned his coat and hat and went out.

The air was crisp as new money.

Hell of a day for a jailbreak, he thought.

He walked down the street taking in the lay of the place, how the roads entered the town, where the alleys were. He went down one of the alleys he judged ran behind the jail. There wasn't any back door or window to the building and the wall looked to be several feet thick. He came back 'round again to the front, continued walking. He passed a hardware store, several saloons, a barbershop, and a land office.

The man he'd seen sitting in the saloon the night before — the one playing solitaire

with the dark eyes and bloodless flesh —
was unlocking the front door of a store-
front. The sign over the door read: DEN-
TIST DOC HOLLIDAY TEETH EXTRACTED.

The man looked up as Teddy ap-
proached. He was thin inside his clothes,
not very big, five-seven, maybe a hundred-
ten pounds. The man nodded.

"You need a dentist?"

"No."

"That's too bad."

The man turned the key in the lock and
went inside without further comment.

Teddy found the telegraph office and
went in and sent George a wire:

*Have arrived in Las Vegas. Too late to
do any good, it seems. Thanks for
your help anyway. Probably won't be
here long. Any news on the case,
send me a wire.*

General Delivery, Silver City. T. Blue.

He walked out again and down to the
livery stables just north of the town proper.

A stout man wearing a leather apron was
shaping a glowing white horseshoe by
striking it hard with a five-pound hammer
against an anvil. The ringing of steel on

67

steel was enough to crack an eardrum.

The man did not alter his rhythm or otherwise acknowledge Teddy's presence until he was satisfied he had the shoe shaped the way he wanted it and thrust it into a bucket of water with a long pair of tongs until the steam it raised evaporated.

Setting the shoe aside the man said, "Help you?"

"Like to buy some horses."

"Take your pick," the man said, nodding toward a small corral around the side of the building with maybe a half dozen mounts. Teddy studied them for a few moments, watched how they moved, how their eyes were, the curve of their backs.

"I'll take that paint mustang and the roan," Teddy said. "How much?"

"Twenty for the paint, thirty for the roan."

"Saddles too."

"You real particular on the saddles?"

"Don't need any the stirrups will bust halfway between here and Arizona." Teddy made it a point to tell the man he was headed for Arizona, knowing Hoodoo Brown would probably be asking questions after the jailbreak. Let him think Arizona.

"That where you headed?"

"It's a tough ride, I know that."

"Got two that ain't nothing fancy, but they'll do for a ride like that. I could let them go at fifteen apiece."

"Give you twenty-five for the pair."

"Done."

"Get 'em saddled, I'll be 'round later to gather them up."

Teddy paid the man and asked for a receipt. Man said, "They ain't stole."

"I know they ain't. I just don't want to be stopped by somebody wearing a badge who thinks they might be. Put a new set of shoes on 'em too."

Teddy walked back up to the jail. This time it was Hoodoo Brown guarding the coffee. Hoodoo looked like he'd been wrenched through a knothole.

"I'd like to meet with my client, Sheriff."

"Client? That what you Pinkertons call 'em who hire you?"

"I'm his attorney too." Teddy opened his coat and handed over his pistol.

"You want me to shake my legs?" he said.

Hoodoo looked at him down the length of his nose.

"You might not be from around here, son. But you don't look stupid enough to bust nobody out of jail."

"You don't have to worry about me.

Hell, I'm afraid of my own shadow."

Hoodoo didn't act like he thought the comment was funny, said, "The door's open, go on back," with a lot of confidence.

John was eating his breakfast, what looked like a plate of mush, a burnt biscuit, tin cup of black coffee.

"I bet it doesn't taste anything like Delmonico's," Teddy said.

"You'd be surprised how good bad food can taste when it's all you got to eat."

"I went to see the judge today," Teddy said.

John just looked at him.

"I wish you'd put this out of your mind."

"You don't have a say in it, the way I see it."

John looked from his plate to the door.

"He'll plant us both . . ."

"You afraid of dying sooner rather than later?"

"I'm all fixed on that part. It's you I don't think should count yourself as ready. Not from where I'm sitting, no how."

"I quit sucking the tit a long time ago, John. Why don't you just let me worry about me."

John stuffed the last of the biscuit in his

mouth, drank some of the coffee.

"Well, sir. If you've got your mind all over this thing, you might as well tell me how you're going to play it so we'll both know."

"I figure simple is best."

"Always seemed to be before. But I'd just soon hear a few of the details."

So Teddy told him and said afterward, "I'll be around this evening when Ramon — is it? — is on."

John stood and came to the bars then and put his hands around them and looked Teddy squarely in the eyes.

"You sure?"

"Yeah, John, I am. By the way, what size boots you wear?"

John told him.

"You staying for the hanging?" Hoodoo said when Teddy went back out into the office.

"No, I don't reckon."

"Friends is hard to come by, that's for sure. I guess you'd hate to see one you got go like that."

Hoodoo seemed to be enjoying his morning, now that he brought up the subject of death.

"See you around, Sheriff."

71

Teddy walked down to the mercantile. They had everything from Mexican blankets to strings of drying chilies. Teddy looked first at the boots, picked out a pair he was sure John wouldn't mind putting his feet in. Then he picked out a hat before looking at the shelf of pistols.

John favored the Birdseye Colt Lightning, like the one Teddy carried in the shoulder rig, but there wasn't any of that model on display.

"Let me see that Schofield," he said to the clerk.

"Forty-four forty," the clerk said, handing it to him. "Russian model."

Teddy broke it down, checked for rust in the chambers and barrel, worked the action, said, "I'll need a box of shells for it too."

Then he went and had lunch before going back to the livery.

"I'll ride that roan out now, want to see how he does," he told the smitty.

He took the road leading south, found a place maybe a mile along where they could cut southwest up through an arroyo and over some hard country. He scouted far enough along the arroyo he could see where they could cross and recross a wide stream and he liked what he saw.

He rested for a time near a stand of cottonwoods where the stream ran clear and the sun shone in it like broken glass and some fish held their place in the current by just shifting their tails slightly as they waited for a meal to come along. Brown fish. He studied on the plan some more; they rode hard they could make it. Most posses would give out after a day or two, he didn't figure any that Hoodoo Brown could raise would be any different. Satisfied, he mounted again and went back to the stables and picked up the other horse and led it down to the hotel where he tied both horses off at the hitch post. He went inside to his room and put together his things, then lay down on the bed and waited.

Somewhere in the middle of the waiting he fell asleep, knowing that if he didn't rest while he could, he might not get to for a while. And if things went wrong he might be resting for a very long time.

He awoke to a shattering sound and came up with the Colt in his hand, cocked, ready, then realized the sound was only thunder and heard the first rain strike against the tin roof above his head, a sound like peas being shelled into a pan. He went to the window and looked, only it wasn't

73

rain, it was hail and the street was nearly white with it.

He saw men ducking in under eaves and awnings where there were some to duck under. The two horses tied up out front were skittish and he went down to calm them. By the time he arrived out front of the hotel, the hail had stopped and was replaced by rain — a light rain at first that grew harder and more steady.

The sky was dark with clouds and the lateness of the hour. Storms were hard things to understand. They could last for hours or they could be over in minutes. Teddy figured the storm presented as good an opportunity as any. *Hell, it might even be some sort of omen.* He went back up to the room and got his things and got John's things, then went back down and untied the horses and led them down the street and tied them off again in front of the funeral parlor, next door to the jail.

Rain was hammering hard now, had a hiss to it and wind whipped and you couldn't ask for things to be much better, the way he figured it. He was half tempted to go on up to the mercantile and buy him and John some slickers, but too late for such luxuries.

Instead, he entered the jail with the

bundle of John's things under his arm in wet butcher's paper.

Ramon was standing at the window looking out at the rain, the way it was pooling in the streets and sluicing down off the eaves and running in small rivers. Wind-whipped rain was always a fascination in that country.

Teddy shook his hat free of water and settled it back on his head.

Ramon looked over at him.

"Some storm," Ramon said, turning his attention to the street again.

"You want to go get my friend and bring him out here," Teddy said. When Ramon cut his gaze to Teddy again, he could see that Birdseye Colt there in his hand, aimed and steady.

"You picked a piss-poor day to die," Ramon said.

"I guess I won't be the only one if it comes to that, but it doesn't have to come to that if you'll just walk on back there with me and open that cell."

Ramon sighed, thought about the fat wife he had waiting for him at home, the one who was always complaining about one thing or another. He thought about how she'd tell everyone what an irresponsible man he had been to get himself killed

over a twenty-dollar-a-month job. It didn't seem worth it. Nothing did lately.

"Hoodoo's dog, that's all he was . . ." Ramon could hear her saying at his funeral to anyone who would listen. Well, he wasn't going to give her the pleasure. He took the ring of keys down from the peg on the wall, thought briefly how long it would take him to reach a little to his left for one of the shotguns or rifles in the gun rack. It took more than a breath it would be too long. *Hell with it,* he told himself and led the way back to the cells.

Ramon didn't have to be told what to do next: He unlocked John's cell and took his place inside and sat down on the cot and waited for whatever else was going to happen.

Teddy handed John the bundle with the boots and hat and gun in it and John put them on without saying anything until he turned to Ramon and said, "I'm sorry about this, you did right by me and I'm sorry it's had to come to this . . ." He closed the cell and locked it.

Then he turned to Teddy and said, "Let's go."

They walked to the front and paused there at the window. The rain still fell hard, like nails and nickels, and John said, "I

don't suppose you were foresighted enough to buy us slickers . . ."

Teddy couldn't see anybody on the streets and opened the front door and John followed him out.

They mounted the skittish horses and John's almost bucked him off, but he stuck and talked to it and stroked its neck as he followed Teddy's lead.

"Don't run 'em," John said. "It will draw attention."

"Might draw more attention if we don't run 'em. Folks will wonder why two fools would be walking their horses in a hard rain."

"Then let's run 'em."

So they did.

Fifteen minutes later they left the south road and cut down into the arroyo that was running a foot deep with red water. They followed it for a ways and came out over a low cut in the bank and rode up it and headed out over a flat. Flashes of lightning stroked the stormy sky.

Teddy looked back over his shoulder and John did too, but there wasn't anybody following them that they could see. They slowed to a lope, John saying, "We don't want to bust these nags out too soon."

They made a stand of junipers and rode up through them and kept going until they came to the stream and crossed it. The rain had soaked them through to the skin and their flesh prickled with goose bumps, but their hearts were pumping hard the hot blood that flowed in their veins.

They rode on, cutting off in different directions when they could, but always taking a southerly course — back and forth, the rain knocking down the brims of their hats, the cold water sluicing down the back of their necks, some of it filling their boots.

They slowed the horses to a walk when they could and ran them when they could and kept on like that until they couldn't ride them any longer.

They found an old cabin, its roof half knocked in on one end, but it afforded some shelter from the rain on the other. They took the horses inside with them and rubbed them down as best they could. John said the horses would give off their heat.

"What time you figure it is?" John asked after they'd settled down, wrapping themselves in their horse blankets.

"Midnight, maybe later," Teddy said.

"You sorry you did it now?"

"No, I'm not sorry, John."

"Hell, I'm not so certain I ain't. I'm about froze, you?"

"Let's try and sleep a couple of hours, then get a shag on."

"Sleep?" John said.

They did their best with the rain coming in one end of the cabin where the roof was gone and dripping here and there in the rest of it. John finally fashioned himself a cigarette as best he could and got it lit and took a deep draw, then handed it over to Teddy.

"I never got the habit," Teddy said.

"Go on, it will warm you some." So Teddy took it and took a draw and held it in his lungs, then let it out again. "Take another," John said. So he took another and handed it back and it did make him feel some warmer, but not much.

"Last week," Teddy said, "I was sitting in a nice warm parlor drinking good whiskey in my mother's house in Chicago."

"Seems like a long time ago, don't it?"

"Yeah."

"She probably wouldn't be too proud of you about now — being a jail breaker and a outlaw."

"She'd probably say I got mixed up with the wrong company."

"She'd be right on that account. Take another draw on this."

They smoked the shuck down to where they couldn't hold it any longer without burning their fingers and John ground it out on an old plank full of rusty nails.

"I guess I owe you," John said.

"You don't owe me."

"I guess maybe I do."

"I thought we were going to try and get some sleep."

"You go ahead, I'm going to just sit here and enjoy this rain."

They fell silent for a time, each trying not to think about how cold and wet they were, then John said:

"They ain't no rain in Hell, that's why I'm enjoying it."

But Teddy didn't say anything.

Sometime over the next few hours they lost the night and first dawn crawled over the land, bringing the hills back to their dull brown color and with it the coo of gambel quail.

Teddy shook himself free from his squatting position and so did John. That's when the first shot rang out, taking a chunk of old wall with it.

"You boys might as well come on out, I

got plenty of guns out here."

There was no mistaking the gravel voice of Hoodoo Brown.

"You ready for this?" John said. "Tell me what you want to do. This is my fight, not yours."

"Way I'm thinking, even if we did give ourselves up, he might well prefer taking us back belly-down. After all, he's got you as a dead man already. One more added to the number wouldn't make anybody any difference."

"I'll tell him he can have me if he'll let you mosey."

"No deal."

"You sure?"

Teddy nodded, shouted through the busted window opening, "Come on in, Sheriff, we're eating chilies and playing whist. There's room for one more in here."

A fusillade of bullets raked the building, some sounding like gravel flung against the walls.

"You're a more experienced hand at this than I am, John. Any suggestions?"

"Fire every now and then, just to keep 'em interested. Maybe we can get them to shoot up their ammunition. Or maybe if we can keep 'em from killing us, they'll give up and go home. Most posse men

ain't professionals, just married fellers and other types thinking they're out on a quail hunt. They get tired and hungry like everyone else."

And so that's what they did, kept up a running gunfight most all that morning and afternoon. The sun struck down through the open roof and once Teddy saw a man running from one juniper to the next and he and John both fired at the same time and the man yelped and rolled like a stone-struck dog.

Hoodoo Brown maintained a running commentary on the situation as well, yelling to them how he was going to kill them and cut off their heads and take them back on the end of a pole and other atrocities he could think to come up with.

Late afternoon found them low on ammunition.

"I've got six shots left, how about you?" John said.

"Three."

"How many you figure is out there?"

"A dozen, maybe."

"Way I see it, we got to shoot Hoodoo. We do him, the others will quit."

"Give me your piece, John."

"What for?"

"You've got more rounds than me and if

I'm going to shoot the sheriff . . ."

"Hell with it, I'll do it."

"No, let me."

Two more shots shattered the wall opposite them. The light was dimming now, the sun sinking low.

"We could just wait till dark and try and sneak out."

"They'd just stay after us, if not here, we'll have to fight 'em somewhere."

Teddy took a silver dollar from his pocket. "Call it," he said.

"Heads," John said.

Teddy slapped it palm-down, showed it to John.

"Give me your gun."

John handed over the pistol and Teddy started to hand his to John.

"How you going to do this?"

"I figure straight on is best, don't you?"

"Best way to get yourself killed, maybe."

"Hell, John, we both know most of 'em can't hit a bull in the ass with a scattergun if they had to, much less a man riding straight into 'em."

"They's always luck. I seen more men get shot lucky than on purpose."

"My luck's never been that bad."

"You'll need both guns, then."

"Yeah, that's what I was thinking."

Soon as the sun dipped beyond the horizon and there was only the last light that lay across the land, Teddy swung onto the back of his horse. "Swing that door open when I say to," he told John.

The two men's gaze held a moment, then Teddy said, "Do her," and John swung the door open and Teddy, lying low over the back of the horse, one hand full of mane, the other full of gun, charged out and rode hard toward the line where he'd heard Hoodoo cussing them most of the day.

It took several moments for the posse to figure it out, and when they did, it was nearly too late, the man with the blazing gun was nearly among them. They opened fire but the rider presented no good target, lying low over the horse's back. He fired left and right.

Hoodoo instinctively knew the score and stood and took careful aim and shot the horse. But rather than it going down it lurched sideways, stung by a badly aimed bullet that struck it high on the rear flank. And when Hoodoo aimed again, he saw fire spit from Teddy's revolver and felt the bullet rip through his thigh. The posse had to hold its own fire until the rider cleared their line, lest they shoot one another. And

by the time he cleared the line, he dropped over a hill and into the brush and none were wont to follow after a man bold enough to charge them.

Hoodoo lay on the ground, cursing and holding his leg that had become a pillar of fire and remorse to him.

" 'At son of bitch shot me, boys."

"He sure as shit did," one of them said.

"We best get you on back to town before you bleed out."

"Boys, I ain't the noble type, carry me back quick before I die out in this chaparral."

Night fell fast over the land and John wondered was his friend lying out there dead, or maybe if he was smart and lucky and hadn't got shot, he'd just kept riding. John wouldn't have blamed him if he had.

Then something stirred outside the cabin, the land in a deep purple dusk now, and Teddy said, "I'm coming in."

And John said, "Come on in. I don't have nothing to shoot you with, even if you was one of them."

Teddy came in with blood on him, but it was horseblood and not his own.

"I shot him, John. They all packed it in and went home, least for now."

"You kill him?"

"No, didn't want to if I didn't have to. I just shot him enough, is all."

Teddy handed John back his pistol. John checked, saw the cartridges had all been spent. "We best get into the wind."

"My horse has been shot, John, but it went clean through and he's stopped bleeding. I think he'll be all right."

"Let's ride 'em as far as we can, walk the rest of the way if we have to."

"They quit hard, John, Hoodoo and them."

"I know it. Best reason I can think of to go on down to Old Mexico so we don't have to fight 'em again."

They rode out into the night, the two of them, just about spent as two men could be, and kept riding.

Chapter 6

Billy rose early. Louisa slept like a rock still. *Poor girl,* he thought. *I put her through her paces last evening.* Billy was almost always pleased with his performance when he coupled with Louisa. He liked to think he still had something of the old mad bull in him yet.

He went to the window, pulling on his trousers and tucking in a fresh woolen shirt. He rubbed away a circle of frost from one of the panes and looked out at the fresh-fallen snow now sun-struck under a gas blue sky.

It was a fine day to go get his skull read.

He left Louisa sleeping and joined his girls down in the kitchen, where they were already preparing their own breakfast. The girls were quite handy and were becoming fine little cooks.

"Oh, Papa," they called when they saw him and rushed to him and hugged him in such a way he almost wept.

He patted each one and gave each one a kiss and said, "Ladies, what will we be having this fine morning?"

"Biscuits, Papa," Arta said.

"And flapjacks," Orra said.

"And strong black coffee with sugar," Irma said.

"Fine, fine," Billy said. "Let's eat."

The biscuits were a little underdone, and the flapjacks a little burnt, and the coffee tasted about like ditch water, but Billy adored his girls such that he never complained and instead complimented them until their cheeks turned red as apples.

"We love you, Papa," they said in unison.

"I love you too, ladies. Papa will always love you."

And when he rose and went and put on his heavy mackinaw coat and his large beaver sombrero, they clung to him, not wanting him to go away and leave them again.

"Mama says you're always gone and have itchy feet and never will settle down," Arta pleaded.

"You pay no attention to your mama," Billy said, looking back toward the stairs that led up to the bedroom. "Now let me go, ladies, I've important matters to attend to in town. And when I return, I'll bring you each a surprise."

They stood in the door and watched him go out across the yard to the barn, and the

air was cold enough they could see their breaths and see his too.

Louisa came up behind them and told them to shut the door. "Honestly," she said in a disturbed way. "You girls act as though you were born in a barn." They all giggled and said, "Yes'm," and ran off.

Louisa watched through the window as her forever-restless husband came out of the barn astride his big white horse and turned its head toward town. She still felt a little tired from last night's adventure. She smiled in spite of everything and went and ate an underdone biscuit and washed it down with some of the paltry-tasting coffee.

"I come to get my skull read," Billy said to Bartlebee Bone.

"Well, sit right in that chair and I'll read it."

"You ain't going to ask me why I want it read?"

"No, that's your business. Now, take off that big Mexican hat or I won't be able to read very much."

Billy took his sombrero off and hung it on a hat tree in the corner and climbed up into the barber's chair that had once been a tool of Bartlebee Bone's former profession.

"Nice chair," Billy said, settling in.

"I cut Clay Allison's hair in that very chair," Bartlebee said, taking a pair of calipers out of a drawer.

"The gunfighter?"

"You could call him that, most just called him a homicidal maniac that would shoot a sleeping man as quick as he would one that was awake. Saw him ride into Mobeetie once buck-naked on the back of a lop-eared mule. Damnedest man I ever met."

"Did you ever read his skull?"

"Just once when I was cutting his hair, only he didn't know I was reading it — it was while I was still perfecting the art and needed the practice."

"What'd you come to conclude?"

"That he was crazy as a crab in a whore's nightgown."

"This before or after he rode in naked on a mule?"

"Before."

"Well, I can tell you with all certainty, I'd never ride into any town in this whole country without my clothes on, not even for all the tea in Chiny."

"Please hold still, if you don't mind," Bartlebee said as he began to take measurements with the calipers.

90

"The points on them things is a bit sharp," Billy said.

"Hold still."

Billy held as still as he could manage while Bartlebee Bone read his skull, jotting down things in a small book as he went, pressing his fingertips here and there all over Billy's scalp. Finally he finished.

"What's the verdict?" Billy said.

"Well, according to my calculations you have a great propensity for wanting to be liked and liking others. You're somewhat more prone to combativeness than the average man, and you are given over to grand ideas but shy away from domesticity. You fear little, hope for much."

"What's all that mean in general terms?"

"That you are a dreamer."

"That's it?"

"That's the gist of it. I mean, I'll complete my findings in greater detail and provide you with a thorough charting, but in a nutshell, that is the stuff you are made of, Mr. Cody."

"I was sort of hoping for a look into the future."

"I don't do futures. You want futures you'd best go see Dora Hand, the palm reader."

"Palm reader? Why, I thought old Dora

91

was a prostitute over to the Yellow Dog?"

"Not anymore. She's given up that particular profession and has taken up the art of palm reading."

"Where's she set up shop?"

"Keeps an apartment above the drugstore."

"Above the drugstore, huh?"

"My charge is three dollars."

"Sorta steep for what little I learned."

"Dora charges less for reading palms, I'm sure."

Billy dug the money out of his pocket and handed it to the phrenologist and went out almost forgetting his hat. He turned back and plunked it on his head and his head didn't feel any different having been read by Bartlebee than it did that morning when he got up and combed his hair.

Billy thought he'd better stop by the hotel and check on Yankee Judd and White Eye Anderson to see how they were making out with getting the supplies for the hunting party. Then he would stop by the telegrapher's and see if there was any new word from Ned Buntline as to the exact date of the hunting party's arrival. He hoped too that Buck Taylor would show up soon, as well as Jane Nebraska. Well, he wasn't so sure about Jane Ne-

braska. A woman so lust-starved as Jane might prove his undoing.

Snow was starting to melt under the warm sun and here and there dripped from overhangs into barrels, and where it melted in the streets it turned them muddy.

Billy met up with Yankee Judd and White Eye coming out of the hotel.

"How you boys making out on that list?"

"Got near everything but the stoves," White Eye said.

"We'll need stoves," Billy said. "This time of year the prairies get mighty cold at night."

"Hardware man said they was a load due in any day from Omaha," Yankee said.

"Everything else in order?"

"Just about," White Eye said.

"Good, good. You ain't seen nothing of Buck, have you?"

"No, sir, we sure ain't. But Jane rolled in just about an hour ago and gave us a list of foodstuffs she'd need. You want us to get what's on her list, charge it to you?"

"Yes. Where's she staying?"

The men shrugged. "Don't know and she didn't say, but she had a peculiar look in her eyes."

"Well, I aim to get on down the street," Billy said. "If she asks after me, tell her you

ain't seen me yet today and that I'll meet up with her later on."

"Where you headed?" White Eye said.

"Down this street here," Billy said, not wanting to say where he was going.

White Eye and Yankee Judd just stood there without saying anything, each curious as to Billy's secretiveness. Billy went on down the street to Dora Hand's apartment up above the drugstore, climbed the stairs to a landing, and knocked on her door.

Billy hadn't seen Dora in perhaps a year, the last time Wild Bill stopped in on his way up to Cheyenne — him and Colorado Charley Utter. Dora was working at the Yellow Dog at the time and though Billy never hired her services, he did buy her a drink or three back in those days. She had a reputation as one of the best prostitutes in North Platte and mostly cowboys who paid for her time went away more than a little happy.

"Why, heavens, look what the cats drug in."

"Dora," Billy said, removing his sombrero. "You mind I come in?"

"Just to let you know, I ain't in the whore business no more, Bill. I found peace with the Lord. And you ought to be

half ashamed, a married man like yourself."

"I didn't come here for no whore business," Billy said. "I come to get my palm read. Bartlebee Bone said you was a palm reader now and could foretell futures. That's why I come. I'm perfectly happy with my Lulu, as far as that other is concerned. I, much like yourself, have given up the whore business . . ."

Dora allowed Billy in to her apartment, ducking behind a dressing screen to put on something a little less revealing than the pink kimono she was wearing. Once reemerged she sat down at a small table and told Billy to do so likewise and he sat across from her and extended his right hand for her to read.

She took hold of it and traced lines with her forefinger, muttering as she went, seeing things he could only imagine.

"What is it exactly about the future you want to know?" she asked.

"I am most interested in how long I got to live," he said.

She traced a line in his palm that went from thumb to forefinger.

"Hmmm . . ." she said.

"What is it, Dora?"

"Can't say with certainty, but you could be in some terrible danger, Bill."

He remembered yesterday, the bullet that almost smashed his melon.

Dora traced another line that ran partway across his palm but was broken in half, intersected by another line.

"This is not good," she said.

"Plain lingo," he said.

"Could be you ain't going to last very long."

"How long?"

"Hard to say, but there is danger everywhere I look. Let me see your other hand."

He showed it to her. She sighed.

"I'd say you need to put your affairs in order," she said.

"That's it, then?"

"Well, there is a chance you could live to be a very old man . . . see this line here, it's your life line and it shows longevity. I just don't know."

"What if you were me, what would you do?"

"I'd hide out for a while, someplace safe."

"I can't," he said.

"You oughter."

"Somebody took a potshot at me yesterday," he said.

"I ain't surprised."

"Hell's bells."

"I'm God-fearing now, Billy, I'd appreciate you not swearing."

"Then I know what I got to do."

"It's fifty cents per hand, Bill, the reading is."

Billy gave her a dollar, then left and went to the telegraph office and sent a wire to Pinkerton's Detective Agency in Chicago — the same ones that had sent a man to protect Wild Bill. What was good enough for Wild Bill sure as hell was good enough for him. Just to see him through until the hunt was finished and he was headed east again with his new combination. What was that fellow's name he'd met up in Cheyenne? It come to him just as he opened the door to the telegraph office:

Teddy Blue.

That's the man he wanted.

Chapter 7

Mysterious Dave Mather had not planned to murder Buffalo Billy Cody. It just worked out that way. Mysterious Dave had mental problems. It was in the late autumn that he first tried to kill Buffalo Bill across three hundred yards of freshly fallen snow. Mysterious Dave did not know that it was Buffalo Bill he tried to kill, nor would he have much cared.

Mysterious Dave's mental problems began when he was a boy and drank standing ditch water one hot summer's day and ended up with a brain fever that ruined his thinking. Before drinking the ditch water and getting brain fever, Dave was a simple charming boy who enjoyed all the usual pleasures of youth. It was only after the brain fever that he acquired the nickname of "Mysterious Dave" and began to engage in bizarre behavior. Dave would often forget where he was or where he'd been or what he was about to do right in the middle of doing it. And when he got old enough, he just got on an old plow

horse one day and rode off and was never seen or heard from again by any member of his family.

Mysterious Dave had his good days and he had his bad days. He was never sure what sort of day he was going to have when he got up in the morning. And sometimes by the time he went to bed at night, he wasn't sure what sort of day he'd just had.

Mysterious Dave tended to forget a lot and he couldn't quite remember such things as when he had left Denver or Dodge City or Arkansas or Texas or any of the places he had ever been, or *why* he had left such places, or why he had been there in the first place.

Sometimes bits and pieces of memory would come to him at the oddest times. These bits and pieces were like little tintypes flashing in his brain: images of himself wearing a deputy marshal's badge, or of him stealing horses, or shooting somebody in the face. Once he had an image of himself on his knees, tossing dice on a blanket with a group of Negro soldiers. And another time he saw himself frolicking in a water tank with several naked whores whose bosoms bobbed in the water.

But such memories would disappear al-

most as quickly and unexpectedly as they appeared, and he'd be left wondering if any of those things actually happened or if they were just dreams he'd had.

So it came to pass that on that particular fine October day, Mysterious Dave saw a man riding a high-stepping horse through the snow. Dave, resting as he was upon a ridge in a stand of willows, withdrew his Henry repeating rifle, having decided on the spur of the moment to empty, what looked to Dave even at such a distance, a mighty fancy silver-studded saddle.

He took careful aim.

But then the rider stopped and got off his horse beside a stringy black creek. Dave saw this as a sign of good fortune; it was much easier to shoot a man who was standing still than one who was moving. Dave took more careful aim but the feller walked about stamping his feet, adjusting the cinch strap on his saddle, and wouldn't hardly stand still for a second.

Stand still, you son of a bitch.

Dave was a bundle of pure impatience, a jittery sort. His finger squeezed the trigger without his complete will.

The shot from the Henry sounded like a tree limb cracking under the weight of ice — a loud unpleasant sound that shattered

the tranquil air. But there was too much working against Dave that late afternoon: wind had come up from the south, and shooting downhill instead of level, and the last bit of afternoon sun glancing off the snow causing his eyes to water.

The feller went down, all right, and Dave was congratulating himself on such a wonderful shot when the feller suddenly got back up. After a few long moments, the feller mounted up again and rode off in haste.

Dave was disappointed, of course. He'd put his mind on possessing that fancy saddle and the high-stepping horse, and whatever else of worth the feller might possess, including the big sombrero the feller wore. Dave often robbed the folks he made corpses of, though he hardly remembered doing such. Most corpses had on them a small amount of cash, a pocket watch, generally a knife and a pistol, as well as boots and hats that were often much better than those Dave wore.

Mysterious Dave determined he'd track the feller and eventually shoot him and acquire his possessions. Once he had his heart set on something it was hard for him to think otherwise.

He mounted his own horse and went

riding down the ridge at a leisurely pace, staying far enough behind his quarry to not be seen. Mysterious Dave's instincts were always good, even if his mind was not. Dave's instincts were as good as a badger's.

Soon enough, the sun fell beyond the horizon and the sky turned a black silver and before he knew it, Dave could see the dog star and the moon and a lot of other stars in the sky, as well. And way up ahead of him, he could see the shadow of a horse and rider crossing the field of snow just like in a dream he'd had a few nights earlier. Dave figured sooner or later the feller ahead of him would stop and make camp, and when he did Dave would sneak up and shoot him in his sleep. It was always easier to shoot a sleeping feller than it was one awake.

But the feller didn't stop and pretty soon Dave could see the lights of a town in the distance. By now, Dave was having trouble remembering why he was following the feller. He remembered something about a fancy saddle, but the rest eluded him. And by the time he dismounted in front of WALLACE & TEAGUE'S BILLIARDS & SPORTSMAN'S CLUB his feet were numb with cold and his mind adrift. The light in-

side the window looked inviting and he went in and straight to the long oak bar, where several customers stood swallowing liquor and conversing with one another.

"Why, I'll have a beer," Dave says to the bartender, a jolly feller in a white apron and paper collar. "Say, where is this place, anyhow?"

The bartender looked at Dave curiously as he poured the beer, then swiped the head off it with a wooden paddle.

"Ten cents," the bartender says. "Why, this is North Platte, bub."

Dave took his beer over by the potbelly stove glowing red as a cherry and had some other fellers sitting around it, some playing whist, and some watching some other fellers playing billiards at the tables.

"Why, this is a damn fine place to be on a cold night," says he to the fellers.

Collectively, they see a stranger among their midst.

"It ain't so bad," says one.

"Oh, it ain't, huh . . ."

Some shook their heads.

Dave drags a chair up close to the stove and sets his feet near it and watches the whist players and the billiard players. A fragment of a memory flashes through his thoughts: two fellers playing billiards; one

suddenly stabs the other through the heart and kills him dead. Some of the dead feller's blood splatters up on the green felt of the billiard table. The stabbing feller looks a lot like Dave hisself, but he can't be sure.

Then he remembers the big hat the feller riding a fancy horse was wearing and says to the other fellers at large: "You boys know a feller what wears a big beaver hat and rides a high-stepping horse at has a silver-studded saddle from around these parts?"

Wary, one of them says, "Oh, you must mean Colonel Cody, what about him?"

"Colonel Cody, huh?"

"Buffalo Bill," the feller says.

One of the fellers playing cards slaps a card down hard on the table and whoops like an Indian, causing Mysterious Dave to jump to his frozen feet and pull one of his pistols: a Colt Peacemaker with worn walnut grips and most the bluing rubbed off.

"What!"

The other fellers pause what they are doing and stare at Dave, who stares back.

"Nothing, mister," the card slapper says. "I was just topping old Joe's hand."

Dave looks at 'em hard. Then looks

down at the pistol in his hand. He isn't sure why he is holding it.

"Nothing, mister," Dave says, then holsters the pistol and orders another beer and takes up the warming of his frozen feet again.

Soon after the place empties out, except for Dave, who is remembering how he was once a deputy marshal in Dodge City, Kansas, and shot three or four cowboys and one or two soldiers and a Mexican vaquero. His memory of this is as clear as rainwater for several long blissful moments. He remembers too that he used to ride out almost every day to a lone soddy, where he fornicated with a woman named Maude, who had a passel of kids running 'round outside screaming the whole time he and Maude were in the bed, and sometimes scorpions would fall into the bed with them from the dirt roof over their heads. Sometimes the scorpions would fall in their hair as they were fornicating.

Then the memory goes away and all Dave knows is that he is drinking beer and warming his cold feet.

Comes closing time. The bartender is tired and wants to go home to his missus, but is cautious about disturbing the mysterious feller still sitting by the pot-

belly. The mysterious feller has kept his boots so close to the potbelly that the bartender can smell his boot leather baking.

The bartender chooses instead to count out the evening's receipts and when finished, he goes to the back room to lock them in the safe. When he returns, the mysterious feller's chair is empty, the front door is left swung open.

The bartender hopes the mysterious feller doesn't come back. He was bad for business.

Chapter 8

They rode toward Silver City cautious, John saying how it was possible Hoodoo Brown could have wired every lawman in New Mexico about the escape.

"I think we'd be wise to keep right on riding clean on down to the Rio Grande and cross it," John said.

"You're probably right, but there's somebody here I mean to see."

"Woman, I'm guessing. Why else would you risk getting shot or jailed . . ."

"Woman's good a reason as any, I reckon. You lost all your taste for women, John?"

"The wrong kinds, yeah. I sorta did when I shot Maria. Least until I can get down to the old place, cross that river where I ain't wanted no more."

"You can go on if that's what you want. Like I said before, you don't owe me anything."

"I reckon I'll ride with you for a while. Least ways until you make up your mind which way your stick is going to float."

They swung down from the dusty hills and onto the south road about a mile from the town and rode like two old hands off a cattle drive.

"I helped bring a herd up into this part of the territory once — little farther east of here, though. Charley Goodnight run 'em out of Belknap all the way to Fort Sumner. Two thousand head of the mossiest longhorns you ever wanted to get behind. Had some high old times in Fort Sumner, though."

The sun was beginning to set throwing shadows over the land. Their horses looked like they had legs ten feet long.

"Might be best if I held up here for a spell and let you ride in alone, then I'll come in after dark," John said. "If Hoodoo did send a wire to the local, he'll be watching for two men riding together."

"Okay," Teddy said. "Why don't we meet up in the morning out front of the telegraph office. I'll need to send a wire to George, let him know the situation."

"Listen," John said. "Things go bad for either one of us, the other should just ride away if he's able. We agreed?"

Teddy nodded.

"See you tomorrow, amigo," John said, and turned his horse back off the road and

up toward a stand of junipers. Teddy watched him for a moment, then rode on.

The last bit of sun glanced off the few metal roofs of the town's buildings and glowed golden in the dust. The mud of the adobe walls looked warm with the fading sun on it. Teddy reined in in front of the first saloon he saw, tied off, and went inside.

It was a small narrow room with a long bar running down one side, a few tables with chairs occupied by that breed of single men who had no home nor wife nor children to go home to at the supper hour. Teddy knocked dust off his coat, what he could that wasn't crusted by the rain they'd ridden through two nights earlier.

He ordered a whiskey and when the barkeep brought it, Teddy threw four bits on the bar. The barkeep said, "It's only two bits, a shot is." Teddy replied, "That other is for a question I want to ask you." The barkeep took up the money and said, "Go ahead."

Teddy asked if he knew of a woman named Kathleen Bonney.

"She'd be fairly new in the area," he said.

"She runs a boardinghouse just off the

main drag," the man said. "Got a boy with her, rough kid."

Teddy nodded, tossed back his whiskey, said, "Which direction off the main drag?"

"West, mister, first cross street you come to, almost right there on the corner. Got flower boxes under the winders. She don't know how hard it is to grow anything 'round here that ain't got thorns."

"Obliged."

The light was all but gone by the time he came out of the saloon. Evening was settling in, easy as a breath. Teddy hoped it stayed that way.

He mounted and rode on down the street, turned onto the first cross street and saw immediately the house — smaller than the one she ran in Cheyenne. He reined in, tied off, tried again to knock some more trail off him, then gave up and knocked on the door.

She looked thinner than before, more pale.

She smiled when she saw him, smiled and stood there without saying anything and he couldn't think of anything to say either right away. It was good just to see her again and he figured she was thinking the same thing.

She looked past him finally, as though

she expected him not to be alone, then she said, "You've come."

"Not exactly the way I planned it, but I'm here and there is only one reason that I am."

He took off his dusty hat and held it down alongside him in one hand and with the other he drew her to him and kissed her and she didn't resist, but she didn't exactly kiss him back either.

"You better come inside, lest we cause a scandal."

He followed her into the dining room, where three men sat at the table, napkins stuffed into the throats of their shirts. They looked up from their plates. One, a man sitting near the head of the table, had long drooping brown moustaches and he looked especially hard at Teddy when Kathleen introduced him. There were two empty chairs and Teddy took one and somebody said, "Would you pass them peas," and another border handed him the bowl.

Kathleen went and took her place at the head of the table and everyone continued eating mostly in silence. Teddy exchanged glances with her and noticed that the fellow with the shaggy brown moustaches kept a close watch on both of them.

It didn't take long for everyone to finish

their supper and for all but brown moustaches to excuse themselves and leave the room.

"My name's Antrim," the man said after a time. "Henry Antrim. I do some mining hereabouts. How is it you and Kathleen come to know each other?"

Teddy looked at this Mr. Henry Antrim with no inclination to explain himself.

Instead, Kathleen said, "We met in Cheyenne, Henry. Mr. Blue was kind enough to take a hand with William and help him out of a jam."

Antrim cut his gaze from her to him.

"He's full of spunk, that boy is. It will take a constant strong hand to keep him in line."

Teddy wanted to say something to the effect that it sounded like Mr. Antrim was volunteering himself for the job, but only because of what was attached to the job. But he refrained for the sake of Kathleen, who looked clearly uncomfortable.

"Yes, sir," Antrim said, almost as if he was answering an unspoken question. He sat back and showed no indication of leaving.

"I could stand to rent a room for a night or two if you have one available," Teddy said at last.

She looked at him and he knew there wasn't any room.

"I'm sorry," she said. "I only have three and they're all rented . . ."

"That's okay, I'll find something at one of the hotels."

"Might try the Fisher Hotel," this Antrim said. "They got good rooms, clean, hardly no ticks."

Teddy stood to leave.

"I'll see you out," Kathleen said.

Antrim started to stand, but Teddy cut his gaze to him — a warning look — and Antrim slumped back in his chair.

When they reached the front door, Kathleen stepped outside with Teddy.

"I guess I came at a bad time," Teddy said. "Looks like you —"

She put her fingers to his lips.

"It's not what you think," she said.

"Tell me what it is, then."

"He's taken to me. He's a good man, Teddy. He cares about William. I didn't do anything to encourage him . . ." She coughed and the cough rattled through her like the sound of breaking glass. He took hold of her and held her until she stopped and he could feel her trembling still.

"I've not long to live," she said. "I need someone to watch after William when I'm

113

gone. He needs a father more than I need a husband . . ."

"I wish you had talked to me about this," Teddy said.

"I wanted to . . ."

Teddy saw the curtain being pulled back slightly from one of the windows, saw Antrim's face peering out.

"He's asked me to marry him," Kathleen said.

"Don't. Not until at least we can talk about this first."

"I didn't know if I'd ever see you again . . ."

"I'm here now. Let me see you to-morrow."

"Okay. But you have to understand the fix I'm in . . ."

He touched her cheek and wanted to kiss her again, but he didn't want to set up a row between her and the man Antrim inside. She waited for him to mount his horse, stood in the doorway until he turned the animal's head back up the street, then went inside and he could hear the door closing and with it his heart.

He found a bathhouse and washed the trail off his hide and paid to have his clothes cleaned. He asked for a hand mirror and shaved while still sitting in the

zinc tub. The face he saw in the mirror was a stranger's face. It was him, but it wasn't him. The eyes were the eyes of an outlaw. He finished shaving and set about drinking from the bottle of bourbon he'd had sent for. And when he about knocked it clean down to the bottom, he lifted himself from the bath and dressed in fresh clothes and then went and found a hotel and fell into a fitful sleep. But soon a knock at the door awakened him. When he opened it, Antrim stood there, fists balled by his sides.

"I want you to leave her be," Antrim said.

"We got no quarrel unless you want one."

"She needs herself a father for the boy, that's one thing. And she needs herself a steady man. You don't look like no steady man to me."

Teddy leveled his gaze at the man.

"I don't need you telling me what I am, or what you think I am. My business is just that. Take a walk, Antrim."

"I'll fight you for her, goddamn if I won't."

"You're interrupting my sleep."

Antrim glared and was still glaring when Teddy closed the door in his face.

He tried going back to sleep, but it was

no good and instead decided to go for a walk, maybe get a drink and weigh the situation. That's when Antrim and some others caught him, just outside the hotel, a knot of them standing there.

They encircled him, Antrim saying, "We decided maybe it was time you just moved on, cowboy."

Teddy sidestepped Antrim but brought a stinging right fist to the side of the man's face, snapping his jaw with such blinding speed the others weren't quite sure what happened. Antrim sagged to the boardwalk spitting blood, a tooth. One of the other men stepped in, swinging both hands like a windmill. One of the flailing fists glanced off Teddy's shoulder, another knocked off his hat, but he battered the man with three fast jabs, knocking him back off the walk and into the street. Another swung a club that missed and Teddy brought up a sweeping left hook that smashed into the center of the man's face and exploded his nose into a bloody pulp of bone and cartilage. The other two danced and feinted like they were going to challenge him, but when he turned on them, they ran.

Antrim was climbing to his feet again and Teddy was prepared to put him down

just as quick. But Antrim held forth a palm, signifying he was finished.

"I'll let it go this time," he said. "But it ain't going to be finished until one of us is left this town. You care anything at all about that woman, you'll leave her alone." Teddy's hands rang with the shock of hitting the men. It hadn't been a contest hardly and he felt half ashamed in some respects. But more so because Antrim was right when it came to Kathleen's welfare. "Goddamn it to hell," he muttered.

The next morning he went to the telegraph office to send George Bangs a wire and found one from George already waiting for him.

Our agency has been employed by Colonel W. F. Cody. He's requested your services in particular. Need you to go to North Platte immediately. If unable or unwilling, send word as to the reason why, otherwise, I'll expect further word from you once there. Cody will fill in the details upon your arrival.

G. Bangs

He debated whether to accept such an assignment. He thought about John, the

law that was probably after them both. They could run to Mexico like John wanted to do, but in truth, he didn't feel like becoming an expatriate. Maybe John did, it would be up to him.

He didn't have to wait long to find out. John was standing out front of the telegrapher's when Teddy came out. John stood there looking up and down the street, his eyes shaded by the Stetson.

"You get to pay your visit?" John said.

"Somewhat."

"You staying or going with me?"

"Something's come up."

"Why don't we cross over the street and have some breakfast and talk about it. That way if the law comes for us and we go down, we'll go down with our bellies full, at least. I'm about tired of running anyway."

"I am too."

They took a seat by the window so they could watch the comings and goings of anyone out on the street. John ordered flapjacks and steak and Teddy did the same. They ate like starved drovers. Swallowed coffee black and hot. Then John took out his makings and rolled a shuck and lit it.

"Let's hear it," John said.

"I've been assigned to go down to Nebraska."

"Goddamn, old son, you must be on the low end of the detective stick to get assigned to Nebraska. Nebraska ain't nothing but grass and empty places."

"Colonel Cody has requested me for a job. My boss wants me to go or tell him why I won't."

"You going, then?"

Teddy thought about last night — Kathleen and Antrim together and how things were.

"I've got to decide quick, John."

"Go ahead."

"What's in Mexico you couldn't find in Nebraska?"

"You wanting me to go with you?"

"That's what I'm thinking."

"What about this woman you came here to see?"

"I guess that isn't going to work out."

"Hardly ever does, I mean women and cowboys."

"It's less likely the law would catch you down in Mexico," Teddy said. "You should think about it."

Two women carrying parasols walked by the window and John took notice of them, then returned his attention to Teddy.

"What about you?" he said. "The law could find you too."

"I don't reckon they'll be looking for me in Nebraska. Why would they?"

"Well, I don't reckon they'd be looking for me in Nebraska either. I don't reckon nobody would."

"I need to say good-bye to my friend," Teddy said. "Why don't you go get us a good price for the horses and saddles. We'll take a train. I'll meet up with you at the depot, say in an hour."

John nodded, said, "Nebraska . . ." as though he was still trying to get used to the idea.

Teddy knocked on Kathleen's door and the boy, William, answered. The kid smiled and showed his squirrel teeth, said, "I wisht you'd come sooner, she's about to marry that dang miner."

"I know," Teddy said. "I met him last night. You keeping your nose clean?"

The kid smirked, said, "Clean as anyone. She's in the kitchen."

Teddy went in and Kathleen turned away from the stove, her hands dusted with flour, a spot of it on her brow.

"I've come to say good-bye," he said.

She didn't say anything at first. Her feelings were evident in the sad way she looked at him. It felt a lot harder than he

120

thought it would, saying good-bye.

"I won't ask you to fight for me," she said. He didn't even consider telling her that he already had fought for her.

"Kathleen. I want you to know . . ."

"We both know what's going to happen, Teddy. I'll most likely be gone by the spring. It wouldn't be fair to you . . ."

"But it would to Antrim?"

"No, not to him either, but he's willing to do it. He knows the situation. I agreed to it already."

He crossed the room and took her into his arms.

"Maybe the doctor's wrong," he said. "We could go back to Chicago, where they have good doctors."

"The trip would only weaken me more."

"Jesus, Kathleen . . ."

She kissed him and held to him.

"You go on now," she whispered. "Go and find yourself someone who you can love for a very long time and who can love you just as long . . ."

He kissed her hair and she turned from him so he couldn't see the tears brimming in her eyes.

"Go on, Mr. Blue. Let me keep my memories of us the way we were the last time we were together. Do that for me, please."

121

He didn't say anything, but turned instead and walked out.

John and Teddy set the bench in front of the depot, waiting for the train to come in. John whittled on a stick of cottonwood and kept an eye peeled on the street for trouble. Teddy fought the urge to go back to the boardinghouse. A lonesome wind blew up the street and a Mexican pushed a handcart loaded with ocotillo and cages of chickens.

"I guess that train ain't ever going to get here," John said.

"It'll get here."

"I wish it would sooner than later, don't you? I keep waiting for the local law to come up the street . . . I sure don't want to shoot nobody else this year."

"Me neither, John."

But the law never came and an hour later the train arrived and they got on it and John said he wouldn't breathe easier till it pulled out again. And when it did pull out, when they felt it make that first lurch, then start to move steadily, Teddy felt his heart abandon him as the little town slowly receded into the distance and with it, his first hard love.

John rolled himself a cigarette and passed the makings in Teddy's direction.

Teddy looked at them and said, "I guess it's time I learned, ain't it?"

"Now you're starting to talk like a true outlaw, old son."

They rode in silence for a time, smoking and looking out the window at the country-side with its hills like brown sombreros.

Then Teddy said, "Can I ask you something?"

John shrugged. "Sure."

"That woman you shot, Maria, did you love her or were you simply jealous?"

John didn't say anything for a moment, but Teddy could see he was studying on the question.

"I don't know," John said at last. "I always figured love and jealousy went together, if you felt one you had to feel the other. But maybe they don't have nothing to do with each other. I guess if I had to put money on it, I'd say it was love I felt more'n the other . . ."

"It all hurts, don't it?"

"Like something's broke inside you."

The conductor came through taking their tickets and after he walked on down the aisle John said, "The worst part was, my love couldn't save her. Nothing could . . ."

It was about as close as Teddy figured he'd ever see a man like John come to

crying; the way his voice broke when he said that, the way his jaw tightened into a knot and how he swallowed hard.

Teddy understood the feeling even as John's words rattled around in his head: *The worst part was, my love couldn't save her.*

Chapter 9

It was later reported in the *Times-Picayune* that the old man's name was Adolphus Fly. The article said that he'd been hauling a load of logs down to a nearby sawmill, and that it was less the case of the train striking the old man, his horse, and wagon that caused the wreck, than it was of the hauled logs becoming jammed under the train wheels.

The newspaper said:

Mr. Fly, local sawyer, and an industrious citizen of our fair community as well as a deacon in St. Andrews Presbyterian Church, was struck and killed just outside of town by the morning zephyr. Mr. Fly, recently widowed by the suicide of his wife, seemed a man of great misfortune. He shall be greatly missed by one and all.

The article was accompanied by an artist's rendition of the carnage.

Bob Parsnip had been reading a copy of

the *Police Gazette* when the wreck occurred. He had suddenly been flung from his seat into a heap of writhing, screaming flesh. A heavyset woman landed across his lower back and he heard a *pop,* this followed by instant searing pain that caused his nuts to shrink and his legs to go numb.

A bloody-nosed porter crawled over seats and bodies, trying to untangle the lot of them. Then the police arrived. A skinny reporter for the *Times-Picayune* also arrived and began questioning anyone who would talk to him. One of the policemen looked down at Bob quizzically and said, "Get up, son."

"I can't."

Then the policeman tried to pull him up and the pain almost caused him to faint. The policeman called for some men to come and put him on a stretcher. The policeman said, "I think he's a Indian, boys," to one of the Negroes who placed him on the stretcher.

He was placed inside a horse-drawn ambulance along with another fellow who looked quite dead — an older man with part of his jaw missing. Somebody had tied a tag to the man's toe. Bob could read the name on the tag: *A. Fly.*

126

★ ★ ★

At the hospital Bob was taken into a room that reeked of medicine. After an hour or so a man in a white apron stained with blood came in and looked at him and said, "I'm Dr. Glass," then started tapping Bob on the knees, then tried to get him to stand. But the pain was too much and this time Bob did faint.

When he woke again, he was in a bed of starched sheets and his back felt stiff as a board and his legs and feet tingled like they were stuck full of needles.

A nurse came over and said, "How are you feeling, young man?"

She was tall with hair the color of the sun.

"I feel fine," he said, because he'd learned a long time ago — before his mother stole him and ran off with the preacher — that an Indian never tells a white person what he is thinking. His father had taught him that: Yellow Hand, who was now in the spirit world and immune to such things as train wrecks and sore backs.

"You don't look so good," the nurse said.

She had green eyes and looked a lot like the sort of sin the boys at the school brought down on themselves by the white

God when they talked about diddling girls. She was pretty for a white woman. She put her hand to his forehead and her hand felt cool and comforting.

"You're running a fever," she said and took her hand away and some of the heat in him seemed to go with it.

She poured water into a basin and dipped a cloth in it and wrung it out and put it over his eyes.

"This will help," she said.

He didn't say anything.

"You don't talk much, do you? Is that because you're an Indian?"

"Careful, I might scalp you," he said.

She blinked, then laughed a little tittering laugh that had the pleasant sound to it of birds chirping in the morning. He figured she was about the age his mother was.

He felt tired and started to drift off, but then had a dream he was falling and started and the pain crawled all over him. His back felt like somebody had hit it with a sledge.

She poured a teaspoon of something from a dark blue bottle and put it to his lips and said, "Drink this, it will help with the pain," and he did and pretty soon he felt like he was floating.

She came to see him the next day and

each day after. On the third day she sniffed and said, "You need to bathe." He looked at her stupidly. "Oh, don't fret," she said. "I've done this before, lots of times. I was a nurse in the war."

She left and returned shortly with a large pan of warm water and a cloth and began to wash his arms and face and neck. Then she helped slide off his nightshirt and he said, "Why?" She said, "So I can wash the rest of you." He replied, "I can do that myself." She handed him the cloth and said, "Go ahead." When he couldn't bend to wash his lower parts, she took the cloth from his hand and washed them for him.

He closed his eyes while she washed him down below and it felt quite pleasurable. Then her hand stopped and he opened his eyes and saw she was staring at him down there.

He said, "You see something you like?"

"As a matter of fact . . ." she said.

She came to visit him again that night and, halfway through the "bath" she was giving him, she paused and said, "You never did anything like this before, have you?"

"No," said Bob. "I haven't."

She smiled and he could see the white of

her teeth in the moonlight that shone through the small window above his bed. Her yellow hair looked white with the moon in it. He wondered how old she was. He reasoned she could be nearly as old as his mother.

"Well, you're sure enough a natural lover," she said afterward.

"I am?"

"Yes."

"I don't hurt so much when you . . ."

She smiled again.

"I wonder why," she said.

"You think maybe you could wash me some more?" he asked.

"Sure," she said, looking down at him. "You look like you could stand a second washing."

She returned every night and Bob seemed to lose all track of time or his central purpose — the one that had got him this far in the first place. He began to realize how easy it would be for him to never leave this place.

She told him her name was Pearl. He told her his was Bob, "But that isn't my real name."

"What is your real name?" she said.

"I don't know."

"How is it a person doesn't know his real name?"

"I don't know."

He thought it too much to try and explain to her; and besides she was a white person and you didn't want to tell white people too much. Not even pretty ones whose hands and body felt like a flock of angels beating their wings against you.

By the following Tuesday Bob was able to sit up by himself and walk around some, but it wore him out to move around too much.

"How long do I have to stay here?" he asked the physician.

The doctor shrugged, said, "Maybe another week. Soon's you're able to get around on your own well enough, I'll discharge you."

Bob took some solace in the doctor's words.

That night after he and Pearl finished their bathing, he said, "I'm leaving out of here the first chance I get. I've got to be somewhere. There's something I've got to do."

"What?" she said.

"I don't want to talk about it."

She sighed deeply and Bob felt a little bad for being so abrupt with her.

131

"I could go with you," she said.

"You could?"

"Sure. I've nothing to hold me here."

"I might have to do something bad when I get to this place I'm going."

"Something bad, huh? You mean, something worse than what we've been doing for the better part of a week now?"

"Something a lot worse."

"I suppose you're going to tell me you're an outlaw . . . a wanted man?"

Bob thought about how he had strangled the schoolmaster. He probably was a wanted man.

"I'm not wanted yet," he lied. "But I will be after I do this thing."

"Oh, dear, perhaps you shouldn't do it."

"You better get off of me now."

Pearl did not come to visit the next couple of nights and Bob missed her company a lot more than he figured he might. But he was concentrating once more on his true purpose — to find Buffalo Bill and end his life. Just as Buffalo Bill had done for his father. It was the way he could get back to being a true Indian instead of a pretend white man.

Pearl finally came to visit him.

"I've thought about it," she said.

"Thought about what?"

"About you and me."

"I've thought about it too," Bob said. "I'm going to become an Indian again."

"I think that's a fine idea."

"Going to let my hair grow long and go live on the land my father's people lived on."

"You mean, on a reservation?"

"No. I aim to take back what was stole from us."

"Is that the thing you have to do — the bad thing?"

"That's part of it, but that's not the main part."

"What's the main part?"

"I can't say."

"Because you don't trust me, isn't that it, Bob?"

He didn't answer her but looked instead through the window above his bed — looked out into the utter darkness of a world of which he knew so little about.

"I think I love you," Pearl said. "I want to go with you."

"Better that you don't."

"A woman should be with the man she loves."

"If they catch me, they will hang me unless they don't want to wait long enough for somebody to fetch a rope and shoot me instead."

"Why would they do that, Bob? Who's they?"

"The white people I'm going to make angry when I do this thing."

"Oh, Bob. You're impossible to figure out."

"Did you want to give me a bath?"

She touched his face with a hand as smooth as porcelain.

"I do."

"Me too."

And later he said, "You're a lot older than me, does that bother you?"

"No, Bob," she said. "It doesn't bother me, does it you?"

"No," he said.

Such was the power of love and desire on dark stricken nights in a world made lonely without those things.

Chapter 10

Teddy and John arrived in North Platte on a day so full of sunshine they had to squint when they got off the train. Wind made the telegraph wires hum and John looked at them and said, "Now I remember why I was only here once and why I left and why I didn't come back till now. That damn wind will make you go crazy."

"Let's go find us a beer, then find Cody," Teddy said.

"I'm all over that."

They walked down the street where they could buy a beer. It felt good to stretch their legs and shake loose some of the train ride from their blood.

They entered a saloon and stepped up to the bar. John ordered two beers and watched as they were poured and had the heads knocked off. Then John said, "I guess I forgot I don't have any money," and Teddy placed four bits on the bar and said, "Whatever that will buy," and they drank and slaked the thirst they'd built up.

"It almost seems like that business back

in Las Vegas never happened," John said, swiping clean his moustaches. "Don't it to you?"

"Yeah," Teddy said. "In a way it does."

The bartender poured them two more and they drank them down and Teddy said, "You know where I can find Colonel Cody?" The bartender told them how to get out to Billy's house: "It's about a mile out."

Teddy said to John, "I reckon we'll have to rent horses unless you want to walk the mile out there."

John shook his head.

"I'm guessing the Pinkertons give you some sort of expense account?"

They found out where there was some-place they could rent horses, then went down and rented a pair of saddle horses and rode out to Billy's house.

Three, four hounds came out baying and the horses got skittish. John's almost bucked him off because John had a knack for riding the most skittish horses, but he stuck and cussed the hounds. Billy came out onto the porch and called to the dogs and they ran back as John and Teddy rode up to near the steps.

"Colonel," Teddy said.

"Mr. Blue. Won't you get off that fine-

136

looking nag and come on in, you and your companion?"

John had heard a lot about Cody, his Indian-fighting skills and all the rest, though he didn't put much stock in a lot of it because he knew from experience that a lot of those fellers with big reputations didn't always earn them. But because of Teddy, John was willing to allow Billy the benefit of the doubt.

It was a large spacious house with mounted heads of buffalo, cougar, antelope, and mule deer hanging from the walls of the room Billy led them into. Teddy and John could hear children off in another room and a woman's voice scolding them. There were cowhide rugs on the floor and a chair made out of steer horns.

"You boys have a good trip out?" Billy asked. "And can I get you a glass of refreshments?"

"I'd not object to some whiskey," John said.

"Whiskey it is, same for you, Mr. Blue?"

Teddy nodded and him and John settled their hats on their knees as they seated themselves in camp chairs.

Billy poured three glasses half full of Kentucky bourbon he had sent to him every few months and they clinked glasses

when Billy said, "To old friends not here to drink with us . . ."

Then John said, "That's some heap good firewater, Colonel."

Billy told him how he came by it. John didn't know whether or not to be impressed.

Louisa came to the entryway of the room and said, "I'd like a word with you, Bill." Billy excused himself and went out with her.

Teddy and John looked at each other.

"What is it exactly you're supposed to do for him?" John asked.

"I don't know yet."

"Well, he serves some damn fine liquor and I guess if nothing else the trip was worth tasting some of it. I don't guess I've ever had any better, you?"

"Believe it or not, yes, but nothing this good west of the Mississippi."

They could hear Louisa talking to Billy, her voice loud but indistinct beyond the walls of the room. They couldn't hear Billy saying much in return.

A few minutes later he came into the room again, his face a little flushed.

"I apologize for the distraction, boys. Family business always needs taking care of, it seems. Either of you lads married?"

They both shook their heads and Billy said, "Marriage is a fine institution, if you know what I mean. We'll have some lunch in a short while."

"George Bangs didn't say in his telegram why you wanted to employ my services," Teddy said.

Billy looked at him.

"We never got to know each other very well that time up in Cheyenne when I was up there trying to talk Wild Bill into joining me and Texas Jack for another go 'round back East, did we?"

"No, sir."

"My misfortune. I heard some good things about you from Colorado Charley . . . after the sad event of Bill's dying. He told me how Wild Bill turned you out, once he learned you were a Pinkerton. Such was his misfortune."

Teddy waited for Billy to get to it. Some men took the long way around things.

"I did what I could for him, Colonel."

"I know you did, and I know too that had he allowed you to go along up into the gulch you might have kept him from getting himself shot. We all make mistakes, some just more fatal than others."

"What is it I can do for you, Colonel?" Teddy said.

Billy rose from his chair and went and closed the double doors to the room, then returned and settled in again. John thought the chair made of steer horns Billy sat in looked damned exotic and not something he'd care to sit in, for fear a feller could puncture himself.

"I've had a bit of trouble. I aim to take a party of some wealthy folks on a hunt to raise money for a new Wild West combination I'm putting together. I can't afford any trouble."

"Trouble, such as?"

"Somebody shooting a hole through me, or one of them."

"You know anybody who'd want to do that?"

"There's lots who would, I suppose, but I don't know any of them personally. Thing is, somebody took a shot at me a few days ago. I was lucky. Else, Louisa might not have found my bones till next spring."

John said, "You couldn't spare another glass of that Kentucky whiskey, I don't suppose, could you?"

Billy went and got the bottle and brought it over and handed it to John and said, "Help yourself."

"Obliged," John said and did.

"You have any idea of who it was took that shot, Colonel?" Teddy asked.

"No, sir, I sure don't. And I didn't wait around in that open country for him to get a second opportunity. Listen, I know one thing, death comes in threes. First, there was Georgie at the Little Big Horn, then Wild Bill. Me and them boys was tight, ran our string together on and off. You might not believe in such things, but fate plays its hand every time and I figure I'm next on the list. I don't want to be next on the list."

Teddy was hesitant to say what was on his mind but he figured that he had no choice.

"Colonel, I've come here reluctantly. I never felt I was any good at this detective business. In spite of what Colorado Charley said about me, the plain fact is, Wild Bill ended up a corpse. I may not be any better at protecting you than I was him."

"I'm willing to run that risk, Mr. Blue. You came at my request, and that shows me all I need to know about you. I'll take my chances with you if you'll accept the job."

Billy cut his gaze toward John.

"Mr. Bangs never said he was sending two men."

"John here is a friend, I'll pay him out of my cut."

"Oh, it's not that," Billy said. "I'm pleased to have the additional help. One of my people never arrived. I don't suppose you'd know much about horses, do you, John?"

"Horses?" John said with a sort of smile, now that he was feeling loose with the good whiskey in his blood. "There ain't much I don't know about horses."

"Well, I'm in desperate need of a wrangler. The good folks I've got coming from the East for this hunt may not be the best riders and they'll require sound horses, nothing too skittish, no hammerheads. Fact is, I'm not sure if any of them have ever been on a horse. How do you feel about rich people, John?"

"About the same as I do everybody else. Just because they got money don't eliminate 'em in my book."

Billy liked John for his open ways.

"I'm paying seventy-five dollars for a week's hunt with a bonus if we have a good trip."

"Sign me up, then," John said, used to more like forty a month, working cattle.

"I've worked out the financial arrangements for your services with your boss,

Mr. Bangs," Billy said to Teddy.

"Yes, sir."

"Good, let's go have some lunch, then."

They followed Billy into the living room and sat around a large table, Teddy and John, Billy and Louisa, and the three girls, who could hardly take their eyes off John's right hand where the thumb was missing. Louisa caught them staring and said strongly, "Girls!"

John said, "Oh, I don't mind, ma'am. Ain't often you see a man without both his thumbs attached . . ."

"I appreciate your candor, sir," Louisa said, "but it is important that they act like young ladies."

John nodded, then dug into the beef-steaks.

Later in the hotel bar where he and Teddy stopped for a nightcap, John said, "She's rather dry, ain't she, the Colonel's wife?"

"I don't guess it's easy being married to a legend," Teddy said.

"I wouldn't know nothing about it," John said.

"Me either."

They drank until it got late enough to go to bed.

John said on the way up the stairs, "This feels like it's going to work out, us going on this hunt. We'll make some spending money and we won't be hanging round town where some local law might get wise to who we are."

Teddy's thoughts had returned to Kathleen; he felt glum about the way things had turned out. Once in his room, he lay on the bed and continued to think about her there in the dark. It felt lonely. He could hear John singing in the next room. Something low, like what a cowboy might sing, night hawking.

Teddy sat up, struck a match to the lamp beside the bed, dug around in his kit, and found the writing paper and pencil he'd brought along.

Dearest Kathleen,

I can't find the words exactly to convey my feelings. Leaving you for the second time was one of the hardest things I've had to do. I can't stop thinking about you, about us and what we might have been for each other. I don't know if what I'm feeling is love. I've never been in love before I met you, so this is all new to me,

these feelings. There is something I must tell you, the true reason why I didn't fight for you so you'll know that it wasn't because I didn't care, or that I didn't love you, for I think I do. I think that is what these feelings I have are — love. The true reason I didn't fight Antrim for you was because I did something wrong, I broke the law and I was worried that the law would find me. That you would come to depend on me, trust me, and then the law would come and take me away from you and you'd lose your chance with Antrim and the security he offered you. I'm sorry it turned out this way. I cannot express to you how sorry I am. But I'm going to set things right somehow, and maybe it's not too late. Maybe fate will be kinder to us in the future.

> *With love & affection,*
> *Teddy*

He read it over several times. He wasn't sure if he would actually send it or not, but it made him feel better having written it. He blew out the flame and lay back again. John's singing had tapered off next door and eventually things grew quiet.

★ ★ ★

He was asleep. How long he couldn't say. There was a noise. Something uncommon. He held his breath even as his hand snaked out for the Birdseye Colt hanging in the shoulder holster at the head of the bed.

Then something hit him hard and lights flashed in his brain and his hand never made the grips of the pistol. He rolled off the bed and came up hard, driving into the shadow with a head butt. He struck belt buckle, a solid belly, felt fists flailing at him as he drove the intruder across the room and hard into the wall, then swung 'round and into the bureau, knocking against it. The water pitcher and wash bowl crashed to the floor. He swung a hard right hand to the stomach, felt it sink into the ample flesh, heard the intruder gasp, the weight of him sink. Then a kick took Teddy off his feet, his head slamming back into the iron bed frame.

He scrabbled to regain his feet.

Suddenly the door was kicked open and someone was standing there holding a lamp forth. It was John.

"What the hell's going on in here?"

The shadow moved between Teddy and John's light. Then there was an explosion and the shadow crashed to the floor.

146

John held the light down close.

"Jesus Christ," he said. "I thought maybe I'd shot you, old son. You okay?"

Teddy felt a trickle of blood down the side of his face.

"Who is that?"

John shook his head.

"Looks rough as a cob, dead as one too."

Teddy took a good look at the man. It wasn't anybody he knew.

"Lawman, maybe," John said.

"Tell me it isn't."

John searched through the man's pockets, came up empty except for a small knife and a set of brass knuckles.

"He's not carrying a badge."

Teddy exhaled.

"We better call whoever the law is."

"You sure you want to do that?"

"We've got no choice, John."

"I reckon not."

They summoned a hotel clerk, who went for the constable, the same one that had found most recent Colonel Billy Cody and Texas Jack Omohundro lying drunk in the street and had begun to wonder just what sort of town North Platte was turning into. When Henry Egg arrived and things were explained and he looked close at the dead man, he said, "That's Dallas Smith. He's a

local mush brain and now former trouble-maker. You boys did the town a good service for putting him out of our misery and his'n too."

"We're sorry somebody had to die here tonight," Teddy said.

"Hell, I am too, I reckon. But by tomorrow after I've gotten the rest of my sleep, I won't be so much bothered. What you boys doing in my town? You ain't from here."

Teddy explained that Cody had hired them to help him with the upcoming hunt.

"Oh, that," Henry Egg said. "The Colonel's always got one thing or another going. Well, wish you all a lot of luck. I'll have some boys drag this one down to the undertaker's. Sorry he cracked your head, son."

Teddy and John just looked at each other and John said, "I wonder if they's a saloon still open, I could stand a drink."

"I could too," Teddy said.

The letter he had written to Kathleen earlier had fallen to the floor and been torn in the struggle.

Chapter 11

Dora Hand soon came quickly to realize that palm reading didn't pay nearly as well as whoring. Her rent had come due and she'd only read two palms in the previous week for a total of two dollars: Billy Cody's and Dallas Smith's. In neither did she see a bright future. Death lurked near for each. She was tempted to lie to the men and give them jolly good fortune readings so that they would tell their friends, who, she hoped, would come to get their palms read as well. But Dora had never been a very good liar while sober and men could generally see right through her, except when she was whoring. Then she could be the best liar in the world and make men believe anything. She could make the ugliest man believe he was handsome, and she could make dumb men think they were smart, short men tall.

Men in heat, especially if they were drunk too, would believe anything. More importantly, drunken men in heat were generous. She never thought she'd miss whoring, but she came to conclude otherwise.

She went to the Yellow Dog and asked the Hunchback to take her on again. The Hunchback — whose Christian name was Willard Simpkins — said, "You'll have to prove to me personal you still got what it takes, Dora."

She never favored sleeping with the Hunchback; he was dirty for one thing and had breath that stank like kerosene. But Dora did what she had to and took the Hunchback upstairs where the cribs were and gave him a ride on the Dora Express, in order to win back her old job.

And afterward the Hunchback got up and tugged up his trousers and said, "You might have forgotten a trick or two, but winter's set in and men ain't got much to do around here but drink and whore. You're hired back."

And so Dora returned to her old life and took up the whoring trade in the Yellow Dog Saloon, third crib from the top of the stairs on your right. And it was here that she learned of the demise of one Dallas Smith, for which she was not ungrateful. Dallas was a lummox that had no way with women whatsoever. He slobbered a lot, for one thing. She wasn't sorry somebody had shot him.

It was on a Sunday that she encountered

150

her next lunatic lover, one Mysterious Dave Mather, who liked doing it with his boots on.

"You're muddying up the bed," Dora said the first time they started to do it. "Take them dang boots off."

"Can't."

"Why not?"

"Might have to get in the wind, burn daylight, hightail it, go quick."

"Ah, jeez," she said. "Another in-a-hurry cowboy."

"No," said Dave. "I ain't no cowboy."

In spite of wearing his boots, Dave proved an amorous lover who did little bragging on himself, and so she forgave Dave his boot wearing. After they made love Dave offered Dora some cocaine pills, saying, "These will make you feel a lot better."

"Make me feel better about what?"

"Just about everything."

So she swallowed some of them and Dave's prediction proved right. Soon the world looked to Dora to be wrapped in blue paper and it did for Dave too. They lay in the narrow little bed naked and giggling like children.

"I think I love you," Dave said. "What's your name?"

"Dora," Dora said.

"Dora," Dave said. "Dora, Dora, Dora . . ."

"That's my name, don't wear it out," Dora said, and then they both giggled some more.

Later, after the effects of the cocaine pills wore off, Dave sat up and said, "I got to go kill somebody." Dora asked, "Who?" Dave said, "I don't know exactly, but I think his name is Buffalo Bill."

"Oh, jeez," Dora said.

"But maybe it's not him," Dave said. "That name just somehow sticks in my mind."

"I wish you wouldn't kill Buffalo Bill," Dora said.

"Why not?"

"Because me and him were once lovers."

"That's too bad, why ain't you still?"

"I don't know. Love is like that sometimes, it just goes away, even though you don't want it to. That's what happened between me and Bill; one day we was in love and then the next he was gone, got himself married and stopped whoring."

"I hope my love for you doesn't go away anytime soon," Dave said, pulling on his trousers over his boots and having a hard time of it.

"I hope not either," Dora said happily

for the first time in many years. She could possibly see some sort of future with Dave, in spite of his odd ways.

"Well, it may not be Buffalo Bill I need to kill, but it sure is somebody."

"Why do you need to kill anybody?" Dora asked, unashamed of her nakedness under Dave's watchful gaze. She liked the way he looked at her, like a starved wolf looking at a recent-killed calf carcass.

"That's what I do," Dave said. "I kill folks. At least I think it is. Seems to me I've been in the killing business as long as I can remember, which sometimes is confusing as to how long exactly that's been."

"I don't believe you," Dora said. "You seem like underneath it all a nice feller, even if you do have some odd ways about you."

"Hey, watch it," Dave said.

"Watch what?"

"Nothing. I forget sometimes."

"You going to come back to see me again?"

"I don't know, how much is it going to cost me if I do?"

"Same as this time, ten dollars."

"Ten dollars, huh?"

Dave dug through the pockets of his trousers and pulled out the loose money

that was in them and put it on the bed and said, "Count that out for me while I put on my shirt, would you?"

Dora counted and then said, "There's sixteen dollars and two bits here."

"Then I'll come see you again if I still have it later."

"Why not leave it with me and set yourself up an account."

"That's a novel idea, but I might need that money for bullets and trail grub if this Buffalo Bill proves hard to find. Or whoever it is."

Dave stood and tucked his shirt into his trousers, then strapped on his guns and pulled on his coat and tugged his hat down on his head until the brim bent his ears over.

"How do I look?" he said.

"Like an outlaw, like a very bad man, like somebody about to go kill somebody."

Dave grinned.

"You got a way of making me feel good, Dora. I bet you like me as much as I like you."

"I like you quite a lot. But a girl hates getting her heart broke. I've had mine broke plenty."

"Here's a dollar," Dave said, taking up the money Dora had counted and peeling

off one of the bills. "As a way of showing my extreme appreciation and undying love."

"That's very sweet of you, Dave, but it would be a lot sweeter if you'd leave me the whole amount."

"I've got to go now."

"Don't you even want to kiss me good-bye?"

Dave looked down at his boots.

"I guess I do," he said.

"Then come on and do it."

"Jeez, Dora, you're quite a gal. I'm surprised you ain't already married."

Afterward Dave rode out from North Platte, not sure exactly which direction he should ride to find the man he was meant to kill, thinking still that it was this Buffalo Bill person whose name kept going 'round in his head.

Buffalo Bill, Buffalo Bill, Buffalo Bill, Buffalo Bill . . .

Dave rode in a northerly direction from town, giving his horse its head and the horse had a hankering for water and sweet grasses that had not yet been killed by the cold nights and so did eventually head toward a river whose water and sweet grasses it smelled. Some of the land looked fa-

miliar to Dave. He'd forgotten that it was the same land he'd tracked Buffalo Bill over but mostly for the reason that much of the snow was now melted and the land looked different without it.

When the horse finally came to a river it stopped and drank and cropped the grasses along the banks and Dave dismounted, feeling the need to relieve himself against the trunk of a tree. He didn't know what sort of tree it was, nor did he care. Types of trees weren't a thing Dave was curious about. To him, trees were simply trees, put there for shade and firewood and to hang a man from if the need arose. And to piss against.

He was pissing against the tree when he saw a rider on the far side of the river headed his direction. *It could be Buffalo Bill, Buffalo Bill, Buffalo Bill . . .* he thought.

He finished up and buttoned his trousers before taking his rifle from its scabbard. This time he was determined not to miss. He already saw himself wearing that big sombrero and sitting in that fancy saddle aboard that high-stepping horse of Bill's.

He took refuge behind the recently pissed-on tree and used one of its low branches to rest his rifle on for a steady

aim. He was still feeling a bit undone by his earlier bout with Dora. She'd about taken all the sap out of him and his arms and legs felt weak still, his aim unsteady.

The rider came on steadily, but as he got closer Dave could see that the rider wasn't wearing the big sombrero, nor riding aboard the high-stepping horse. And the saddle he was sitting was just a plain old saddle without any silver studded into it. The rider's hat was a simple-looking affair with the front brim pinned back and the horse was a chesty mustang that looked bluish under the noonday sun. Dave was sure as anything the rider wasn't Buffalo Bill.

Dave shot him anyway.

The rider flopped back off the hind-quarters of his horse as though he'd been swept off by an invisible tree limb. The horse kept on walking toward the smelled water.

Dave put away his rifle and mounted his cayuse and forded a shallow place in the river, then rode out to meet the riderless mustang. He approached it cautiously, speaking to it soothingly in much the same way he had spoke to Dora earlier at certain times during their lovemaking. The mustang nuzzled noses with Dave's cayuse and

Dave leaned and scooped up the reins and said, "You're mine now, meet your new owner. I think I'll call you Old Blue."

Then Dave walked the horses back to where the rider's body lay sprawled upon the earth. Both the rider's eyes were open and staring at a perfectly blue sky that the eyes would never actually see. Dave dismounted, careful to hold tight the reins of his new horse and his old one and knelt by the body.

There was a red wet flower of blood near the throat of the man's shirt. Dave congratulated himself on such a fine shot. Other than the bloody stain, the man simply looked dusty, like he'd ridden a long ways, gotten tired and lay down for a rest, perhaps to look at the sky with all its nicely shaped clouds.

"For nothing," Dave said. "You've come all this ways for nothing."

The man did not quarrel the fact.

Dave searched through the man's pockets to see exactly who it was he had shot. He found a wallet and opened it up and several pieces of paper money fell out like dry wings of some long-dead birds and there was a name written on a piece of paper that fell out too. Dave read what was on the paper: *If this wallet is found, please*

*return to its rightful owner: Buck Taylor,
Ulm, Montana. Thank you.*

"I sure will," Dave said with a grin that
caused him to look possumlike.

He tossed away the paper and kept the
rest.

Then he took a swell-looking Smith &
Wesson pistol from the dead man's waist-
band. A forty-four forty, it looked like.

"I guess this didn't do you as much good
as it was meant for," Dave said.

Still, the dead man did not quarrel.

Dave pulled off the dead man's boots
and tried to put them on his own feet but
it proved impossible. The boots where
about half as long as Dave's feet.

"You got the smallest dang feet of any
man I ever saw," Dave said.

The dead man's feet were small and
white as flour when Dave peeled off his
socks.

The dead man's hat was too small for
Dave's head as well, so Dave left it, taking
with him the wallet, the pistol, and the
socks, which Dave figured could stretch
well enough to fit his own feet. He dragged
the dead man to the river and dumped him
in and stood watching as the body was
carried downstream past a stand of bull
rushes and around a bend. The last Dave

saw of the dead man was his bare feet bobbing in the water. Then Dave mounted his nag and rode away wishing the dead man had been named Buffalo Bill instead of Buck Taylor from Ulm, Montana.

Buffalo Bill, Buffalo Bill, Buffalo Bill . . .

Chapter 12

Teddy rose early and walked over to the telegram office and sent a wire to George Bangs.

Have met with Colonel Cody, will be joining him on big hunt. He has explained the details. Expect the assignment to last not more than one to two weeks. There is something I need to tell you but will do so in a letter. You might have already heard by way of city marshal Brown of Las Vegas. Will explain my side of the story soon.

T. Blue.

He had the torn letter he'd written to Kathleen in his pocket, still unsure whether to send it or not.

He started back to the hotel and saw Cody riding down the street.

"Mr. Blue," Billy said, touching the brim of his sombrero. "Glad to see you're up and about. The train comes in an hour,

and on it will be our hunting guests. I'd like you and John to join me for breakfast and then we'll all go over together and meet the flier, how will that be?"

"That will be fine, Colonel."

"Good, good. Now I must go and find our other companions who I will introduce to you and John at breakfast before I send them forth to set up an advance camp. We'll meet you at the Platte Café. Just up the street yonder."

Teddy nodded and went back to the hotel and rousted John, who answered the door with his hair askew and his eyes somewhat red.

"Colonel wants us to meet him for breakfast."

"Let me get my boots on. I had a hell of a dream last night," John said as Teddy followed him into the room and went and stood by the window, looking down on the street.

"I dreamt I was making love to a woman in a rainstorm and lightning struck us."

"That's some dream. I guess good liquor will do that to you."

"I guess maybe it will," John said, tugging on his boots. "I guess my system needs to get used to the good liquor over all the years of the bad I put in me." John

strapped on his pistol belt, then shucked on his coat over it and his hat.

"I'm set. I hope the Colonel's buying."

They made the Platte Café and Cody was sitting there with two other men.

"Boys, this is Yankee Judd and White Eye Anderson. Boys, this is Teddy Blue and John Sears."

The boys shook hands all around and commenced eating slabs of ham and fried eggs and flapjacks from various platters and washing it down with lots of hot coffee.

"Where you boys from?" White Eye asked. "Me and Yankee is lately from up in Deadwood."

"Deadwood?" Teddy said.

"Yes, sir. We was gold panning, but that mountain water gives you arthritis of the joints, lumbago, and worse if you stay in it too long."

"White Eye here buried Wild Bill up in that country," Yankee said. "Din't you, old son?"

"Buried him deep and pretty."

Teddy felt a twinge of something thinking about the dead Wild Bill compared to the last time he'd seen him so alive and confident, those piercing clear eyes.

Billy didn't say anything.

"I'm from Texas," John said.

"Same here," Teddy said, feeling it was best not to give away too much information to men he didn't know.

"Me and Teddy were drovers," John said.

"I did some droving myself once," White Eye said, "before I took up gold panning and burying folks." Teddy made note that White Eye was tall and cadaverous with a singed eyebrow and Yankee was short and dark and youthful-looking. White Eye seemed like the sort of man who would not take umbrage at burying people, whereas Yankee seemed more serious.

"I never did no cowboy work or grave digging," Yankee Judd said. "I don't consider myself above such work, it just ain't for me, is all."

They ate more and soon John rolled himself a shuck and smoked it while Billy gave White Eye and Yankee instructions.

"Go on to Dismal River and set up a camp," Billy said. "And take Jane with you."

"We ain't seen Jane since yesterday," Yankee said.

"Well, find her and take her with you."

"Jane?" John said.

164

"She's our cook on this foray," Billy said. "Good one too."

John liked the sound of her name.

"Then we'll see you boys, when?" White Eye asked.

"Tomorrow late, I reckon," Cody said. "The whole lot of 'em is being brought in on the morning flier. We'll give them time to settle a bit, then start out in the morning and arrive at camp late day tomorrow."

"Well, we best go round up Jane then and get started," Yankee said. "You got molasses in your moustaches," he said to White Eye, who didn't seem to mind that he did.

"Interesting fellers you got there, Colonel," John said after Yankee and White Eye left.

"They're good boys. Now, sir, if you don't mind, here's a list of the horseflesh and equipment we'll need to get the tenderfeet out to the camp and for the hunt after." He handed John a list that had a total of four horses and two pack mules and included saddles and pack trees.

"I'll trust your good judgment, but just remember, these tenderfeet probably haven't ever been on a horse, so we'll want ones with a gentle nature. Best place to go

is over to Ash Upsom's. He runs a fairly good stable, thinks he's a writer of some sort and works ofttimes when he's not selling horses as a stringer for some of the back East newspapers. You might mention that I'm leading a big hunt, he'll get it mentioned in places like New York and Boston."

John took the list and folded it and put it in his shirt pocket, then made his leave, saying, "You want me to bring them horses out to the house, or where?"

"The house will be fine," Billy said.

Teddy and Billy walked over to the train station and waited the arrival of the flier.

"The gentleman we're waiting on," Billy was saying as he pulled a silver flask from his pocket, "owns a string of banks in New York. Big money. I don't know much more about him than that. Ned isn't always the most reliable when it comes to getting information straight. Odd thing is, the man's name is Banks, Rudolph Banks." Billy looked 'round to make sure he wasn't being observed, then put the flask to his lips.

"It'll be easy to remember," Teddy said. "The name, I mean."

Billy held forth the flask, but Teddy waved it away.

"Best I stay alert," Teddy said.

"Yes, you're right, but if you was to look at it the other way, a bullet might not hurt so much if it was to find you with a bit of old tose in you."

"Might not hurt at all if there was enough in you," Teddy said.

"I'm hoping if a bullet does finds me, it won't hurt."

They stood then in silence and after a few moments they could hear the low long whistle of the train off in the distance.

"I'm counting on you not to let a bullet find me, Mr. Blue. I'd appreciate very much if one didn't."

"I'll do my best, Colonel."

"You mind if I say something?"

"No, sir."

"You look troubled, son. What's bothering you, besides the fact you've been hired to wet-nurse me?"

"It's nothing to do with you, Colonel."

"Has to be a woman, then. Hell, anybody knows about women troubles, it'd be me."

"It's nothing I can't handle," Teddy said.

"Just wouldn't want you overly distracted from the task at hand."

"No, sir, I won't be."

They saw the black shape of the train's

engine, the chuff of black smoke from its stack.

"Here they come, old son. We'll ride 'em out, shoot a few antelope and deer, maybe a bear if we get lucky, and ride 'em back."

John Sears purchased a string of riding stock that were gentle in the eyes and gait. He tested them by stepping inside the corral and waving a blanket around their heads. Those that didn't shy he cut out from the others and paid the man for four horses and two pack mules, including saddles for the horses and pack trees for the mules. Then he rode them out to Billy's house.

Louisa was out in the yard beating hell out of a throw rug. The girls were off running 'round the chicken coop, running and squealing like girls their age do. John rode up and Louisa stopped her rug beating and looked at him, then at the string of horses and mules.

"You can put them into the barn," she said.

John took them into the barn and put them up in some empty stalls and then grained and watered them before stepping outside again, sidling over to where the sun fell against the barn door, enjoying its

warmth. He rolled himself a shuck and watched the woman beat the rug.

He warned himself against having some of the thoughts he was starting to have about her after he'd stood there ten minutes smoking and watching her.

She's a married woman, old son. And you best remember what happened up in Las Vegas, even if she wasn't a married woman.

He smoked the cigarette down, then rolled himself another. The girls had run off up a hedgerow chasing after a wild hare.

Louisa finished her rug beating and carried it back inside the house and came out again a few moments later and stood there on the porch, looking John's direction.

Hell, she's a dry one, he thought.

Then she came down the steps and over to the well and lowered a bucket down into it and then worked at lifting it out again full of water. John went over and said, "I can do that for you if you'll let me." She handed him the winch and he pulled up the bucket, water sloshing over its sides.

"You want me to carry it somewheres for you?" he said.

"I need to fill some wash tubs out back," she said.

He carried it out back and poured it into a galvanized tub resting on bricks that had wood for a fire built under it.

"Looks like you'll need a few more buckets of water," John said.

"Looks like," she said.

He went and hauled maybe ten buckets of water for the big tub and several more for a smaller one sitting off to the side. Louisa started a fire under the big tub, then put bed linens into it and soap shavings she cut from a bar with a knife.

"Thank you, Mr. Sears," she said.

"You can call me John," he said. "I prefer being called John."

"John," she said.

He liked the way she said it.

She took a large wood paddle once the water began to boil and stirred the bed linens with it. He said, "That looks like gruesome work."

"It can be."

He watched her stirring for a few minutes, then said, "You mind I try my hand at it?"

She looked at him cautiously, then handed over the paddle. He took hold of it and felt the pleasure a man can get from doing work for a woman.

He stirred for a time and then she said,

"That should do," and took the paddle and lifted the sheets out of the water and dropped them into the second tub to be rinsed. Then she showed him how to take one end of the linen and her the other and twist out the water. Afterward she strung them across rope clotheslines.

The bed linens fluttered in the wind.

"I like the smell of the wind in them," she said when she'd finished.

"I do too," he said.

"Do you like tea, Mr. Sears?"

"Yes'm," he lied. "But you can call me John," he reminded her again.

They went around front again and up on the porch. She told him he could have a seat in one of the ladder-back rockers while she prepared the tea. He did and rolled himself another cigarette and smoked it and looked out on the land, the buildings, the trees off in the distance. He could hear the girls calling to one another way up the hedgerow and he could hear a dog barking somewhere too.

He reasoned to himself that a man could get used to sitting on his own front porch and overseeing his holdings. Then he thought about the woman inside.

I guess she ain't nearly so dry, after all.

It wouldn't be all that bad a thing having

such holdings, he reasoned. It wouldn't be bad having a wife and children who laughed and chased wild rabbits up a hedgerow and sleeping in beds with sheets that had the smell of the wind in 'em.

Louisa came out with the tea. Had a small porcelain pot and two little cups, a bowl with cream in it and another with sugar and everything resting on a nice little silver tray that she set on a small table between the rockers.

She asked John if he liked cream or sugar in his tea. He didn't know since he'd not drank any tea for years and years, so he told her he liked both and she put some of each in a cup, then poured the tea and handed him the cup. He felt special, her doing that for him.

She poured herself some tea and sat in the rocker next to his and sipped the tea without saying anything. He looked over at her and he could see her eyes were looking out over the same thing his eyes had been looking over.

"This is good tea," he said.

"Thank you, Mr. Sears," she said.

"I sure wish you'd call me John."

"It wouldn't pay to get too familiar, would it, John?"

"No, ma'am, I reckon it wouldn't."

172

They sat and drank tea like that and listened to the sounds in the distance.

John closed his eyes and felt the pleasantness of it.

Chapter 13

Bob figured the night storm was an omen. He awoke to the sound of thunder and climbed out of bed and went to the window to watch the sky. Shattering bolts of lightning snaked across the black cloth of night. The light flashed into the room, as well. Pearl slept soundly. Bob wondered how a woman could sleep through all that noise.

Bob hadn't seen such a storm since he was a boy. Out in the country where his father's people lived there were wondrous storms that charged the imagination. There were great fires that swept over the prairies in tall walls of flame. There were floods, and all manner of natural events that could be as dangerous as an enemy.

But Bob had not seen a truly good storm since his mother stole him and took him east.

Rain lashed at the window and the thunder shook the whole building. Bob imagined this was what it was like when his people fought the white soldiers. Bob

thought he heard the thunder speak his name.

Bob!

He went and woke up Pearl.

"What is it?" she said.

"The storm is telling me to go."

She sat up and rubbed her eyes.

"What time is it?" she said.

"It's time to go," Bob said.

"Oh, Bob, come back to bed, we can go in the morning."

"No, we have to go now."

Pearl lay back, still tired. She and Bob had made love several times that afternoon and evening. She'd remarked to him: "Bob, you're the most insatiable lover I've ever had."

"That's the Indian in me," he said.

She laughed and said, "I guess you're the Indian in me now."

But now she was exhausted and didn't want to get up and get dressed and leave in the middle of the night during a storm.

Bob began to dress. Pearl could see him dressing in the explosions of lightning that lit up the small apartment of Pearl's they'd moved into upon his discharge from the hospital. Pearl insisted they live there until Bob felt good enough to travel. Bob didn't argue with her, but now the

storm was warning him it was time to go.

Lightning flash one: He was naked. Beautiful and naked before Pearl's eyes. Flash two: He had his trousers on. Flash three: He had his shirt on.

Reluctantly Pearl pulled herself from the bed and began to dress.

"You better wear something you can ride a horse with," Bob said.

"Why not the train?"

"You forget that's how come I ended up in the hospital?"

"You forget that's how we ended up meeting?"

"Okay, we'll take the train, but when we get close to where we're going, we're going to get some horses. Real Indians don't ride trains, they ride horses," Bob said.

Pearl dressed quickly because she knew Bob to be a wild impatient boy who might run off and leave her behind. She didn't want to be left behind. She'd been left behind too many times by men. She didn't want to be left behind by another one.

Pearl took a valise down from a shelf in the closet and put some extra clothes in it.

"What will we do for money?" she said.

"I don't know," Bob said. "I guess we'll have to go and get some."

"Where?"

"The bank, maybe."

"The banks are closed, Bob."

Bob thought as he pulled on his boots. His back hurt from all the lovemaking he and Pearl had done earlier. He remembered his grandfather saying one time how he could tell when a storm was coming, even though the sky was clear.

"How, Grandfather?" Bob asked.

"When you get pretty old," his grandfather — whose Indian name was Stone Knife — said, "the storm comes and gets in your bones and makes you feel like winter."

Bob didn't understand his grandfather's stories. He hoped the storms would never get in his bones and make him feel like winter.

"I could go and see if there is any money in the drugstore downstairs," Bob said.

"Mr. Dalrymple is a sweet man, Bob. I'd hate to see you rob him."

"Okay," Bob said.

They dressed and went out into the night, the rain soaking through their clothes, and walked briskly to the train station and sat on the hard bench outside, just under the little roof the benches sat under.

There wouldn't be a train until morning.

But Bob didn't care. When morning arrived and the train with it, Bob would be ready.

"You wait here," Bob said after they waited about a half an hour.

"Where are you going?" Pearl asked.

"To get some money."

"Where?"

"I don't know."

The pistol Bob had stolen from the headmaster's house had been pressing against his ribs there underneath his shirt and it seemed to Bob there was only one reason it was nagging him. What good was a pistol if you never used it?

"Oh, Bob. Be careful."

"If I am not back by the time the train gets here, go home and forget everything about me."

Pearl got the same feeling she'd gotten before when men left her. It was a feeling she didn't like.

"We could just go home right now and forget all this," Pearl said. "We could just go on being lovers, Bob . . ."

"No, we can't. I already told you, I'm going to become an Indian and settle some scores."

Pearl fell silent and for a time the only thing either of them could hear was the

178

hissing rain as it fell hard from the terrible stormy sky.

"Don't worry," Bob said. "I'll be back."

Bob was gone a short while and then he was back. Pearl saw him walking through the rain; his hat knocked down over his eyes, his hands in his pockets.

"Well?" Pearl said.

"I've got us enough money for some train tickets," Bob said.

"Where'd you get it from?"

"It doesn't matter."

"Is that the Indian in you — that secretive part?"

"Maybe it is," Bob said.

Bob and Pearl sat there until morning arrived and brought with it the flier that would take them west a little farther than they were now.

Pearl wasn't as sure about things as Bob was. But she loved him more than she'd ever loved anyone, and neither rain nor Bob's secret side or the difference in their ages would prevent her from going with him.

"I'd follow you to the moon," she said.

"I don't guess we have to go that far," Bob said.

The porter brought them a nice big blanket to wrap up in and they fell asleep

like children to the pleasant rocking motion of the train. Bob dreamed about his father and a white high-stepping horse. Pearl dreamed about Bob, that they were getting married in a lovely church in San Francisco.

Bob woke once briefly and shifted the pistol so it wouldn't press against his ribs so hard and remind him of what he'd done to get the train money.

Chapter 14

The gentleman Billy and Teddy were waiting on stepped forth from one of the cars. He was well dressed in a fine gray suit, over which he wore an open black overcoat. He was hatless and his hair was as dark as his coat, parted down the middle. His equally black moustaches were neatly trimmed, his shoes polished. His posture was that of a man confident as to his own power and he turned and extended his hand to a woman wearing a fine plumed hat, long coat, and gloves. She had skin the texture of cream.

"I'm guessing that's Mrs. Banks," Billy said out of the side of his mouth. "Damn good-looking woman."

The woman was followed by a second who was nearly a copy of Mrs. Banks, except she was a few inches shorter and younger and her hat was different. She wore a powder gray coat trimmed in black satin and fastened by a row of black buttons. Following her was another man equally well dressed and wearing a bowler.

Slim and tall, with pale skin that looked like it never got the sun on it.

"Let's go greet them," Billy said.

Billy stepped lively, dressed as he was in his finest buckskins, and greeted the party, extending his hand to each one of the group whom Rudolph Banks, the first man, introduced in turn, beginning with his wife, Emma Banks, followed by her sister, Anne Morgan, and her fiancé, Edgar Rivers. Billy in turn introduced Teddy.

"Mr. Blue is my trusted companion, anything you need if I'm not immediately available you can consult with him on," Billy said.

"Why wouldn't you be immediately available, Mr. Cody?" Banks wanted to know.

"Well, sir, sometimes I'll need to scout out the land to find the best game. It's always best to keep one good man in attendance with the party at such times. Not to worry, everything is in order. Shall we ride out to my ranch?"

Billy had hired a stage to take the party in tow. He and Teddy would ride their mounts — one on either side of the stage in ". . . order to give 'em a little taste of the Wild West."

182

Billy was magnanimous with helping the ladies into the stage, doffing his sombrero gallantly. Teddy tried not to read too much into the look that Anne Morgan gave him as she settled into her seat and looked out the open window of the stage.

Billy told the driver — old Nate Hays — to give the pilgrims a little show of it, once they got out of town a little ways.

"Not too hard or too fast," Billy said to Nate. "Just enough to let 'em know they ain't riding a cab in New York."

"I'll do her," Nate said through a fence of crooked teeth.

And so they journeyed forth toward Billy's house, toward the waiting Louisa, whom Billy was quite sure would play the begrudging but polite hostess. Billy dreaded seeing her again, wished instead he could bypass the house altogether and head straight for the camp on Dismal River.

Billy swung his horse wide behind the coach at some point and pulled alongside Teddy and said, "I guess I don't have to ask whether or not you're keeping an eye out for assassins."

"No, sir, you don't have to ask. It's the reason I'm hanging back some."

"Good, good. I wasn't worried, mind

you, just wanted to make sure we had our ducks lined up together."

"We do."

Billy touched the brim of his sombrero, then swung back around and rode up alongside Nate, who was riding high up in the driver's seat, and said, "Go on, let 'em run for about a hundred or two yards, then rein 'em in."

And with that Billy spurred his mount and Nate cracked the reins over the rumps of the double team and Billy felt like a sure-shot showman.

John and Louisa were finishing their tea when John saw the dust rising far out on the road and said, "It looks like the hunting party is arriving."

Louisa didn't say anything but gathered up the teacups and silver tray, then started for the front door.

"I hope I wasn't bad company to you, ma'am," John said.

She paused and looked at him and said, "You weren't bad company, Mr. Sears. But I'd ask that you not mention our little respite to my husband. He can misinterpret even the most innocent situations."

"Yes'm," John said and watched her go

inside the house and wished they'd had a bit longer to sit and have tea together.

Cody and Teddy rode up and dismounted and Nate drove the stage up and brought the team to a halt. John descended the steps and watched as Billy opened wide the doors and gave a hand to the ladies.

"It's just about raining good-looking women," John said to Teddy in a low voice.

"Best we keep our minds on the business at hand," Teddy said.

"I ain't saying nothing but what I'm saying."

Teddy noted again the look Anne Morgan gave him when she stepped from the stage. It wasn't a long-held look, but one that didn't need to be.

Billy led the party into the house.

"You get the horses and mules the Colonel wanted?"

"Yes, sir."

Teddy looked at him.

"What's going on with you?"

"Nothing. What do you mean?"

"You're acting funny."

"Hell, I don't know why you'd say a thing like that."

Teddy looked toward the house.

"All right, then, maybe it's just me."

"It probably is just you."

"I guess so. Let's wash up and go in and eat."

"You go on," John said. "I think I'll just check on the horses, then head on back to town."

"You in a drinking mood, John? Is that it?"

"No, well, no more than I usually am."

"He wants me to hang close," Teddy said.

"You staying the night?"

"Says I should stay the night. I think he's concerned someone will sneak up on him in his sleep and assassinate him. What can I say, he's paying for my services."

"Okay, then, I'll see you in the morning. He say what time he wants to strike out?"

"Early, before sunup."

"I'll be here. And if I ain't go on without me, for if I ain't, I'm either dead or in jail."

John started for the barn.

Teddy said, "Hey."

John turned.

"What?"

"It's just a few more hours before we're in the country again, try and keep out of trouble, okay?"

John turned, waving as he did, and went to the barn.

Not long later, Teddy could see John riding off toward town as he stood at the window inside Billy's big house. There was a piano in the corner unplayed and he stared at it and wished he hadn't forgotten the few lessons his mother had made him attend when he was a boy. He felt like maybe a bit of piano playing might ease some of his burden. He would have liked to have played the piano for Kathleen, perhaps heard her sing, or danced with her to music.

Too late for any of that, he told himself.

Louisa announced that supper was being served and Teddy went and washed his hands in a basin and dried them with a towel before joining the others. He was seated directly across from Anne Morgan. To her right was her fiancé, Edgar. Next to Teddy on his left was Rudolph Banks, followed by his wife, Emma. Billy sat at the head of the table and Louisa at the far end. The girls sat on either side of Billy.

They ate with the gentility of people who were wealthy and Rudolph Banks kept the conversation engaged by asking Billy what sort of game could they expect to take and would they get a chance to shoot any buffalo.

Billy's girls watched their papa wide-

eyed as he explained about the business of shooting buffalo and how they were practically all killed just a year or two previous.

"We might come across a few strays," Billy said. "And if so, I'll make sure you get a good crack at 'em, sir."

"Good, good," Banks said.

Teddy caught Anne twice looking at him.

After supper the men retired to the porch to smoke cigars from Billy's humidor he kept on hand for special visitors and drink some of Billy's imported Kentucky whiskey.

They stood on the porch and watched the sun sink off to the west and watched the sky take on a purple hue.

"I'm anxious for the hunt," Rudolph Banks said, his face eager, his eyes full of that last bit of sun.

"Yes, I am too," said the other man, Edgar.

Billy made casual inquiries of their riding and shooting skills and both men professed to be quite capable of both.

"And what about the ladies?" Billy asked.

"Oh, my wife is a lovely shot," Banks said, "and a terrific horsewoman."

Billy looked toward Edgar, who said, "I

188

must confess, I'm not at all sure how Anne will do."

"Not to worry," Billy said.

They drank some more, until the land fell into the maw of darkness and stars began appearing. Lights were turned on inside the house and Teddy could see through the windows the women moving about before eventually settling into the parlor. He took his eyes away from the scene and said to Billy, "I think I'll retire."

The guests said they would as well and went into the house to join the women.

"I had Louisa fix you up the spare room in the back of the house," Billy said.

"I was thinking it might be better if I slept out here where I could keep an eye on anyone who might come around."

"There's the barn."

"I was thinking that wagon," Teddy said nodding toward a buckboard that stood alongside the barn.

"It gets damn cold nights this time of year."

"I'll borrow some blankets."

Billy went inside and came back out again with three nice blankets.

"You change your mind middle of the night, come on in."

Teddy said goodnight and Billy went back inside the house and Teddy could see him joining the others in the parlor through the window. He could see too the profile of Anne Morgan.

He went and threw down his blankets in the wagon, then climbed in. He removed the shoulder rig and placed it near his right hand so the pistol would be handy, then lay there looking at the stars.

He knew he was waiting for something, he just wasn't sure what that something would be.

What he'd been waiting for came sometime between dusk and dawn — he guessed around the hour of three in the morning. It was just a sound at first, something a man not on his vigil might not have heard at all. The crack of a dry twig, the sound of a footstep on hard soil, the slightest creak of boot leather.

He rose quietly from the bed of the wagon, shucking off the blankets, bringing his gun to bear in the sound of the noise.

Something was moving out there by the barn. The moon was only quarter full, the light poor. He closed his eyes and held them shut for a moment, then opened them again and let them adjust to

what little light there was. *There.* Something moved between barn and house.

He fired.

The muzzle flash ruined his sight momentarily.

There was no gunfire returned.

He slipped from the back of the wagon, staying low, he made his way to the area where he'd seen the movement. A light went on inside the house, then another. The light fell through the windows and into the yard. Whatever had been there was gone. There wasn't even a drop of blood.

Billy came out of the house with his hands full of Winchester.

"What in God's name!"

"It may have been nothing, Colonel. But still, it would be best if you went back inside and stayed there until I can check the grounds." Louisa came out onto the porch carrying a lamp.

"What's going on?"

"Lulu, give Mr. Blue your lamp and go back inside, dear."

Teddy declined, said, "Best you dampen it, it makes too easy a target. Go back inside. You too, Colonel."

Reluctantly Billy went in.

Teddy scouted the grounds but found

only a single boot print that looked like it could have been freshly made. Whoever it was could have gone off anywhere. Whatever fears Cody had seemed suddenly justified. Somebody was obviously out to do him in.

Teddy kept a steady vigil the rest of the night, his thoughts alternating between assassins and the curious glances of Anne Morgan.

Chapter 15

White Eye and Yankee Judd and Jane Ne-
braska had set up camp along the Dismal
River right about where it curved around
several sand hills and flowed deep and
swift.

"I ain't much on rivers," White Eye said.
"Rivers and water in general tends to give
me the willies."

"Why, there ain't nothing more beautiful
than a river," Yankee Judd said.

"I've seen too many men drown in 'em
to find 'em beautiful or otherwise in-
viting."

Jane had been listening to the two of
them talk ever since they lighted in this
spot. She had helped them pitch the tents
and set the camp and gather firewood. The
sun was starting to sink low beyond the
sand hills and several times they saw
cranes flying overhead following the course
of the river. They were enormous birds
with long legs and sometimes they had fish
in their beaks. Their long legs reminded
Jane of Wild Bill's long legs, how pale they

were when he wasn't wearing pants.

Jane prepared a supper of rabbit stew with the two rabbits Yankee had shot a little ways from camp earlier. He came walking into camp holding them by their ears in one hand and the needle-nose gun he'd shot them with in the other. White Eye had heard five or six shots before Yankee came into camp with the rabbits.

"I guess you ain't nearly as good a shot as Bill Cody," White Eye said, for he couldn't stand not to have something to talk about when he was out on the prairies.

"I left them others for you to go find and bring on in," Yankee said, dropping the rabbits by Jane's cooking pot. They were jackrabbits.

"Humph! I just bet you did," White Eye said.

Jane skinned the rabbits easily and cut them into nice pieces and dropped them into her pot, along with a bucket of river water and some salt.

Jane was hoping one of the boys would take a direct interest in her after supper. She hadn't had the sweet pleasure since Wild Bill had made overtures to her on that hunting trip with the Grand Duke Alexis. It had been a long time since then. She still thought about it almost every day;

how he come to her tent in the moonlight and stripped himself down to the bare essentials, his long white legs like a crane's as he stood over her. He still had some scar marks on his body from where a bear got to him years earlier and had wandered onto her daddy's property and they nursed him back to life and health. That was when she lost her virginity and she remembered that time fondly.

Bill was half clawed up and wrapped in bandages, but it didn't seem to hinder him none.

She'd said, "I never had a feller before," and Bill laughed and said, "Well, that makes us even because I ain't ever had one either."

Bill kissed her tenderly and she swooned and gave up all hope she'd be a virgin on her wedding night. Bill was equally tender and gentle with her and he felt a natural blessing, like rain or sunshine.

She and Bill met many moonlit nights during that time, meeting mostly out in the meadows. She could still smell the way the meadows were with evening heat in them and the wildflowers dozing.

Then after Bill got well and went off, Jane went a long time without knowing the company of another man until Billy came

calling on her to be the cook for their
hunting party with the Duke. But that was
now several years in the past and she
hadn't seen a man's bare legs in the moon-
light in all that time.

Yankee Judd came over and looked into
the pot and said, "Is that rabbit stew about
ready?"

Jane saw a big fat moon rising over the
sand hills.

It made her feel melancholy.

"You know, if you wanted, we could take
a walk after supper," Jane said.

"Walk?" Yankee said. "Why, we best not
go for any walks. There could be cougars
or worse out there. Grizzly bears even."

"Why, a big strong man such as yourself
wouldn't be afraid of any cougars or bears,
would you?"

"I ain't afraid of anything I can see,"
Yankee said. "It's the things I can't see that
cause me the most concern."

"I wouldn't let nothing happen to you,"
Jane said.

She could see the light of recognition
slowly seeping into Yankee's eyes.

"Well . . . I, er . . ."

"This sure is lonely country, ain't it?"
Jane said.

Somewhere an owl hooted.

White Eye came over to the pot and joined them.

"I'm so hungry my belly's shaking hands with my backbone," he said. "Smells delicious."

Jane, standing between the two men, thought she might faint at the prospects.

She looked at Yankee, but his eyes were cast down into the bubbling stew.

She remembered something her aunt had told her once when she was a little girl still and her mama had run off. "The way to a man's heart, little Jane, is through his stomach, Janey deary."

Maybe if I feed these boys they'll be more in a mood to take notice of me, she thought.

So she dished them up each a plate of stew and herself a plate as well and they sat around the campfire and ate with yellow light and shadows playing on their faces.

Yankee finished his grub and went down to the river to wash out his plate.

"Sure is a lonesome night," Jane said to White Eye, who was gnawing on a leg bone.

"Sure is," he said.

"A body would do well to keep company on a night like this."

White Eye licked his fingers and looked

across the fire at Jane and said, "I reckon a body would, right enough. You feeling sorta lonely, Jane?"

"I am sorta."

"I reckon I am too."

White Eye wasn't Jane's first choice of the two men. She favored Yankee more for his dark youthful looks; White Eye was a lot older than she preferred, maybe as old as her daddy. But on such a lonesome night a girl couldn't be too choosy.

"I was thinking of taking a little walk," Jane said.

White Eye looked 'round.

"It's real dark."

"I know it is."

"You figure you might like me to accompany you along, in case there might be a cougar lurking about, or something?"

"I'd surely hate to get eaten by some old cougar," Jane said.

"We'd be hard to find another cook on such short notice," White Eye said.

"Billy would sure enough hate it if you were to let anything happen to his cook," Jane said.

"He'd be all-fired mad."

Jane stood up and White Eye stood up with her, wiping his greasy fingers down along his trousers. Jane walked off into the

darkness and White Eye followed her.

Yankee came up from the river with his clean plate and saw that the camp was deserted.

Oh, them two's gone off together. He had been down to the river washing his plate and trying to work up the nerve to go off into the darkness with Jane and had accomplished both, but now Jane had gone off with White Eye.

"Rolling stones don't gather no moss," he could hear White Eye saying, if ever the subject was brought up.

Yankee looked up at the stars flung across the sky and thought: *It sure is a lonesome night.*

Chapter 16

The hunting party arrived midafternoon of the next day.

Billy rode in the lead along with Rudolph Banks, who insisted he ride in Billy's company. Emma Banks rode alongside her sister's fiancé, Edgar, with Anne riding a little behind on a little sorrel horse. Teddy and John trailed behind the lot of them, Teddy wanting to make sure he kept an eye on things from a discreet distance.

The party stopped several times along the way for the women to rest and stretch their legs and the horses to water and crop grass. Once they came across a herd of pronghorns grazing off in the distance and Banks wanted to shoot some of them, but Billy politely suggested that the animals were too far away for any sort of shot.

Everyone was watching the herd except Anne, who turned to look back at Teddy standing off a ways, holding the reins to his mount. John was occupied checking the shoes on his horse. This time Teddy didn't

look away when his and Anne's eyes met; they held their gaze for several seconds before she returned her attention to the antelope herd.

Teddy wasn't sure how to respond to Anne's glances, but he knew what he was beginning to make of them.

When they mounted up and rode on toward the camp, John rode alongside and said, "That's trouble."

"What is?"

"You know what is the same as I know what is."

"It's nothing."

"Boys like us," John said, "are just trouble bound."

"It's not trouble unless it happens," Teddy said. "And there isn't anything that's going to happen."

"You and me both know what it is when it comes to a woman."

"You maybe, not me."

John sort of shifted so he was riding a little off to the side, then spat some of the dust from his mouth before kicking his horse into a little trot and rode on up to the front, where Cody and Banks were riding, saying as he passed the two of them, "I'll run on up ahead a little and see how things are looking."

Teddy watched the backs of the riders ahead of him, especially the V-shaped back of Anne Morgan.

He's right, he told himself, hearing John's words ringing in his ears. *That's trouble.*

White Eye and Yankee stood at the edge of the camp and waved their hats as the party approached. Jane was nowhere to be seen.

The riders dismounted and Teddy and John unsaddled the horses and rubbed them down, then led them down to the river to drink before stringing them to the remuda.

"I could about use me a siesta after such a long lazy ride, couldn't you?" John said after they finished tending to the horses.

It was that hour of day when the sun had the most strength to it but would lose it quick once it fell beyond the sand hills.

"You do something last night in town to wear yourself out?"

"No, sir, other than stay up too late drinking."

"No dance hall queens?"

"No, sir."

"I still say there's something going on with you."

John looked at him as he untied the bandanna from around his neck and dipped it in the river and brought it up again and wiped his face with it. Then he strung wet fingers through his hair and put his hat back on again.

"I guess there is more to life than dance hall queens, is all," John said. "I reckon it's time a feller like me took a hard look at what's ahead of him and made some sound decisions. I can't always be drifting; none of us can."

Teddy followed John up to the heart of the camp as Bill was asking the boys where Jane was.

"She's taking a nap," White Eye said.

"Nap?" Billy said looking at the sun, judging the time.

"I guess she's a little worn out."

Yankee and White Eye exchanged looks.

Billy knew better than to pursue the matter for details. He'd recalled what Jane had said to him that day back at her father's place about how a gal needed to be molested every now and then. *Lord,* he thought.

"Well, go wake her and tell her our guests have arrived. You boys shoot any game for supper?"

Yankee went over and drew back a small

tarp and under it lay a half dozen pheasants.

"Shot these," he said.

"Those will do," Billy said. "You boys pluck and clean them for Jane."

Yankee felt a snit coming on. He hadn't hired on to clean no damn birds.

But White Eye started right in, taking no offense at the request. He was feeling quite content after last night's stroll in the dark with Jane. Jane had been about the most pleasant female company he had had since before he reached Deadwood and took up the practices of gold panning and grave digging. There weren't any pleasant women like Jane in the gulch. All the females in the gulch were hard-bitten and ugly and unpleasant and charged way too much for their company. He'd foregone the females in the gulch because they were disturbing to his nature to be around. White Eye couldn't understand how a man with Yankee's disposition could have fallen in love with someone like Calamity Jane, who was about the bottom of the womanhood barrel in the gulch, but he had. White Eye thought he'd prefer to fornicate with a tree knot than an ugly and unpleasant woman.

So all them months in that gold country had left White Eye a man who practiced

celibacy, which was further against his nature, and it was under such circumstances that he found Jane Nebraska's company last evening to be of supreme pleasure. He'd pluck all those pheasants and more if the Colonel wanted him to, just to be in the same camp with Jane. There wasn't nothing he could foresee the Colonel asking him to do he'd take offense at.

John found himself a spot on the sun-drenched side of one of the sand hills and lay down and took a nap with his boots crossed at the ankles and his hat pulled down over his eyes.

The guests were shown their tents, Billy saying, "I'm sure you all have found the ride today arduous. Now's a good time for a siesta for everyone."

Yankee, still in a snit, said to White Eye, "I shot them damn birds, I sure as hell ain't gonna clean 'em too," and stalked off following the path of the river.

Once everyone had settled in Billy said to Teddy, "You go on and take a siesta too. I'll stand watch."

"I'm feeling plenty good, Colonel. I don't mind sitting up while you catch a little shut-eye."

"You sure?"

"Yes, sir, go ahead. I'll alert everyone in an hour."

"I can't tell you how good it is to have you in my hire, old son."

Teddy watched Cody retreat into his own tent, then climbed one of the taller sand hills where he could have a good view of everything for several miles in any direction.

The sand hills stretched out for some distance and between them ran the blue green Dismal River where, here and there, he could see white water churning into rough rapids.

He took the makings from his pocket and rolled himself a shuck, like John had taught him, then twisted off the ends and put match to it and took a long deep draw.

He sat there reclined on the hill smoking and became lost in his thoughts of Kathleen. He tried not to think about her off in New Mexico being courted by the man Antrim. He tried not to think of Antrim kissing her as he promised her a good life, once they were married. He tried not to think anything at all about her as an Antrim.

He could see Yankee walking down by the river in one direction and White Eye sneaking into Jane's tent.

Something moved in the grass behind him. Instinct brought him around, reaching for the Colt in the shoulder holster.

She stopped suddenly.

He let his hand drop away from the gun.

"I didn't mean to disturb you, Mr. Blue," she said.

"It's no problem," he said.

She stood there with the wind streaming through her light brown hair, the sun awash on her face.

"This is beautiful country," she said.

He nodded, started to stand.

"Oh, please don't get up on my account," she said.

He looked back down toward the camp. Nobody else was moving about.

"You want to sit?" he said.

"Yes, if you don't mind."

He shook his head and she knelt there in the dry grass beside him, so close he could smell the sun in her hair.

They didn't say anything for a time. The wind sang its song to them.

"You must think me bold," she said at last.

"No, ma'am."

"I'm not a shy person, Mr. Blue."

"I didn't get that impression."

"Sometimes things happen we don't plan for or have any control over."

Her fingers touched his.

"This isn't a good idea."

"I know it isn't," she said.

"What about him, your fiancé?"

She looked down at the slumbering camp.

"Edgar knows I'm not as content with him as he'd like for me to be."

Her fingers went from his own to his wrist, lingered there.

"This sort of thing can't work out."

"I know it," she said. "Will you kiss me?"

He studied her face, the intent way she was looking at him, then how she closed her eyes.

Before he could say anything more he was kissing her.

She made a little sound when he kissed her and her lips nibbled at his mouth and he knew that they could fall off the edge of the world easily if they let themselves.

He withdrew his mouth. She opened her eyes and looked at him.

"Thank you," she said. Then she stood and turned and walked back down the gentle slope of the sand hill. He could see her from where he was as she went to her tent next to Edgar's tent. She turned and

looked back in his direction momentarily, her hand shading her eyes, then climbed into her tent and he did not see her again until that evening when Jane served them all plates of roasted pheasant.

Chapter 17

After Mysterious Dave rolled the dead man into the river he headed back to North Platte. Within an hour he had forgotten the shooting incident. He was hungry for ham and flapjacks and some more of Dora Hand. It was hard for him to concentrate on too many things at once. He rode along quite leisurely, pleased to have in his possession a new horse, pistol, and a pair of socks.

"This is some lonesome country," he said to the horse. "Why, the damn wind blows constant. I've never been in no country where the wind blows as constant as it does in this country."

Dave thought of flapjacks smothered in molasses, and he thought of Dora's naked ample flesh, warm and soft as flapjacks. The sweet thoughts of how flapjacks would taste and fornicating with Dora made his mouth water.

Then he saw something on a dun-colored bluff that made him lose his thoughts about flapjacks and Dora Hand.

Three or four Indians were sitting on

horses, maybe a quarter mile distant.

Indians were never a good thing to see in lonesome country. Dave sort of remembered that most of the Indians had been rubbed out and those who weren't, were put onto reservations in various unhappy places. But sometimes some of the Indians got off the reservations and went wild and killed and scalped folks and burned their houses, if they had any.

These looked like those kind of Indians to Dave, the kind that would scalp and murder you and burn your house.

He drew back on the reins of his cayuse and sat studying the Indians on the bluff and could see they were studying him, as well. They circled around a bit and their circling made Dave more nervous. He decided he better run for it and, as soon as he put spurs to his cayuse, the Indians came charging down the sand hill, just like he was hoping they wouldn't.

He had a pretty good lead on them if he could maintain it.

He looked over his shoulder several times and he could see the Indians were gaining on him. Their horses were mustangs and could run faster than the one he was aboard, a big chestnut gelding he'd stolen from an army sergeant.

This is turning into a piss-poor day, he thought.

It started out well enough, but now I wish I hadn't never come to this country, he thought. *Goddamn wind, and now Indians!*

Pretty soon he had to turn loose of the reins to Old Blue. Old Blue was even slower than Dave's cayuse.

"I'm sorry," he shouted into the wind. Old Blue just stopped running once Dave turned loose of his reins and stood waiting for the Indians to catch up.

Then the wind snatched Dave's hat away and it tumbled along the rugged ground like a pie plate before snagging on a bush.

Dave felt the wind streaming through his hair and stinging his face. His cayuse began to labor. He looked back and saw that one of the Indians had gathered up Old Blue and another had leaned way over at a full gallop and snatched up his hat and plunked it on his own head.

They yipped like coyotes.

What little lead he had on them he was losing.

Dave couldn't tell if the sound thumping in his ears was his cayuse's hoofs or his own heartbeat. He whipped the flanks of

the gelding hard with the ends of his reins as he remembered the stories he heard about what Indians did to white men if they caught them: how they cut their eyelids off so they were forced to stare at the sun till they went blind; how they cut their pizzels off; how they staked a man out on ant hills. None of it sounded like a pleasant way to die.

He looked back once more and the Indians were maybe a hundred, two hundred yards behind. He could see their teeth. They had good teeth.

Some buffalo hunters came into Dodge City once and said they'd found a buffalo skinner with so many arrows in him he looked like a big porcupine.

I don't feature becoming no porcupine, Dave thought.

He was looking back over his shoulder at the Indians and figured he didn't have a hell of a lot more time before they caught up with him. He was mostly right. He rode right off a cliff, still looking back at his pursuers.

For a few wondrous seconds Dave felt like he was flying. It was the goddamnedest feeling he ever had and there was something thrilling about it until he hit the river forty yards below.

Then it was like somebody smacked him with a bunch of frying pans.

Dora Hand was entertaining a blind man, Old Judge Harris, the day Mysterious Dave showed up in North Platte for the second time.

The judge had been a regular of Dora's, but this particular day he'd come to visit her for the purpose of celebrating his one-hundredth birthday. He was skinny and wrinkled as an unmade bed when he took off all his clothes. His eyes were like mother-of-pearl where they had once been as green as spring grass. His mind was partially gone, but some of it was still intact. He had been a widower for nearly forty years and frequently sought the companionship of the various whores who came and went over those years. Dora was among the latest of his paramours, and one of his favorites.

"It's time," he said, handing Dora the money. "I figure I won't live to see another winter. I aim to try and go out of this world by the same route I came into it."

Judge paid Dora twenty dollars — twice her normal fee, because, as he said, "I'm old as rocks and know I'm not easy for a handsome young woman to look at, much

less bed." Soon enough he was in the bed with Dora and feeling around on her until he found what he was looking for.

"That's it," he said, feeling her. "The road to El Dorado, the path of my final escape."

His fingers were as cold and hard as roof nails.

I wish it was me that was blind, Dora thought as the judge rooted against her. Fortunately the judge's rooting did not last long. He died before he finished.

Dora wasn't sure at first if the judge was dead or merely fainted.

She climbed out of bed and dressed in her kimono and waited to see if he would come 'round again.

It was an odd thing, but Dora hadn't been able to stop thinking about Mysterious Dave ever since she'd met him. She wished it was Dave on the bed instead of the old judge. But if the old judge was dead, she was glad it was him instead of Dave on the bed. She could see after more careful examination that, indeed, the old judge had taken the same route out of the world as the one he'd arrived in it.

She went downstairs and had the Hunchback pour her a drink of whiskey

and swallowed it before she said, "You better call the undertaker."

It was about then that Mysterious Dave walked in. His clothes were torn and he was bleeding from several places. And he walked with a limp.

"Oh, dear," said Dora. "What happened to you?"

"I rode off a cliff and fell into a river."

"Oh, that's terrible."

"Accident?" the Hunchback said.

"No thanks, I just had one," Dave said. "But you can pour me a double shot of that whiskey."

"Why'd you ride off a cliff and into the river, hon?" Dora said. "Weren't you watching where you was riding?"

"I was looking the wrong way when it happened."

The Hunchback poured Dave his whiskey and he and Dora watched as Dave drank it down before nodding for the Hunchback to pour another.

"It sounds like you were damn unlucky," the Hunchback said.

"No, it was a lucky thing for me I rode off that cliff and fell in that river," Dave said, "or I might not be here now telling you about it."

"Lucky?" the Hunchback said. "I don't

see nothing lucky about riding off a cliff."

"You would if you was being chased by a bunch of goddamn Indians wanting to cut off your eyelids and shoot you full of arrows when they caught you."

"Indians!"

"Don't worry, they're all dead now."

"They ride off the cliff and into the river too?"

"No, they saw what happened to me and stopped short of riding off the cliff," Dave said, drinking his second whiskey a little more slowly than his first.

"Then they was luckier than you, hon," Dora said.

"No, they was unlucky. For I tracked them later on and found that they had foolishly ate my horse and fell asleep with full bellies. I shot 'em in their dreams."

Dave winced when he turned wrong. "I think maybe I sprained an ankle. I also lost my wallet in that river. Dora, honey, I sure could use a free one."

Dora was so happy to see Dave again that she quickly consented to giving him a free one.

"But first, I'd like me a stack of flapjacks with lots of molasses on 'em. I've had a hankering for molasses for two days running."

Dora took Dave over to the restaurant and bought him a platter of flapjacks, which he devoured, declaring they were about the best flapjacks he could ever recall eating; allowing, of course, for his memory being sometimes faulty.

Once back at the Yellow Dog, as Dave was following Dora up the stairs, some fellers were carrying a corpse down the stairs.

"That's a very old dead man," Dave said.

"Yes," Dora said. "It's Judge Harris."

"Old and dead," Dave said. "Bad combination."

Dora didn't have the heart to tell Dave how the corpse came to be carried out of the Yellow Dog by some fellers.

Once in Dora's crib, Dave took his torn shirt off and washed up under his arms and across his chest and belly with a washcloth Dora gave him and rinsed out for him repeatedly in a small basin.

"You know something," he said in the middle of his toilet. "If it wasn't for hitting that hard water, the fall wasn't all that bad. It was sort of like flying, the way you'd imagine it would feel if you was a bird and had wings and could fly. It just didn't last long, is all . . ."

"I don't reckon I want to give it a try,"

Dora said. "Riding no horse off a cliff into a river."

"It was the river that saved me. Otherwise I'd been smashed on rocks and hard ground and those Indians would have desecrated me and left me for the crows to plunder."

Dave finished his washing and said, "I was real hungry for flapjacks before I seen those Indians, and I was real hungry for you too, Dora."

"Well, let's do a little cooking, then," Dora said with a warm smile. She was just pleased to have a feller in her bed that didn't have a hunched back or one that would likely die halfway through the fornicating.

Dave limped over and fell on the bed and gave her a big kiss.

"It's amazing to me what a difference a little time can make," he said.

"Two days ago I had me two horses, two guns, and two pairs of socks. Then a few hours later, I didn't have nothing and was about to be scalped and mutilated. Then today, I've got myself five horses, a belly full of flapjacks, and a willing woman. It's some life, ain't it?"

"It sure is," Dora said, noticing how Dave had taken his boots off this time.

Dora felt very happy.

Dave was acting almost civilized.

It was that very same night he slipped off while Dora slept and went looking for Buffalo Bill, only to be shot at in the dark once he'd found the ranch and run off by someone he didn't know and back to the safety of Dora's bed. He told himself if he hadn't been so bunged up he'd shot whoever it was that had been shooting at him and he'd shot old Buffalo Bill too.

Well, there was still plenty of time to shoot Buffalo Bill, he reckoned, and fell asleep dreaming about such a glorious time when he would.

Chapter 18

There was a dusting of snow fine as sugar on the ground that morning. Billy had shucked on a bear coat and raised the others from their tents. Normally he would have been on the scout for game much sooner, but he understood about rich people who enjoyed a more leisurely time of it. He figured they'd easily find some game farther up the river in one of the canyons — mule deer or maybe even a bear.

White Eye and Yankee Judd had built a fire and Jane prepared a breakfast of hoe cakes, fried bacon, red-eye gravy, biscuits, and plenty of hot coffee.

Teddy and John had taken turns standing watch throughout the night, like they used to do riding nighthawk on the cattle drives. They had watched the sky turn a soft red, saw the spitting snow, felt the cold deep in their bones, then later John had seen the moon come out and Teddy the stars.

"It's a lot easier watching over humans than it is gnarly cattle," John said.

"Except the cost is more dear if we lose one of them."

"I saw White Eye going into Jane's tent last night," John said.

"That's something you ought to keep to yourself."

"I just thought you should know the lay of things. Nobody else needs to know, unless you think I should mention it to the Colonel."

"No. I'm sure the Colonel doesn't much care, as long as the hunt goes well."

They had gone down to the river's edge to water the livestock. John smelt the food and said it put a gnaw in his belly, so they went up and joined the others for breakfast.

Teddy took his plate and went off by the chuck wagon and stared out across the river toward some trees in the distance. He hoped things didn't get like they did last time in Cheyenne. Trees made good cover for a man with a long gun if such a man wanted to shoot somebody. Still, the threat Cody had revealed to him didn't seem like that great of a threat somehow. Cody did not have the same reputation as a mankiller that Wild Bill had.

The others finished eating and Jane and White Eye took the plates down to the

river to wash them. Yankee refused to wash dishes or pluck the feathers from pheasants or most other tasks he deemed undignified. White Eye didn't mind, as long as it was a task he and Jane could do together.

"I think I'm clear in love," White Eye said as he scrubbed the plates with sand and Jane rinsed them.

"No feller's ever told me that," Jane said.

"I'm glad I'm the first, then."

John and Teddy began saddling the horses and getting the pack mules ready.

"We'll ride up river a ways to some canyons," Billy told the party. "I think we'll have some good luck today. The fresh bit of snow will make tracking easy."

"I'd like it if we got a bear or two today, Colonel," Rudolph Banks said. "A nice bear rug would look swell in my office."

"I'll do my best to get you a bear, sir," Billy said, quite accommodating.

"I'd like one too," Edgar said.

The women stood huddled inside their woolen overcoats. They'd tied scarves over their western hats and stood in tall riding boots. Teddy did his best not to make eye contact with Anne. But at the last moment, as everyone was saddling up, their eyes did meet and he saw a slight smile play at the edges of her mouth.

John saw it too and when he and Teddy mounted up and lagged behind the others he said, "I guess my little speech went in one ear and out the other."

"I don't know what you are talking about," Teddy said and rode on ahead a little ways.

Yankee Judd had chosen to go with the party, thus leaving Jane and White Eye behind to tend to the camp, which suited White Eye as fine as a can of peaches.

John looked back just as they rounded a bend in the river and saw the two of them entering Jane's tent again. It caused him fleeting thoughts of his afternoon tea with Louisa.

I guess it ain't none of it right, he thought.

The weather was proving to be more ominous than first thought. Low dark clouds were being buffeted by stiff winds out of the north and it began to snow when they were about ten miles from the camp. The river looked black and treacherous. Snowflakes fell in it and disappeared.

Billy picked up bear signs leading into one of the canyons — not the canyon he'd had in mind that morning. He dismounted and knelt to examine the tracks. It was a

big bear, probably a grizzly. He waved the others up, said to Rudolph Banks, "We might have found your bear."

The man looked eager, his young assistant less so.

John rode up and Cody repeated the situation. John got down and checked the sign too, walking up a ways farther, he turned and said, "This bear ain't walking the way it should."

"How so?" Cody said.

"He's not putting half as much weight on that left front paw as he is the other three. Might be he caught it in a trap or got something stuck in it."

Cody looked at John.

"He's ailing, he's probably a lot more dangerous than regular," John said.

"We best go find him then and put him out of his misery."

"I don't want a cripple," Banks said.

"They won't anybody know his paw is bad, once you've turned him into a rug," John said.

Cody could see it didn't sit well with Banks, the way John said it.

Teddy had stayed with the women but they didn't speak, just waited until Cody waved them all forward.

"Yankee," Cody said. "You want to ride

out ahead or you want me to send John instead?"

"I'll take the lead," Yankee said. "I've killed lots of bears, both good ones and bad."

"Go on, lead out, then."

"I'd like to ride along with him," Banks said.

"That might not be the wisest thing," Cody said.

"I'm paying for this trip, Colonel. I am entitled to do it as I'd like."

"Yes, sir." Cody looked at Yankee and Yankee didn't say anything except, "Okay, then."

"Edgar," Banks said to the other man. "Care to ride along? We might get first crack at this old surly bear."

Edgar did not look as het up about it as his boss, but assented with a strained smile. The others waited for a few moments to give the lead riders time to scout the canyon ahead.

"Is it very dangerous, Colonel?" Emma Banks asked. "Bear hunting?"

"More so than mule deer, but Yankee knows how to hunt 'em."

They moved on at Cody's command, Teddy hanging back still to watch the rear of the party. He expected John to ride back

and join him, but John rode alongside the Colonel with Emma Banks riding between.

Anne rode by herself a little behind Cody and Emma. It didn't feel right that she should; she seemed abandoned by the others somehow. Teddy spurred on ahead until he came alongside her.

"You doing okay?" he said.

"I'm a bit cold, but yes, I'm doing fine, Mr. Blue."

"I'd think after yesterday you could call me by my Christian name."

"I could," she said. "But others might see that type of familiarity as untoward."

"You could call me Teddy when the others weren't around to hear."

She looked at him. Her cheeks were red with the cold and she was beautiful.

"It's none of my business," he said. "But when is your wedding day?"

Looking straight ahead she said, "We're scheduled to be married upon our return from this trip, the first of November."

"You don't mind my saying, it doesn't sound like it is something you're looking greatly forward to."

"We can't always have life the way we'd like it, Mr. Blue. The world isn't perfect."

"I won't argue with you on that account. He seems a decent man, your fiancé."

"He is a very decent man. He's very kind to me, very considerate of my every need."

"Then can I ask you why that visit with me yesterday?"

"You may, but I'm certainly not obliged to answer. Not just yet anyway. Do you think we should catch up with the others?"

"Is that what you'd like to do?"

"No, not really."

"You're a mystery to me, Anne."

"Am I? I'd think you'd be able to see right through someone like me."

"No. I can't, quite the opposite."

The others rounded another bend and were momentarily out of sight. Teddy drew back on the reins and Anne walked her horse a few more steps, then turned its head back around until she sat facing him.

"I find that I am sometimes a mystery to myself, Mr. Blue. I find that sometimes I'm not at all sure what I want, I'm only sure of what I don't really want. Can you understand that?"

"Yes. I can."

"Then you will be considerate enough, I hope, not to make me try and explain it to you further why I asked you to kiss me."

"Put that way, I've no choice. I won't press you for any explanations."

She rode her horse against his until their

legs brushed and she reached out and put her hand on his wrist. Her breath came in sharp little clouds of frosty air.

"It isn't love between Edgar and I," she said. "It is on his part, not on mine. That's all I can tell you."

Her fingers tightened and he looked down at the small gloved hand.

"I want to kiss you again," he said.

"I'd like that as well, but . . ."

She turned and spurred her horse up the canyon in pursuit of the others.

He sat there breathing hard, confused. He loved Kathleen, he told himself. At least he thought he had. Anne's effect on him had been like a knife, quick and sharp and unexpected. It had cut through muscle and bone and reason. *What the hell is going on?* he asked himself.

He heard shots up the canyon, heard the echo of shots ringing off the sandstone walls. He spurred on, hoping the hunters had found the bear and not the other way around.

Chapter 19

They got off the train in Omaha; it was as far as their tickets would take them.

"I should have got more money," Bob said.

"You did what you could," Pearl said. "Don't blame yourself for everything."

They stood there for a time.

"At least it's not raining," Bob said.

"That's a good sign, don't you think?"

They could see the wide brown Missouri River after they wandered around for a time and found themselves down on a street that ran along the river.

"You hungry?"

"No," Pearl said.

"You're not being truthful, are you?"

"Well, what if I was hungry? We don't have any money."

"I got some before, I guess I can get some again."

Pearl had seen the pistol in Bob's waistband on the train when he was asleep and his coat had fallen open.

"I don't want you to take anymore risks on my behalf," she said.

"I'm hungry too," he said.

"Then let *me* get us something to eat."

"How you going to do that?"

"I've got my ways, just like you got your ways."

It was late afternoon and the sun was partially blotted out by mother-of-pearl clouds, thin and streaky, and they could smell the dank wetness of the river as they went down along the street with wharves and saloons and warehouses on one side, the river on the other. They could see ships anchored with long thick ropes tying them to the docks.

"Why we down in here anyway?" Bob said.

"This looks like the sort of place we might be able to get something to eat without too much trouble," Pearl replied.

"I don't like it."

"Nothing's happened yet to like."

They came to a sign hanging out over a building that had a blue parrot painted above the words THE RIVERHORSE.

They went in, much to Bob's reluctance, and took chairs at a table near the door where the light fell in through the dirty windows flat and dull.

The place was full of men, sailors and dock workers and other salty types,

judging by their dress. Eyes from along the bar noticed them in that dim oily light. Bob's hand sought the comfort of the pistol underneath his coat.

Pearl said, "Wait here," and stood up and walked to the bar and Bob could see that the men watched her like a pack of hounds watching a rabbit.

Pearl spoke to the bartender. They talked for a few moments and Bob could see the man nod as he wiped out a glass he held in his large fat hands. Then the bartender put two glasses of beer on a tray and handed it to her and she brought it back over to the table.

"I thought we were going to try and get something to eat?" Bob said.

"We are. It's coming."

"What'd you say to him?"

Pearl looked back toward the bartender, who was working on something behind the counter. She smiled.

"To us," she said, lifting her glass and waiting for Bob to lift his so she could clink glasses.

"I want to know what sort of bargain you struck with that man."

"I struck the only kind a woman can strike with men like him," she said.

"I won't allow it."

She looked intently into his face.

"Bob, it's nothing, really. It's probably a lot less than what you had to do to get us this far."

"No," he said stubbornly.

"Yes," she said.

The bartender brought over a platter of sandwiches and set them down.

"Here," he said.

"This your boy?" he said.

Bob felt a fast hard anger rise in him. He had his fingers around the grips of the pistol. It wouldn't take very much more for him to pull it and shoot the man in his goddamn face.

"Yes, this is my son," Pearl said.

"I'll be waiting when you've finished," the man said and went back to the bar. He was wide as a barrel from the waist up. Short stubby legs. He was like a stump Bob imagined shooting for target practice.

"Eat," she said.

"I'm not hungry."

"Yes, you are."

He watched her eat. He saw the red wet mouth of hers devouring the sandwich. Her eyes watched him until he picked up one of the sandwiches and ate. They ate until they were full and they washed the meal down with the beer.

"Now I have to go," she said. "Meet me back at the train station in thirty minutes."

"I'm not going to leave you and I'm not going to let you do this."

"Yes, you are. We're in this together. All the way. You want me to go with you, then we're partners. If not, you can leave me here and I'll fend for myself and you go and do whatever it is you have to do."

"What if I just go shoot him? That would take care of things, wouldn't it?"

"And you'd be arrested, or some of these men would kill you in turn. Is that what you want? Did we come all this way to have it end here? I thought you said there was something you needed to do, that you wanted to return to your people's land, to become an Indian again."

"Don't do this, Pearl. Please . . ."

"Go on, Bob, I'll be okay. I'll meet you at the train station shortly."

He felt tears burning his eyes. *I should just leave her,* he told himself. *To hell with her. She's just another damn white person.*

"I don't know if I'll be there or not," he said, then stood and rushed out the door.

Bob was sitting in front of the train station, the sun all settled down beyond the

234

horizon, the sky the color now of a dying flame. It felt like he had swallowed busted glass, that it was in his guts, cutting them apart.

"Bob," she said.

He looked up. She didn't look any different than when he'd seen her last, except maybe her eyes were a little different, a little older.

She handed him a fold of cash.

"Go buy us some tickets to North Platte," she said. "There's twenty dollars there, take it."

"I don't want it."

"Fine," she said and went into the station and bought them two tickets and put the rest of the money into her reticule, then came out and sat on the bench next to him.

"The next train for North Platte leaves in the morning," she said. "Let's go get us a room for the night."

He shook his head.

"Look at me," she said.

He refused.

"Look at me!"

He looked and when he did he saw tears spilling from her eyes.

"I need you to hold me and tell me you love me," she said. "I need you to lay in a bed and hold me."

He felt her tears in his own eyes.

"Please, Bob."

"Everything feels crazy," he said.

"I know it."

She leaned against him and he put his arm around her and said, "Don't cry, Pearl."

And later in the room they rented she undressed and got into the bed next to him and he held her some more and she cried some more.

"Make me a promise," he said.

"I won't do it again, Bob. I won't. It was just this time, just because we needed to. I needed to show you I'd do whatever it takes to keep us going, to keep us together. That's what love is, helping each other . . ."

"I don't know if I'm a white man or an Indian," he said. "Sometimes it feels like I'm not either."

"It doesn't matter to me what you are. You could be a Chinaman and I'd still love you."

"There's something I've got to tell you, Pearl. Something you need to know before you get on that train with me tomorrow."

"Tell me later. Just hold me right now. Hold me and kiss me and make love to me."

He swallowed hard. He didn't know if he

could do it, make love to her, knowing what she'd done to get the money. He saw in his mind that short stocky man with her, doing with her what he had thought was sacred between them. He saw that man's fat lips kissing her, pushing his tongue inside her mouth. He didn't know if he could love her again because of it.

But she kissed him softly and touched him tenderly and whispered to him how much she loved and needed him and it caused some of those visions to fade, like when darkness comes and hides the ugly things a person sees in the light.

She kissed him and touched him and urged him to love her and pretty soon he did and it felt like it always felt with her — like beauty itself.

Afterward she lay in his arms.

"You make me feel loved, Bob. No woman can ask for more than that. Nothing matters outside of us. We have each other; we'll always have each other."

He could hear the clanging of ship bells off in the night when he'd gotten up later after Pearl had fallen asleep. He got out of bed and went and opened the window and felt the cold damp air on his skin.

The bells reminded him of the wharves and that street and the saloon and the man

in the saloon. He dressed and went out again quietly, as quietly as the Indian he was becoming, and made his way down to that same street again.

He waited there in the shadows until he saw the stocky man leaving the saloon. He followed the man up the street. The street was deserted at such a late hour. There was just the sound of the man's boot heels on the cobblestones, the creak of ropes that held ships tied to the docks, water lapping at their hulls.

The night smelled of dark water and dead fish.

Bob came up close behind the man, said, "Hey, do you remember me?"

When the man turned Bob gave him a chance to get a good look at him.

"What?" the man said, shrugging his shoulders.

Bob could see the man did not recognize him. Could see he was more than a little drunk, could smell it on his rank breath.

"Go in there," Bob said, pointing with his chin to an alley that ran dark between a pair of old brick buildings.

"What for? You going to rob me?"

"No."

"I ain't going in there."

"Okay, then."

Bob punched the pistol barrel in the man's belly and pulled the trigger. The man staggered backward, stumbled, fell, struggled to get up again. Bob stepped up to him and shot him again. The man fell half into the street; his right hand dangled in the gutter that ran with putrid water.

Bob stood looking at him for a moment. He didn't feel any better. He thought he would, but he didn't.

When he slipped back into the bed Pearl was still asleep. She turned toward him, put her arm across his chest. Her breath was warm against his skin. He closed his eyes.

I am the son of Yellow Hand. I am Indian. I am coming for you, Cody.

Beware! Beware! Beware!

Chapter 20

Teddy came up the canyon in a hurry. Ahead, he saw the party gathered around in a circle, something big and brown in the center. Banks's bear. Teddy dismounted and walked over.

John said, "You boys ruined that bear for a rug. It's shot so full through with holes you'd be lucky to get half a rug out of it."

Teddy could see the Colonel was not amused, and neither was Rudolph Banks. Yankee Judd said, "You want it skinned?"

"No, not if the hide is ruined," Banks said. "Do you reckon there will be more bears up this way, Colonel?"

"There likely could be," Billy said. "Generally where you find one, you'll find others. Especially when it's a sow like this one."

Billy pulled a pocket watch from his coat.

"It's just a little before noon. I suggest we locate a spot for lunch, perhaps on ahead a bit, and give the horses a blow."

Everyone seemed in agreement.

Teddy noticed how Anne stared at the dead bear, the ribbons of blood flowing from it, the way the wind ruffled its fur.

"What about the bear, Colonel?" Yankee said.

"Take the claws, then drag the carcass down to the river and leave it. It'll make a feast for the other critters."

"You want to help me with this?" Yankee said to John.

"Sure, I reckon," John said.

"We'll be up ahead a ways," Billy said. "We'll wait for you boys."

The clouds lay low in the sky. Dark and low like the swollen bellies of beasts. The sand hills protected the party from the brunt of the cold wind. Edgar had ridden his horse close to that of Anne's, saying, "Darling, are you all right?"

"Yes," she said. "It just seems so senseless to shoot something that magnificent for no reason."

"Rudy wanted a nice rug," Edgar said.

"As though that justifies anything."

"Please, darling, he is after all your brother-in-law and my boss."

"Oh, Edgar," she said, frustrated.

Teddy watched John and Yankee Judd remove the long claws from the bear, cutting them out, John saying, "This ain't the

241

same bear we was after earlier. This bear's got four good feet."

"She stood her ground," Yankee said. "She was ready to take us all on, wasn't she. Hell, I thought my nag was going to toss me in the rocks when we came up on her."

"Mine too," John said. "Nags is just naturally fearful of bears, can smell 'em as good as they can water."

"Hell, I know it," Yankee said, cutting out the last of the claws and wrapping them in a bandanna he took from around his neck, then tying it into a nice little bundle that he put in his pocket.

"She may have had cubs around somewheres. Maybe that's why she was willing to take us on."

They looped ropes around the bear's hind paws and dragged it off toward the river, up through some sand hills, and the wind stung their eyes with loose sand when they came out the other side and dragged the bear's carcass down to the water's edge.

"Fucking wind," said Yankee.

"Fucking wind is right," John said. "I ain't seen nothing like it, except in Kansas. Me and Teddy once't found a woman wandering the plains who had gone mad from the wind."

"How do you know it was cause of the wind she'd gone mad?" Yankee said, untying his rope from the bear's paw.

"I don't know, that's all any of us could figure. We took her to a madhouse in Lawrence."

"That was a kindly act."

"I don't know if it was kindly or not."

"I don't guess it made no difference to her."

The party found a spot to lunch near a little creek by some sandstone bluffs that protected them from the wind and as though Cody himself had ordered it, the clouds parted and the sun broke through and, with no wind to trouble them, their respite became pleasant enough.

Billy broke out the lunch Jane had prepared: sandwiches of beef, sliced apples, and a jar of tea. He shook a couple of blankets over the ground and everyone sat Indian-style while they ate.

Banks retold everyone how he had put the kill shot in the bear.

"Oh, of course we all had a hand in bringing it to bay," Banks conceded, "but it was this that did the trick." Banks patted the checkered stock of his thirty-forty Krag. "It was given to me by my old friend President Grant."

"Mighty impressive," Billy said.

"The gun or the presenter?"

"Both. I know the General, as well."

"Yes, he spoke highly of you when I mentioned I'd engaged you to lead me on a hunt."

"Well, that's mighty pleasing to hear."

"What do you think, any chance at all we'll get another shot at a bear? I'd really like it as well if we could come upon some buffalo."

Billy knew they'd have to go much farther out onto the prairies than he'd planned if they were to stand any chance of spotting even one buffalo.

"Well, there is a place we might find a few woollies," Billy said without an over-abundance of enthusiasm. "But it would be a hard ride to get there. I'm not sure the ladies would manage a ride of that nature . . ."

Banks looked around at his Emma, then over to where Anne sat, delicately eating her food.

"We could leave them at the camp and just the men strike out, Colonel."

"No, Rudy," Emma said. "I'm quite up for such a ride."

"Oh, come, dear. No point in turning this into a dreadful experience for you, just

because Edgar and I want to shoot us a few buffalo. You heard the Colonel."

"I would like to shoot a buffalo, as well," Emma said.

Teddy wished he hadn't been there listening to it, this disagreement between husband and wife. He glanced in Anne's direction, their eyes met for a flicker, and Edgar seemed to catch the passing look between them but said nothing.

"No, I won't risk your discomfort," Banks said. "You and Anne can stay at camp, where it will be nice and safe. The Colonel here can tell you how dangerous it is to try and ride up to a buffalo and shoot it. Isn't that so, Colonel?"

"Well, if we ride in on 'em and not shoot 'em from a stand, it is mighty dangerous. Yes, sir."

"You see."

Emma gave him a cold look.

"Well, then, let's all get going and not waste the rest of the day," Banks said.

Teddy, John, and Yankee moved over to the saddle horses and tightened the cinches, then John and Yankee helped the ladies mount. Teddy stood aside, not wanting to make any gesture that might be misconstrued as paying special attention to Anne.

"We'll have about two hours to hunt," Billy said, "then we must head back to camp before darkness sets in on us."

"Fine, lead the way, gentlemen," Banks commanded.

Billy nodded at John and Yankee and they led out ahead of the others at a good lope with the two gentlemen in tow.

Billy swung his horse around to Emma's and said, "Your husband is probably making the right decision about tomorrow, ma'am. But from what I've seen of you, I'd personally not have any worry about you being on the hunt." Billy touched the brim of his sombrero gallantly. "You sit a good horse and I've no doubt you're an equal shot. Just wanted you to know."

"Thank you, Colonel."

"Yes'm."

Teddy fell in alongside Anne.

"You're not enjoying this at all," he said.

"Not very much."

"You like, I can lead you back to camp."

"No, I'll stick it out."

"You don't have to, that's the thing. Anyone would understand."

"Edgar wouldn't."

"Maybe you should not worry about what he'd want right now."

"Maybe you're right."

Anne spurred her horse and caught up to Billy and Emma. She told them she wanted to go back to camp, that she was feeling a terrible headache and that the cold wasn't helping any.

Teddy held back away. Saw Cody and Emma both half turn in their saddles to look at him, then Emma nodded and Anne rode back.

"Would you be so kind as to escort me back to camp, Mr. Blue?"

"Hold on a second, let me talk to the Colonel."

"Of course, but he's already agreed . . ."

"I know."

Teddy rode ahead and asked Billy for a private word.

"Who's going to keep an eye on your backside if I take her back to camp?"

"We'll catch up with the others quick. I'll tell John. He can cover me for the rest of the day."

"You sure?"

"She's a guest, old son. The guest always comes first."

"Okay, but tomorrow, you leave Yankee or John with the women. I've got a job to do, as well."

"Good enough. I appreciate the loyalty."

Teddy rode back to Anne, said, "Okay."

"Can we run the horses for a little?"

"Sure."

So they ran them and it felt good to run them and Teddy could see after they'd run them for a while that Anne's features took on a softness again. It was as though she'd been locked up in a cell and had just broke free. Like when he broke John out of jail in Las Vegas, how good it felt running and free. He understood.

They rode at a good clip, then slowed the horses to a walk.

The sky began spitting snow.

"What are you thinking?" he asked Anne.

"How I'd like to just keep riding forever."

"And not go back to New York?"

She didn't say anything for a while but rode along silently; again she became a mystery to him.

"I wonder what is up that canyon," she said when they came to a break in the sand hills. It was a side canyon they'd passed earlier before they came across the bear tracks.

"I guess it's just another old canyon," Teddy said.

"Let's go see."

"For a short ways."

"For a short ways," she said.

They rode up through the canyon and pretty soon the walls narrowed down to nothing. It was an old box canyon. Well protected from the wind.

"I'd like to get down for a moment," she said.

"Okay."

They dismounted. There was a hollow that was not quite a cave there under the sandstone, a small shelter where Teddy could see some old fires had been built because of the way the ceiling and the walls were smudged black and old chunks of burnt wood were lying scattered across the floor. She went and sat in the hollow and seemed to him like a child curious about the world and everything in it. He went and knelt beside her.

"We shouldn't stay too long," he said.

"I know. Listen," she said.

"What am I supposed to be hearing?"

"Listen to the way the wind sounds."

"It sounds like a whisper," he said.

"Yes."

Then he was kissing her. Her mouth warm and sweet against his. Her arms wrapped around him, clinging to him.

And for a long time they didn't hear the wind whispering, but only the sounds of

their own murmuring. Her flesh was warm against his and they didn't feel the cold nor see the dark bellies of clouds or taste the spitting snow on their faces.

Time and everything that went with it seemed to stop and when they fixed their clothes again, the world seemed different to them.

After they started back up the canyon she said, "I know I am not supposed to feel happy, but I do."

"I do too," he said.

"Don't think me awful."

"I don't think you awful, Anne."

"I can understand how you might think that I planned this, but I didn't, really. I mean, I wanted it, I'd thought about it ever since I first saw you. But I didn't plan for it to happen."

"I know you didn't. It was me who suggested you return to camp, remember?"

"How far are we from camp?"

"I guess half an hour now."

"Kiss me again, Teddy."

He drew his mount near hers and kissed her. He didn't want to turn loose of her.

She stared into his eyes intently.

"Thank you," she said.

He felt suddenly a sense of betrayal to

everything he believed in — to Kathleen and to Edgar.

He started to say something but she pressed her fingers to his lips.

"Let's just leave it as it is this very moment," she said.

But he couldn't simply put it out of his mind. If he wasn't careful, he knew, not only would he become the sort of man he didn't like, but he'd fail his job at guarding Cody.

He swore to himself then and there as they rode back to camp that he would not be distracted again.

Chapter 21

Mysterious Dave took respite for several days and nights following his mistimed foray out to Cody's ranch; the whine of the bullet that came out of the dark still hummed in his ears like a worrisome bee. It had been a surprise, one that he hadn't expected, like riding off the bluff and falling into the river. He was wary of any more surprises and twice as determined to kill *Buffalo Bill, Buffalo Bill, Buffalo Bill.*

That next morning he sold the Indian ponies and bought himself two new pistols and a new rifle and a new hat, as well. He bought three apples to feed Old Blue, then remembered that them buck braves had eaten Old Blue and it made him angry because he sure enough liked that horse plenty. His own nag, having broke its neck when it fell from the cliff into the water, left him without a mount.

He'd told the feller at the livery he wanted to buy a horse.

"Why not just keep one of them Indian nags?"

"I don't want no reminder of how them nags almost chased me down," Dave said. "I see them as disloyal."

"I only got one horse to sell," the man said. "One of Buffalo Bill's men came the other day and bought about every horse and mule I had for their big hunt up on the Dismal River."

"Buffalo Bill, eh?"

"The one and only."

"Well, I need a horse at ain't belonged to some Indian, it don't matter what sort of horse, as long as it can run fast and a long ways."

"Oh, this one is a mighty good horse. I 'spect he could run a hundred miles nonstop."

"Then why ain't you already sold him?"

"It's his looks mostly. Horse buyers don't care so much for the looks of him, is all. But he's a good horse."

"Let's have a look at him," Dave said. "I ain't particular the way a horse looks."

The man brought him out and Dave looked at him and said, "What's wrong with the way he looks? I don't see nothing wrong with him."

"Why, he's only got one ear," the man said. "That's about all's wrong with him."

Dave counted. He only counted one ear.

"Where's his other ear at?"

"Got chewed off, I reckon. Something chewed it off, a bobcat or cougar maybe."

Dave looked closer. The place where the ear should have been looked chewed off, all right.

"Maybe it was a bear chewed it off," Dave said.

The man raised his hands in supplication.

"Maybe."

"How much you want for him?"

"I'd take twenty dollars."

"Knock off five for the missing ear and you got yourself a deal."

"Okay," the man said. "But you'll need a saddle and I got one I could let go for forty." When Dave's nag broke its neck and floated away, his saddle went with it.

"Forty-dollar saddle, twenty-dollar horse," Dave said. "That's what all those woolly cowboys used to say who came into Dodge. I used to lock some of 'em up, and I shot a few too."

"Forty-dollar saddle, fifteen-dollar horse," the man said. "You're getting quite a bargain, I'd say. I must look like a sucker to you." The man grinned foolishly.

"Go on put that forty-dollar saddle on him," Dave said. "I'll be back shortly."

Dave went over to a little shop that had LADIES FASHIONS painted on the window-glass in gold lettering and bought Dora a velvet dress. It was green with black trim. Then he stopped downstairs in the bar of the Yellow Dog and bought several bottles of whiskey from the Hunchback and carried everything up to Dora's crib.

"This is for you," Dave said, handing her the package with the dress in it. "I didn't know what size you took, so I sorta guessed. And these are for me and you," he added, dropping the bottles of whiskey on the bed. "I'm in the mood to celebrate our love. I never celebrated being in love before."

"I'm sorry, Dave," Dora said.

"Sorry about what?"

"About you feeling in love."

"Why, love's a good thing, the way I see it."

"I know what it is to give your heart away to another," Dora said. "But I've come into some money. You remember that old man you seen carried out the other day — Judge Harris? He left me a nice stake and I intend to start a new life, one that don't include outlaws and mankillers and dirty saloons and whoring. And to be honest, it don't include you ei-

ther, Dave because you are what you are and I don't expect you to change on my account."

Dave sat down on the bed and opened one of the bottles and took a long pull from it, trying to figure out exactly what Dora was saying.

"Where are you going if not here?" he said.

"I always wanted to see Paris."

"What in hell do you want to go there for, Dora? There ain't nothing in Paris to look at except a couple of old buildings and a three-legged dog."

"Why, that is simply not true. You're telling me that because you don't want me to go."

"Hell, it is true, I've been to Paris plenty of times. Last time I was there I shot out all the windows along main street."

"Dave, are you a complete fool? Paris is a big city with thousands of people!"

"No, it ain't! Why, they ain't fifty people in the whole town, and one's a three-legged dog, like I said."

"Dave, I don't believe you ever been to Paris, France. I believe you're just trying to get me not to leave you."

"Paris, France! Who the hell's talking about Paris, France? I'm talking about

Paris, Texas; that's what I'm talking about."

Dora rolled her eyes and said, "Hand me that bottle."

"Who's Old Judge Harris to you anyhow?" Dave asked.

"Just a lonely old widower who took a liking to me."

"You were cheating on me with that old feller?"

"I'm in the whore business, Dave. It ain't cheating, it's just business."

"It feels like you was cheating."

"I've got to start packing."

Dave became quieter and quieter as he drank and thought about Dora leaving. He was feeling as low and unhappy as he reckoned a man could feel.

"I should have known better than to give my heart to a whore," Dave said. "But I guess you can't help what you are any more than I can help what I am — a two-gun killer."

Dora let such comments alone, knowing that Dave was bitterly disappointed.

"I got to go shoot somebody now, Dora."

"Okay, Dave." Dora no longer cared much who Dave shot or who he didn't, even if it was Buffalo Bill he shot. She

wouldn't be around to care; she was going to Paris, France. She recalled what the judge had once told her about having money: "It changes you," he said. He was right, she felt changed instead of short-changed all the goddamn time.

"I think it's Buffalo Bill I am going to go shoot."

"Oh, Dave, I wish you wouldn't shoot no more folks, Bill included, but if that's what you've got your head set on doing, I won't try and change it."

"Well, I was going to shoot him because he has a nice hat and a high-stepping horse and a pretty silver saddle. But now I'm going to shoot him because you and him used to be lovers. I might shoot him twice I'm so damn mad."

Dora started to offer Dave some friendly advice, but Dave waved his arm and said, "See you around, Dora. I hope you enjoy Paris, France, and have lots of laughs over there at my expense."

Dora could hear Dave's boots stomping all the way down the stairs.

"Well, so much for true love," she said.

"Well, so much for true love," Dave said as he stepped into the street, trying to re-member if he had bought a horse yet or if he still needed to buy one.

The man at the livery said, "I've got your horse saddled and ready to go."

"I owe you anything for him, do I?"

"No."

"Why's that horse only got one ear?"

"Like I said before, I think a cougar or something chewed it off."

Dave looked at the ear.

"You could be right," he said.

"You ever hear of Buffalo Bill Cody?"

"Yes, sir," the livery man said, confused because he'd had nearly the same conversation earlier with this funny feller.

"One of his men bought up all my stock, except for this one-eared horse, for the big hunt the Colonel is taking some rich folks on. Rich folks from back East."

"Where they hunting, out near his place somewhere?"

"The Colonel's man said they were hunting along the Dismal River, like I said before."

"Which way is it?"

The man pointed toward the north.

"I think that's the river I rode off a cliff into," Dave said.

"Oh, you were the feller I heard about."

"How much you want for that one-eared horse?"

The livery man shook his head.

"You already paid for him."

"That's good, then. See you around."

"See you around," the livery man said and watched Mysterious Dave ride off to the north in search of the Dismal River and Buffalo Bill and whatever else he was looking for.

I sure hope I don't fall into that goddamn river again, Dave thought to himself. *It's bad enough I ain't got true love no more. I hate fucking rich men and fellers named Buffalo Bill.*

Dave's fingers were cold and he put them in his pockets.

It had been a purely frustrating last several days, all in all, what with being chased by Indians, falling into the river, almost getting shot in the brains, and having Dora leave him.

Once forked on the one-eared cayuse, he said to it rather roughly, "I don't give a good goddamn if I ever see any more of this country once I leave it, and if you was smart, you'd not want to see any more of it either; why, look, something's chewed your ear off." Dave and his new-bought horse soon became just a speck on the landscape to the livery man's eyes.

Chapter 22

White Eye felt plum in love. He watched Jane lasso a stump. All the dishes were washed and the food for the supper prepared, potatoes boiling in a kettle, a fat ham ready to go on the spit, apple pie for supper baked in a dutch oven. The air was cold but White Eye's mood pleasant nonetheless. It had been a lot colder up in the Deadwood Gulch. Him and Yankee had shared a bedroll whilst panning for gold, had slept with their clothes and coats and hats on and near froze to death two or three times. Had woke up with their teeth chattering and looking at the stars and praying for day to break and a little sun to come out and warm them.

Why, this little bit of spitting snow, these gray fat-bellied clouds, the harassing wind weren't hardly nothing at all compared to weather up in the Deadwood Gulch.

And having a big strapping gal like Jane to share his bedroll with was almost like what he thought dying and going to heaven would be like. Jane was warm-bodied and

big-boned and strong. She could cook and ride a horse and shoot and do just about anything a feller could do, except pee standing up.

"I'm asking you to marry me," he said, watching her lasso that stump. They'd spent the better part of the day fornicating and White Eye was just about wore down to the nub.

"Why, I can't marry you, Willy." She had taken to calling him Willy, said it was her pet name for him, and he sort of liked it better than White Eye.

"I don't see why not. I'm a decent hard-working feller," he said. "Why, I used to bury folks for a living. That ain't exactly the sort of work a slacker would do."

"It ain't you, Willy. It's my daddy. I need to take care of him until the Lord comes and takes him to his heavenly reward. My daddy would never stand for me to have a man around him. He might shoot you and chop off your head. He's gone a little soft in the brains."

"I knowed Wild Bill," White Eye said. "I helped bury him. I ever tell you that?"

"Yes, about ten times now."

White Eye wasn't sure why he was mentioning Wild Bill's name, other than Wild Bill had his ways with women and White

Eye figured some of his ways might rub off on him if he mentioned his name often enough to Jane.

"I knew Bill too," Jane said. "He was a very good friend of mine."

Jane's rope fell over the stump for about the hundredth time and for about the hundredth time she went over and shook it loose. Wild Bill was younger and prettier than White Eye Anderson was, but Wild Bill was dead and White Eye, she reasoned, was better than a dead man if she had to be with someone, so it all worked out pretty even.

"I reckon we ought to walk down to the river and bring up some more buckets of water so when the party comes in they'll be able to wash their faces and hands," Jane said, weary of lassoing the stump. "We'll heat some for the ladies, in case they want to take a bath."

White Eye rose from the blanket and grabbed two buckets and Jane took two and they went down to the river's edge and began filling them.

"You think you'll be up to any more romancing before the party gets back?" White Eye said.

Jane had lost a lot of interest in White Eye, for she liked the handsome dark looks

of the more aloof Yankee Judd and had pretty much decided she'd do her best to win his attention if she could. But it would be tricky, the two men being friends as they were.

Jane sighed and said, "I think we would do best to stick to our camp duties, Willy. I think Bill would be displeased if he knew we weren't minding after him and his guests." Dipping them buckets in that cold water reminded White Eye of panning in the icy creeks of Deadwood. The cold water hurt his fingers. His pard, Yankee, wasn't keen on kneeling in those cold creeks and oft complained about them. Yankee wasn't much on forced labor or any labor that proved a hardship to his person or sensibilities.

"What's that floating?" Jane said suddenly, looking out toward the middle of the river.

White Eye stood up to get a better look.

"Lord, that's a corpse," he said.

"You sure?"

"I've buried enough fellers to know a corpse when I see one . . ."

Jane quick ran back to the camp and got her lasso and returned to the river's edge.

"You ain't going to rope it, are you?" White Eye said.

"It wouldn't be right to just let it float on and not bury it," Jane said, letting out a good length of rope. "I reckon that feller needs a decent burial like anybody else."

Jane spun the rope several times over her head, trying to gauge the right distance. The rope hummed in the cold air. Then she let it fly and it sailed out over the muddy brown river like a coiled snake and *plop!* landed just so. The corpse drifted into it and Jane drew tight her end.

"Easy," White Eye said. "We don't have any idea how long that feller's been floating; he might be waterlogged and if you tug too hard, he might come apart."

Jane played the corpse about like she would a big fish, brought it in toward shore steady and easy.

"Help me pluck him out," she said.

"Lord Almighty!" White Eye said.

"What?"

"It's Buck Taylor."

The corpse was bluish and a bit bloated, but White Eye knew Buck Taylor well enough to know it was him and not some other.

"Wasn't he supposed to meet up with us and buy horses for Bill?" Jane said.

"He was, but it looks like he ain't now."

The body was heavy as an old log.

"He's been shot," White Eye said, rolling Buck onto the muddy bank. "Look it that hole in him."

"Poor feller," Jane said.

White Eye didn't have a shovel to bury Buck with, so he went and gathered rocks, him and Jane, and they buried Buck under the rocks up under a big cottonwood tree; high enough away that the river wouldn't come and claim him when it flooded in the spring like it usually did every year.

"You think that's enough rocks?" Jane said when they'd built a fine cairn for Buck. "I mean, enough so's the wolves and bears don't get to him?"

"I reckon maybe it is," White Eye said. "I'm no expert on burying fellers atop the ground, but I reckon it is."

They stood for a second, breathing hard from the labor of hauling so many rocks, and finally White Eye said, "You know any prayers?" Jane said, "Just one." White Eye said, "Go on and say it, then," and Jane did.

"Dear Lord and God in Heaven, take this poor feller's spirit, if you ain't already, and forgive him whatever sins he may have committed . . . and amen."

"That's it, then," White Eye said.

"I reckon it is."

They both stood looking at the river for a time, the way it flowed smooth and brown with the snow starting to fall into it.

"It's snowing again," Jane said. "It's a pretty snow."

"I know it," White Eye said.

They walked back to camp, both bereft now of any earlier joy at having been part of such a fine adventure as they'd had to that point. Lassoing and burying a corpse they found in the river just ruined the mood for anything happy or pleasurable.

"Billy will be sorry to hear about Buck," White Eye said as he and Jane sat around the fire, drinking hot coffee in order to warm their cold hands and hearts.

"Who, you reckon, was it that shot him?" Jane said.

White Eye looked out across the land, the sand hills, the broken canyons, said, "It could have been anybody. Probably somebody just wanted to rob him, for you notice he didn't have no hat nor boots nor pistol on him."

"This is hard times," Jane said. "And these folks around here, some of 'em, are hard folks."

"I know it," White Eye said.

"I wish it hadn't happened."

"I'm sure old Buck wishes it hadn't either."

"I feel bad for him," Jane said. "And I feel bad for us too for being the ones to find him. It started out such a nice day and now my mood is all black, ain't yours?"

"It sure enough is. I guess the happy times never last too long, do they?"

They both looked glumly into the fire's flames.

Then Teddy and Anne rode in and were followed by Billy and the rest of the party two hours later.

Snow fell nicely from the sky, but that was about all any of them could say about it.

Chapter 23

There was a heavy knock at the door and Bob opened his eyes.

"Mr. and Mrs. Smith," a gruff voice said from the other side. "I need to speak to you-all."

"Who is it?" Bob said.

Pearl's eyes fluttered open.

"It's Sheriff Mudd," the man said.

"What do you want to see us about?"

"It's a private matter. Would you open the door, please?"

Bob felt his heart thumping.

Pearl looked at him. She was naked, her skin a nice pink.

"Give us a second, if you would," Bob said. "We'll need to dress."

"Make it quick," the voice said.

"You think that man at the tavern said something?" Pearl whispered.

"Get dressed," Bob said, sliding out of bed and struggling to put his clothes on.

"We didn't do anything wrong," Pearl said.

"I know it."

The knock came again in a few seconds.

"You folks about dressed in there?"

"Just a moment," Pearl said.

"Yes'm," the voice said. "But hurry it up in there."

Bob finished dressing before Pearl did. He took out his pistol. There were two spent shells, leaving him three that weren't spent. The pistol only had five shells in it when Bob took it from the headmaster's drawer; the hammer had been resting on an empty chamber that Bob figured was for safety reasons.

"What are you going to do with that?" Pearl whispered.

"Whatever I have to."

Bob plucked out the two empty cartridges and dropped them in his pocket, then stuck the pistol in the waistband of his trousers and buttoned his coat over it.

"Let him in," Bob said. Pearl opened the door.

There was a big oafish-looking fellow with a mule's face standing under a plug hat.

"I'm Sheriff Mudd," the fellow said again. Pearl and Bob didn't say anything.

"You'd be Mr. and Mrs. Smith, as it states on the register?"

"Yes," Bob said. The man looked at him curiously.

"Actually, Sheriff," Pearl said. "This is my son. He wasn't quite sure how he should sign our names. We're on our way to San Francisco to meet my husband."

"I see," the sheriff said.

"How can we help you?"

"Well, ma'am. There's been a body found — local feller, shot dead."

"I don't see how that has anything to do with —"

Sheriff Mudd cut her off with a wave of his hand.

"This particular feller was a barkeep at one of the waterfront bars and it has been reported to me by several witnesses that you and . . . Mr. Smith here . . . were seen with the deceased as of yesterday evening, and that there was some sort of transaction that took place between you and the deceased, one Harry McGrew."

"I don't know quite what to say," Pearl said.

Bob felt the handle of that pistol there against his side under the coat. He sure didn't want to kill another man if he didn't have to but he might have to, he told himself.

Sheriff Mudd cleared his throat roughly, said, "Perhaps it would be better if you and me spoke without the boy being present,

ma'am, considering the delicacy of what I have to ask you."

"Yes, perhaps that would be best," Pearl said.

"Bob, why don't you go down to the dining room and order us some breakfast and I'll be along shortly."

"Oh, Mother, I am a full-grown man now, there's no need for me to leave the room."

"I insist."

"No, Mother, I'd like to stay and hear what the sheriff has to say."

"Son, go on do as your ma says," the sheriff ordered. He was wearing a large sidearm in a holster high on his left hip. He had the eyes of a man who'd never spent one happy day in his entire life.

"Go on, Bob," Pearl said, trying to get Bob to read her expression, that plea in her eyes, the same look she had when she insisted he leave the tavern the day before.

"We've got that train to catch this morning, Mother. We can't be late," Bob said.

The sheriff pulled a pocket watch from his waistcoat, glanced at it, and said, "The flier don't leave until nine, you've got a good hour still."

"Why don't you take our valise, Bob,"

Pearl said. "That way we'll be all set to go as soon as I come downstairs."

Bob picked up the valise, looked at the unmade bed, their warmth still in it.

"Don't be too long, okay, Mother?"

He put enough edge on his voice to let Pearl know he wasn't happy with the situation.

"No, I promise," she said. "I won't be detained long, will I, Sheriff?"

"No, ma'am."

Bob saw it then, the sheriff reaching out and taking Pearl by the elbow, the hungry look in his eyes as he did. Bob jerked the pistol free of its hiding place and aimed it at him, thumbing back the hammer as he did.

"Turn loose of her, you son of a bitch."

"Easy, boy."

"Back on up," Bob said.

Pearl started to say something but Bob jerked his head toward the door.

"Go over to the train station and wait for me there," he said.

She saw the look in Bob's eyes and did not quarrel with him but instead took the valise and went out, closing the door behind her.

Soon as she left the sheriff said, "What you gonna do, son?"

Bob told him to ease the pistol out of its holster and toss it on the bed, and when he had, Bob cracked him hard on the back of the skull and the big bastard dropped like a shot horse.

"Goddamn!" the lawman gasped from his hands and knees.

Blood trickled from the place where the iron split his head. It dribbled through his fingers and onto the floor.

"Shit!" he said.

Bob took the sheriff's gun and aimed it at him.

"You ever think of what it would feel like to get shot in the face by your own gun?" Bob said.

The man was trying to stanch the flow of blood with his fingers but wasn't having very much success. His blood leaked down through his hand and dripped off his bony wrist.

"I know now you killed that barkeep," the sheriff said. "It could have been self-defense. I could let it go as self-defense. It ain't too late for that. Hell, I can write it off as *unsolved,* but you're going to have to put that gun down."

Bob hit him again, this time hard enough over the skull to knock him senseless. The sheriff moaned and rolled onto his side

and Bob hit him again and again until he stopped moaning and just lay there bleeding.

Bob tied him up in bedsheets and gagged him with his own tobacco-stained kerchief and rolled him under the bed after he took the wallet from his pocket and the money in it.

"You're just another white man who is paying for your sins," Bob said. Only the sheriff wasn't conscious to hear it.

Bob found Pearl sitting there on a bench in front of the station.

Pearl said, "Please tell me you didn't kill him."

"I did what I needed to so he won't follow us."

They got on the train when it came and sat in silence.

The train rumbled along and after a time Pearl said, "I can't be part of killing. I can't be an accomplice to it, Bob."

"Don't tell me nothing about it, okay," Bob said.

"Why are you angry at me?"

"I don't need a mother," Bob said. "Especially one that's white."

"Fine. But tell me, did you go back and murder that barkeeper the way the sheriff said?"

Bob didn't answer.

They watched out the windows. It had begun to snow and the snow fell among the sage and into the bare trees and into creeks that cut crooked scars in the land. Here and there they saw small herds of cattle, looking forlorn, standing in the snow.

"I didn't kill the sheriff," Bob said at last, "but I should have."

"I just don't want them to catch you and hang you," Pearl said.

"It's too late for that."

"That saloon keeper last night. Did you . . ."

"No," Bob said. "I didn't kill him either."

She touched his arm.

"There is no place we can go where they won't find us if you killed someone."

"I know it," Bob said. "The whites are everywhere. But I didn't kill anyone."

"I'm sorry if I've hurt you," Pearl said.

"You can strike off on your own if you want."

"We don't deserve this. Let's try not to be mad at each other, Bob. Let's try and love each other while we can. Everything I do is for you. Tell me that you believe me."

The snow fell on the plains and in the old grass that would become new again in the spring.

"Love is a strange word," Bob said.

"It's all we have left to us."

Snow fell from the sky and fell and fell and fell.

Chapter 24

White Eye warned Jane that they probably shouldn't tell Billy in front of the hunting guests about finding Buck's corpse.

"The Colonel wouldn't want us to shine a black light on things," White Eye said. "Those rich folks might decide to call off the hunt and return back East they know there's dead men floating in the rivers out here."

Jane was in complete agreement.

"It's a bad sign all the way around," she said.

Soon as supper was finished and the talk of the day's hunt — how they'd killed one bear but not another — and tomorrow's plan to ride out and find a few buffalo had been discussed and everyone made for the tents as night fell early, White Eye said to Billy, "They's something me and Jane need to tell you."

"Don't tell me you two have fallen in love and aim to get married," Billy said with a wide grin. He had been drinking heavy blackberry wine and was in good

spirits, in spite of the relative unsuccessful day they'd had hunting.

Teddy stole a final glance at Anne as she prepared to enter her tent. Edgar had gone off into the brush.

"No, sir, I wish it was that good of news," White Eye said.

"Spit it out," Yankee said. Yankee was still irritated about the entire affair between Jane and White Eye; he wasn't sure why he was irritated about it, he just was.

White Eye told them about finding Buck Taylor, how they buried him under a cairn of rocks. He and Jane walked Billy, John, Yankee, and Teddy up to the cairn. Billy took off his sombrero and closed his eyes. The wind fluttered his hair and snow fell in it and caught on his eyelashes.

John and Teddy stood somber until Billy finished his silent prayer.

"He was a good hand," Billy said. "A good hand and a good man."

"He had a big hole in him," White Eye said. "Somebody shot him and tossed him in that river. He didn't drown. It wasn't no accident or anything."

"This ain't good," Billy said.

"Maybe you should consider canceling the hunt," Teddy suggested.

"This," Billy said, nodding toward the

cairn, "might not have anything to do with us."

"No, sir, you're right. It might not, but still, you could be in some danger and so could your guests, if there's a killer roaming loose." If Teddy had been forced to be completely honest, he would have told Cody that one of his concerns was especially for Anne's safety.

"That's why I hired you, old son, to make sure that bad things don't happen to any of these good folk, or to me."

Billy's breath smelled like the fruit wine.

"You think you can handle this for me while I go and worry about where we'll find some buffs tomorrow?"

"Yes, sir."

"Good."

Billy said to the others, "Best we keep this piece of news among ourselves."

They looked back toward the tents, some of which had oil lamps lit inside them.

"They're the reason we're all here," Billy said. "We can't afford anything to ruin this hunt and the bonus money that'll come with it."

Billy and the others walked back to the camp and Teddy pulled John aside, said, "Let's talk."

John and Teddy walked off a distance.

John rolled himself a shuck and lit it.

"This is some bad business," John said. "You just don't find dead men floating in rivers, most generally."

"I've got a bad feeling about it too, John. I think whoever took the shot at the Colonel the other day shot Buck Taylor. It just doesn't wash that the two events would be unrelated."

"What you want to do, old son?"

"I think we take turns standing watch from here out."

John shrugged.

"Whatever you think."

"I'll stand first watch," Teddy said.

John smoked some more, then started back to camp.

"There's something else I guess you need to know."

"You don't have to say it," John said. "I seen the way you two were. I guess if I seen it, maybe her fiancé saw it too. Wake me when you need relief."

John walked down to his tent and climbed in.

Teddy went to the wagon and took out a Winchester and an extra blanket, then went to the fire, where Yankee Judd sat wrapped up in a big coat, sipping a cup of coffee.

"That coffee any good?" Teddy asked. Yankee looked at him, shadows playing over his face.

"It'll do if you've got paint you need removed," Yankee said.

Teddy poured himself a cup.

"Me and John are going to take turns standing watch tonight. Just so you know."

Yankee nodded.

"Finding Buck like he was is a bad omen," Yankee said into his cup.

"I don't expect any real trouble. And if there is, there are plenty of us that can shoot well enough to handle whatever comes our way."

"I didn't come on this hunt to shoot no humans," Yankee said.

"None of us did."

Teddy sipped the coffee; it warmed him some, but not as much as his thoughts of Anne.

"This is some lonesome country," Yankee said.

"I've been in just as bad."

"I guess we all have. You want me to take some of the watch too?"

"Not necessary," Teddy said. "Me and John can handle it. We put in lots of time night watching herds we run from Texas up to Kansas."

Snow fell into the fire and was eaten up by the heat.

"I wish it would quit snowing," Yankee said.

"I do too."

"Bad bears and now a dead man in the river," Yankee said. "I don't care for none of it."

"I'm going to go off up yonder and stand my watch," Teddy said and tossed the dregs of his coffee into the snow, then walked off toward some sand hills a hundred yards from camp; a place he could see but not be seen. The snow was almost blue in the darkness, and the sky was the red of a bloodstained shirt.

Teddy scaled the slope of the hill and found a notch just below the top. He settled into it and tried not to think too hard on the falling snow and the cold and Anne and Kathleen or the dead man. The only thing he needed to concentrate on, he told himself, was the Colonel's safety and that of the party.

He heard the river slip its banks; the way it moved gave it the sound of an eternal whisper. He saw White Eye Anderson go inside Jane's tent, then saw the lamplight go out. He turned his attention to Anne's tent, saw her shadow moving around in-

side, felt drawn to go to her, knew that he couldn't.

One by one the lights flicked out inside the tents until there was just the campfire and Yankee Judd still sitting close to it. Then finally Yankee stood and went to his tent and went inside without bothering to turn on any light. The horses in the remuda stood sleeping. Teddy took out his makings and rolled a shuck, taking his time as he did. He'd stand watch four hours, then go wake John for the last watch. The Colonel would want to get an early start, probably before daylight. Teddy debated about what to do. He didn't think it wise to divide the camp, leave some behind while the others went on the hunt. Not now, not with one man already buried.

He twisted the ends of his shuck and struck a match, cupping it in his hands, and lowered the end of the cigarette to it, then snapped out the flame as he drew a lung full of smoke.

Somewhere far off a wolf called, then fell silent, then called again. There wasn't an answering call. *That old wolf is looking for its mate,* Teddy thought. *Everything's lonesome.*

He thought of Kathleen back in Silver City. Was she sharing her bed with

Antrim? Had they had a quick marriage so Antrim could bed her before it was too late? Was she lying awake now, thinking of him and not Antrim?

He smoked and held the Winchester across his lap and brought the blanket up over his shoulders.

Well, come on if you're coming.

He would have preferred for whoever it was that was out there to make his play, but he knew it wasn't going to happen that easy. The snow eventually came to an end and off to the west he saw a piece of moon carved out of the black sky, then some stars and pretty soon more stars and with them came the cold, hard, and bone-deep and he had to roll himself another shuck and smoke it. Time went by slow as death.

When he figured his watch was up, he stood on stiff legs and made his way back down to camp and tapped John on the soles of his boots and John came awake, saying, "Huh, okay, I've got her," and climbed out of his tent and said, "Jesus Christ, it's cold."

Teddy handed him the blanket and the Winchester, said, "I was sitting up yonder in that notch; it's out of the wind." Then he went over and stirred the fire and threw more wood on it and warmed his hands

and John came over and said, "I reckon that coffee's about burned to tar, but pour me some anyway, would you?"

John rolled himself a shuck and sipped some of the coffee and said, "I hope they get a buff or two tomorrow so we can get the hell on back. I need to get myself on down to some warm country; I ain't been warm since I left Texas."

"John, you're not obligated to stay," Teddy said. "Nobody, especially me, would read anything into if you want to get on down the line. Fact is, I think it would be a smart thing for you to do. You want, head on down to Juarez and if things work out for me, I'll meet you down there by the spring."

John swallowed the last of his coffee with a grimace, set the empty cup in the snow.

"I appreciate the sentiments, old son. And maybe I will and maybe I won't. But not tonight, okay. Go catch you some shut-eye."

Then he watched John stand and walk off toward the rise, the shadow of him plain against the snow, the crunch of his boots sinking down in it.

Teddy climbed in his tent and pulled the blankets around him and immediately wished that Anne were there with him.

Stop being a damn fool, he told himself.

He thought he heard something, footsteps outside his tent. He held his breath. But then there wasn't anything more. He felt a deep disappointment, knowing it wasn't her, then closed his eyes and pretty soon John was tapping on the soles of his boots, saying, "Colonel's up, he wants to talk to us."

Teddy crawled out of the tent. Billy was squatted by the fire, his hands extended toward it. Teddy saw a wolf's footprints in the snow by his tent, walked over to the fire with John, and squatted down near it for some warmth to come into them.

"If we're to locate buffs today we'd best get an early start," Billy said.

"I don't feel good about us dividing the camp," Teddy said.

"I know it. I thought about that too. I'm going to leave Yankee behind with White Eye and Jane. They're all three good shots."

"What about the women?"

"I'll leave that to their men," Billy said.

"I don't care for it much. I think it's best we keep everyone together, in light of what's happened."

"It'd slow us down too much if we're to make that buffalo jump I've got in mind.

It'll take us half a day's hard ride to get there as it is. The weather's turning bad, as well. Wouldn't do for us to get caught out on that open country in a bad storm. The women would be better off here and I'll recommend the same to Banks."

"What if we left John behind, as well?"

Billy looked at John.

"All right," he said.

"I ain't for it," John said. "But I'm just the hired help and if you want me to stay here, I will."

"Four of us riding hard, we could make good time," Billy said. "That suit you okay?"

Teddy nodded.

"Then it's done. Let's go roust them out of their nests."

After they'd gotten the others up, Teddy and John saddled the horses. John said over the back of his, "You know I ain't for this, me staying behind to wet-nurse the women."

"I know you're not, John. I'm asking you to do it on my account."

"You think something bad's going to happen, don't you?"

"Anything does, it's you I'd trust most to handle it."

John looked at the sky. It was a terrible

shade of gray, like a dirty rag. He could feel more snow in it too.

"Goddamn, but I bet it's plenty warm down in Mexico about now," John said.

"I bet it is too."

They finished saddling the horses and brought 'em into camp and the men mounted up — Billy, Rudolph Banks, Edgar Rice, and Teddy. Then Billy said, "Let's get to the chase, boys!" And they rode off.

John rubbed his chin and thought to himself he could use a shave one of these days.

Chapter 25

Mysterious Dave made sure to skirt wide the ranch of Buffalo Bill and eventually arrived by the more circuitous route the same river in which he'd fallen in and lost his horse, gun, and saddle. The river looked like it wouldn't hurt a flea; it moved slow and brown as molasses.

"I'll just follow along it, but not too close," Dave said to his horse. The horse flicked its one ear. Dave was in a sulky mood. The thought of Dora leaving him for a dead rich man's money didn't sit well. It was all because of that goddamn Buffalo Bill, the way he saw it. If Buffalo Bill hadn't come riding along that day with that big sombrero and that fancy silver saddle on that high-stepping steed and tempted Dave to take a shot at him, he'd never met Dora and fallen in love with her, only to lose her love to a dead man's money. Life just didn't seem fair; it seemed downright cruel and mean as a rattlesnake sometimes.

Well, the river was floating brown and

peaceful and slow under the gray skies. He'd just have to follow it until he found Buffalo Bill and then dust him front and back and take his big sombrero and silver saddle and high-stepping horse. He'd look a lot better riding Bill's high-stepper than he would a horse with one ear gnawed off.

Dave rode along until he rode clean out of daylight. He made camp, gathering dry wood and setting it ablaze with a kitchen match from several of which he kept in a tobacco can. He chewed some old beef jerky he found in one of his pockets that he forgot was there. He thought it might be some of the same jerky from that time him and Bat Masterson were buffalo skinners back around 'seventy, in along there.

Buffalo skinning was about the worst job he ever had as far as he could remember. A lot of his life — the parts he could recall — had not worked out very well.

"I should have planned things out better," he said. The horse cropped some old brittle grass it had pawed snow away from and swished its broom tail back and forth and flicked its ear, oblivious to Dave's conversation.

"That's always been my problem, I never was a good planner."

Dave remembered a time when he was a

lawman — he never knew why he remembered certain things and not others — it might have been in Kansas, or it might have been in Wyoming. He wore his gun backward then because this Texas Ranger came along and said wearing your gun backward on the opposite hip made you a lot faster on the draw. So Dave took to wearing his that way until a freed slave named Nigger Nate shot him in a gambling den with a gun worn in the regular fashion. After that, Dave wore his gun the way he always wore it before the Texas Ranger came along. Dave thought that Nigger Nate's bullet was still in him somewhere, that the medico never did get it out. Somewhere in his lung, because his left lung hurt when it got cold or there was to come a storm. His left lung hurt now. Dave looked at the dirty-cotton-shirt sky.

"I was a lawman, onc't," he said to the horse that continued to paw the ground for old grass.

"I think I was pretty good at it too. I reckon, I should have stuck with it. I might not be here now camped along this river, looking to shoot a feller I never met. It's going to snow. I can feel it in my lung."

Dave rubbed his jaw and in his mind he saw a little cabin and sitting inside was a

nice woman who was sort of big and plump and had lots of long black hair.

He chewed his jerky and tried to look inside the vision in his skull.

It was a nice big room with a big warm fireplace and he could hear the fire crackling and popping from the sap that dripped out from the logs burning. He could smell bread baking and there was some kids — two of them — sleeping in a bed in the corner behind a blanket hung up for a curtain. They were sort of pudgy and cute and slept like little fat kittens.

Dave had rested his boots near the campfire and he had to shift them back away because they'd grown too hot.

The woman was reading a book and she had big pillowy bosoms Dave thought would be nice to go and lay his head down on and just close his eyes. Which was exactly what he did in the vision that turned into a true dream. It felt good and restful and the woman stroked his hair and sang softly to him.

Next he knew, Dave awoke under a blanket of snow. The fire had gone out and was just a circle of gray ash. He cursed the dream that wasn't in his head anymore. He looked all around, but didn't see any cabin with any woman or kids in it. All he saw

were sand hills and that muddy brown river he'd fallen into once and near drowned.

He undid himself from the ground and it felt like all his bones were breaking and he was so mad he went over to the river and shot it three or four times, trying to kill it.

He shot the air too, trying to kill the sky.

"I'm in a killing mood," he said to the one-eared horse. The horse simply stood there looking at him with a curious wet brown eye.

"I'd kill you, except I'd have nothing to ride."

Dave finally mounted up, hateful of the fact he was reduced to riding a one-ear horse and not the high-stepper of Buffalo Bill's. He rode along, following the course of the river with the searching instincts of a badger. Such instincts had made him a superior manhunter when he was a lawman and later a Class A bounty hunter. And when he turned bad, his good instincts made him a very elusive man.

He rounded a bend and rode up through a canyon and past some sand hills before the canyon emptied out again near the river. It was confusing country. He rode a little farther before he spotted a small cabin, about the same as the one he'd seen

in his dream the night before. Smoke fluttered out of its stone chimney. If it hadn't been for the ache in his lung, he would have thought he was dreaming still. He stopped the horse and sat a moment, looking at the cabin. When he was sure he wasn't still dreaming, he rode up to it, dismounted, and went and knocked on the door.

An old woman, bent as a bad-struck nail, opened the door instead of a plump woman with large bosoms.

"Yaas," she said.

A mangy little dog stood by her feet growling, its hackles raised, but Dave could see it hardly had any teeth and looked old enough that a good wind would knock it over.

"What would you be needin' here, mister?"

Dave didn't like the sound of her; she had an accent: Irish. Dave recalled how the whole goddamn West was littered with immigrant types, as though they'd been blown onto the prairies by the winds of hope: ragged Irish and Germans, who talked funny and ate strange foods and played polka music and danced jigs whenever several of them got together and one had an accordion and another a fiddle.

Dave didn't care much for the Irish and Germans he'd met thus far. Two such had chopped off the head of a friend of his, Bear River Tom Smith, outside of Abilene with a hoe. A Irish and a German. Dave almost could imagine her distracting him and whilst someone took to hitting him across the neck with a hoe.

"Well, what is it?" she said impatiently.

"I seen your cabin, is all," Dave said.

"And what would it be to you?"

"Anybody living here but you?"

He saw the startle in her eyes.

"Oh, me mister will be back soon, anytime now, he's gone to town and on his way back. Why, I think I see him now." Dave looked back over his shoulder where the old lady's eyes went — toward a ridge of sand hills, but he didn't see anything.

Dave looked past the old crone into the room behind her. He didn't see a plump young woman with dark hair or any plump little children either.

"Nothing," Dave said. "Your cabin or you don't mean nothing to me."

"Well, then, you best be going along before me husband gets here. He's the jealous sort, he is. Awful mean too when it comes to strangers."

Dave turned to leave, disappointed that

the woman in his dream was not the same as the one standing in the doorway: small and dried up like a fig, with no bosoms to even speak of, much less rest his head on.

"Oh, by the way," he said, putting one foot in the stirrup and grabbing the horn of his saddle. "I come across a war party of bad-looking Indians back a ways. They had their faces painted for war. I outrun 'em, but I reckon they'll plunder and rape and scalp everything in their way. I was you, I'd get on to a town somewhere and take that mangy dog with you."

The old thing gasped.

Dave forked his cayuse and rode off with a happy grin. Let all them immigrants go on back to wherever it was they came from; they was just dirtying up the prairies.

The mean mood was still on him like snow was on the land. On him like brown was in the river. It was on him in the worst way and he sure enough wanted to kill somebody, Buffalo Bill most especially.

The bullet ached in his lung like someone was probing around in it with an awl and he had to piss and that was about as much as he could stand.

Chapter 26

The hunting party rode at a good clip, up the canyons until the canyons opened out onto a broad prairie that looked stark and dead under the winter sky. They rested for short periods of time, enough to give the horses a blow, then rode on and on. They crossed the river at a shallow place and then rode on, and in the distance they could see some low-lying bluffs that looked as bleak as an old abandoned fortress.

They topped a rise that looked down onto another plain and this came just after noon when the sky looked like steam and spread out before them was snow drifted in places and poked through in other places with bunch grass. And there in the distance they saw a herd of buffalo — less than a dozen in all — browsing, their dark shapes starkly contrasted with everything around them.

"There's your buffs," Billy said to Banks.

"How do we do it, Colonel, go after them?"

"Well, sir. We can ease down and set up

a stand and shoot them as many as we can before they get wise to our game, or the wind shifts 'round."

"Hardly seems sporting."

"Or we can ride in on 'em and shoot them running."

Banks smiled.

"Let's do that," he said.

Edgar looked pale at the prospect but did not say anything.

"What about you, Mr. Blue?" Billy said.

"I'll let you gents do the shooting," Teddy said. "You tell me where you want me and that's where I'll be."

"You boys make sure you've got a shell in the chambers of your rifles," Billy said. "We ease down off this rise until we get close. We'll try and get as close as we can — wait till they start running, then we'll run with 'em."

Even their mounts seemed eager for the hunt.

Teddy rode alongside Cody.

"Keep an eye for trouble," Cody said, shifting his eyes to indicate he meant trouble with either of the two men. "You ever do this sort of thing before?"

"No, sir. I never had any reason to shoot a cow from the back of a horse."

Cody smiled.

"They're a little ranker than a cow," he said.

"Can't be much ranker than those Mexican longhorns we used to pop out of the brush."

Cody said over his shoulder to the other two, "When you get a shot, make sure and aim either just behind the head between the shoulders, or just behind the shoulder into the heart. Don't shoot 'em in the head, it won't do no good."

They approached the herd with stealth and got to within about a hundred yards before one of the large bulls raised his head and looked 'round at them, watched them for a moment, then commenced to run, the others running with him.

"Go!" Billy shouted and they spurred their horses into a gallop.

The thunder of hooves drumming over the hard ground was the sort of thing that stirred a man's soul and caused his heart to beat fast. John had picked out some good horses and it didn't take much to gain on the herd and finally catch up with them. Cody swung 'round to the right and shouted for the others to swing to the left.

Next thing Teddy knew, he was running alongside a cow and her calf. He had no heart to shoot either one and wouldn't.

But then he heard the crack of a rifle and saw the cow stagger and looked 'round and saw that Banks had caught up to her and fired into her. She ran a few more feet, then stopped, her calf too. Banks swung his mount around and rode up to her as she stood facing him, her head lowered. Banks fired again, this time a direct shot to the skull and Teddy could see the dust spank up but there was little or no effect otherwise.

Rapidly levering another shell into his breech, Banks fired a third time, this time striking the calf, which toppled over — its skull not so thick or invulnerable. The cow turned its head to look at its calf and Banks shot the cow again through the neck and a fountain of blood arced forth before the cow too toppled over.

Teddy felt disheartened. Banks was off again after the others and the rest of the herd, happy, no doubt, he'd gotten his buffalo, but not content with the kill.

The chase lasted nearly thirty minutes. Half the buffs were killed when Cody reined the hunters in.

"We've got enough," he said. The horses were nearly staggering, their chests lathered.

Banks and his assistant rode back to the

carcasses and got down and looked at them close and grasped the horns of the dead buffalo and shook them and ran their hands through the thick coats.

Billy sat his horse next to that of Teddy's and watched them.

"They got their buffs," he said.

Teddy didn't say anything.

"I guess those are the last buffs I'll ever shoot," Billy said. "They've about gone the way of the Indians — at least the wild ones has, anyway."

Billy took off his sombrero and wiped a forearm across his brow.

"It's sort of sad for me to see," he said.

"What now?" Teddy said.

"Now? Why we head back to camp."

"Just leave them for the wolves?"

"The wolves, or if there's some stray band of Indians, they'll be thankful for the bounty."

"Seems a waste, Colonel."

"I know it."

Banks insisted that one of the buffalo be skinned and that the head be cut and wrapped in the hide.

Billy shifted his weight in the saddle.

"We don't have time if we're to make it back to camp by nightfall," he said.

"Then we'll camp where we can for the

night and make the rest of the trip in the morning, Colonel."

It was starting to spit snow again.

Teddy could see that Billy was against skinning one of the buffs, that it wasn't a job a man like him would normally do.

"I'll be glad to lend a hand," Teddy offered. He could see how utterly unhappy Billy was with Banks's request. Billy finally consented to skin the big bull that had an hour earlier been supreme among his fading breed and now lay growing stiff upon the dead grass, its hide dusty and bloody.

Billy showed Teddy where to cut and when they'd made their cuts, they punched ropes through the neck of the hide and wrapped the other ends around their saddle horns and peeled off the hide with the strength of their mounts. Then Billy cut off the magnificent head of the bull and wrapped it in the hide and tied the whole thing together into a bundle.

It took the better part of an hour and they tied the bundle on the back of Billy's horse and then started back for the camp, knowing that they would not make it before dark.

Teddy could smell the blood of their journey following them, could smell the

death of the hide pursuing them like a bloody ghost of the past.

And when at last they made a camp by the river as the gray afternoon sunk to a darker hue and snow began to fall more in earnest, there seemed to have fallen with it a pallor over Billy.

They ate jerked beef around a quick fire and Banks and his assistant sat together, talking about the hunt, Banks doing most of the talking. Teddy realized Banks wasn't a bad sort, neither of them was. They were just wealthy men who wanted more of an adventure for a little while than making money. That soon enough, they would return East and whatever they left behind in this country, whether it be the corpses of buffalo or bear, would soon enough be forgotten and that they had no real affinity for this country, that they were just visitors and little else.

Soon enough, both men rolled up in their blankets and fell to an exhausted sleep.

Billy sat with his arm resting on one raised knee, the light of the camp's fire darting in his dark eyes.

"You sorry you did this hunt, Colonel?" Teddy said.

Billy glanced over at him.

"Seems like everything is different now than what it used to be. Seems like it all just changed sudden over this past year. I lost me two good pards. We about run off all the wild Indians and the buffs are all but gone, as well . . ." Billy's voice had a lonesomeness to it.

They sat for a time longer without saying anything, then rolled up in their blankets. Teddy figured that such a lonesome place late at night with no light — not even moon or stars — that they didn't have to worry about assassins, at least for this one night.

They lay there and listened to the stars falling.

Chapter 27

The telegram arrived just as the blizzard began.

Henry Egg was standing in his small office watching it snow in earnest when he saw Karl from the telegraph office coming across the street, his hat brim like a plate of snow. Karl came in and shut the door behind him, trying to keep the wind out.

"Wire for you, Constable," Karl said, then went and helped himself to the coffee heating in the pot atop the potbelly.

"Sounds like we got us some criminal element coming to town," Karl said.

"I don't know why you bothered carrying this piece of paper with writing on it," Henry said. "Why don't you just tell me what it says, since you already know, and save me the trouble of wearing out my eyes?"

So Karl told him that the wire was from the city lawman in Omaha, warning that there were two people — a woman and a young man, probably an Indian — most likely to pass through North Platte on the

next train. That the woman and Indian boy had killed a feller in Omaha and that when Sheriff Mudd went to arrest them, he was pistol-beat near to death. Karl went on to say that these two individuals were thoroughly dangerous types and should they be spotted they were to be arrested and held until Sheriff Mudd could arrive and take them into custody.

"Say, this ain't bad coffee," Karl said upon finishing telling what the wire said.

Henry Egg read the telegram anyway.

"It looks like one of them hell fire storms," Karl said, stepping close to the window. "Like that time in 'sixty-nine when half the livestock in the county froze and Ed Franklin was lost and never found."

Henry took out his pocket watch and checked the time. It was a quarter past noon, about the time he normally went home to have lunch with his wife. It took him fifteen minutes to walk home and another thirty minutes to eat his lunch. He was generally back at the office by quarter past one. But with the snow falling hard as it was and with the noon flier past due, Henry figured he'd be a little late for lunch this day. He put on his hat and coat and took his Whitney shotgun from the wall

rack and jacked two shells of double-ought buck into the chambers, then snapped it shut again.

"You gonna have to kill you something to eat for lunch?" Karl said.

"Gonna wait for the train," Henry said. "Gonna see about arresting them desperados."

"You want me to round some of the fellers up to deputize?"

"No. It's just a woman and a boy," Henry said. "I've been doing this business a long time. I don't see where's I'll need any deputies, for a woman and a boy."

"The snow'll be ass-deep by evening if it keeps on like this," Karl said.

"That don't mean nothing to me."

"It don't to me either."

"Well, I got to get on. Close the door when you leave," Henry said, knowing how Karl liked to take his time enjoying his coffee. "And shuck some more wood in that stove before you leave, we might be having guests."

Karl watched Henry going down the street through the window, the snow gathering on his black hat and coat. Karl knew Henry as one tough old bird. *Like a big old blackbird,* Karl thought. *Just like a big old mean blackbird.*

Bob was watching out the passenger car's window as the train eased into the station of North Platte. He figured it was possible that the lawman back in Omaha might have gotten free in time to wire ahead. Pearl had made the mistake of telling the lawman they were headed west. It wouldn't take a genius to figure where their next stop would be.

Bob saw a lone figure standing in front of the station with a shotgun cradled in the crook of his arm. He had broad shoulders with snow collected on them and a black hat with a snowy brim.

"We've got trouble," Bob said to Pearl.

Pearl saw the man Bob was looking at.

"What should we do?"

"You get off first," Bob said. "Go up to him and do what you're best at."

She felt the sting of his comment.

"I won't do it if you're going to shoot him."

"Well, I'm sure not going to invite him to join us in our hotel room," Bob said.

"I'll distract him if you promise to sneak off the train and meet me somewhere."

"Like the last time?"

"You promised me we wouldn't fight any more about that."

"Yes, you're right."

The train screeched to a halt. Bob could see the man with the gun watching the cars. The porter came through announcing they were in North Platte, that there'd be a thirty-minute delay while they took on water and passengers.

"Why don't we just stay on the train?" Pearl said.

"Because if he's looking for us and doesn't see us, he'll come aboard. I'd rather take my chances out in the open than trapped in one of these cars."

"Where will you meet me later?"

"Go to one of the hotels, sign in as Mrs. Bob Parsnip. I'll find you."

Henry Egg watched the passengers disembarking from the train. He didn't see anyone that matched the descriptions of the desperadoes. He was hungry and his feet were getting cold.

A handsome woman in a gray capote disembarked, looked around. *That could be her,* Henry told himself. Then he watched as she walked right up to him and said, "Excuse me, sir, but might you direct me to some local lodging?"

Henry touched the brim of his hat, an old habit of addressing women. He looked

her over good, could see she had lovely yellow hair bunched under her eastern ladies' hat that had a big plumed feather sticking from it.

"You traveling alone, miss?"

"Why, yes," she said.

Henry looked past her toward the train.

"I don't believe you're traveling alone," he said.

"Why, sir. What would cause you to doubt that I am?"

"Maybe it's because I been in the law business a lot longer than you been in the lying business. Where's your young partner?"

Pearl hissed and fumed appropriately, hoping that Bob had slipped off the train through another door.

"Just don't move," Henry said, then opened his coat enough to show her the badge he wore pinned to his vest. "Henry Egg, ma'am, town constable."

"I don't know what it is you think I've done," Pearl said. "But I assure you —"

"Please, miss, I'm trying to concentrate on them cars."

"Well, then, arrest me if you must."

"I intend to."

Henry saw that no more folks were getting off the train.

"Come on," he said and took Pearl by the arm. They boarded the train and walked down through the four passenger cars, all the way to the caboose. Henry didn't see anyone else.

"He slipped off, didn't he?"

Pearl remained silent.

"Don't worry, I'll find him yet. I'm good at this," Henry said. He took Pearl to the jail and locked her in a cell.

"How long do you intend to hold me on these foolish accusations?" she demanded.

"I'll wire Sheriff Mudd in Omaha, tell him to come down and take a look at you. It shouldn't take him more than a day or two to get here. If you ain't her, I'll let you go with my apologies."

"I can't believe this is happening," Pearl said as she began to weep. *Her act is a good one,* Henry thought, *but I'm not buying any of it.*

"I need to go look for your partner. I'll see Clark brings you some grub."

She didn't know who Clark was, nor did she care to know. The jail seemed a cold lonely place. She was starting to have misgivings about her love for Bob.

Henry felt grouchy at having to miss his lunch and go in search of the young villain. It was bad enough a man had to miss his

lunch, but to have to go tromping around in a blizzard searching for desperadoes made it all feel that much more onerous.

As it turned out, Henry didn't have to search long.

He came upon the young man in an alley not ten minutes later. The alley ran between two brick buildings that muffled the sound of the shot. The muffle of the shooting was further abated by the howling wind of the snowstorm and the fact that hardly anyone was out on the streets at that hour in such bad conditions, or else someone might have come to Henry's aide.

Henry felt horse-kicked. The bullet flung him back onto a heap of trash and he lay there for several moments, trying to get the weight off his chest. Only there wasn't any weight to get off.

So this is what it is like to get shot bad.

In all his years as a lawman, he'd never taken a bullet, but had delivered several — most of which were fatal.

His blood flowed warm and thick between his fingers when he placed his hand over his chest to try and stopper the leak. The snow fell onto him and melted in the blood.

The young dark stranger stood there looking down at him. He sure enough was

Indian, Henry could see that plainly. Just a boy.

"I . . . I . . ." Henry wasn't sure which words he wanted to say, but he felt the need to say something. The dark face leaned closer. Henry Egg could see snowflakes on the eyelashes of his assassin.

"You should have left it alone," Bob said. "You white people just can't leave anything alone . . ."

Henry was thinking about his wife, Cora, back at the house waiting lunch for him, wondering why he was so late and probably getting upset that he was, not knowing Henry was never going to have lunch with her again.

Henry looked down at his fingers. The blood was freezing on them. The weight on his chest heavier now.

"You should have just left it alone," Bob said.

Henry didn't know what the boy was talking about.

Snow fell into his eyes, then melted and it felt like tears.

Henry gasped, the way a fish out of water would do. Bob looked away and when he looked back again Henry's eyes were just staring up at the snow that fell into them, his gasping stopped.

Bob searched through the dead man's

pockets and found a set of keys. Then he took Henry by the boot heels and dragged him farther back up the alley and left him there, knowing the snow would soon cover him up.

Pearl was there, locked up in the little jail, when Bob came in and unlocked the door and said, "We can go now."

"Where will we go?" she said.

"We will go and pay this Indian Slayer, Cody, a visit."

"How will you find him?"

"I'll ask somebody," Bob said.

It was about as simple a plan as Pearl had ever heard of. Pearl saw blood on Bob's fingers.

"I can't go with you," she said. "I can't be part of any more killing."

"I know it. I didn't want it to be this way, but I'm not completely sorry either. I figure those men are just paying the price for being what they are. The whites have killed a lot more of my people than we've killed of them."

"I'm going back on the next train," Pearl said.

Bob nodded.

"I knew it was too good to last forever," he said.

"That's the way love is," she said. "Too good to last forever."

Pearl's lip trembled when she said it. Bob didn't want to see her that way. He took the money out of his pocket and handed it to her.

"I'm sorry," he said.

"I am too, Bob. I'm sorry for you and for me and for the men who died. I'm sorry for everything in this miserable goddamn life . . ."

"Go on home, Pearl. You'll find you a man you don't have to be sorry for."

She stood on tiptoes and kissed him lightly on the cheek.

"It was good for a while," she said. "It was the best."

Bob walked out of the jail with her, the snow falling so hard neither of them could see as far as across the street.

"I guess this is it, then," he said.

She blinked back the tears.

"Run, Bob, run."

He shook his head, then walked off down the street and she saw him disappear in the falling snow. He became like a ghost.

Chapter 28

They awoke to howling winds and a driving, blinding snow.

"Damn it," Billy grumbled. The others shook themselves loose from their ice-caked blankets. Teddy had already arisen and was saddling the horses. It was the most ferocious storm he'd ever witnessed.

Billy came over and began to help with the horses.

"We're liable not to make it back to camp today," Billy said.

"We'll have to stay close together so nobody gets lost in this."

"I know it. We'll ride single-file."

The wind raked their faces and they did their best to talk above it.

Banks came over and said, "What do you think, Colonel?"

"I think we're in for a hell of a time."

"We should try and find some cover out of this," Banks said.

"We need to get back to the others at camp," Teddy interjected.

"Seems to me they are in better shape than we are," Banks said.

Edgar Rivers came up and joined them.

"Jesus, this storm . . ." he said.

"Saddle up," Billy said. "I'll ride lead, Mr. Blue, bring up the rear if you will. Everybody stay close together, don't let the man ahead of you out of your sight."

And so they rode into the teeth of the storm, unable to see more than a few feet ahead of them. Billy knew the land, had a map of it etched in his brain, but the storm made the going tricky at best, wiping out landmarks, confusing his sense of direction.

I can't help wondering if the Creator is taking out his vengeance on us all for killing the last of his great creatures, he thought. He knew it was foolish to think in such a manner, but things were disappearing fast in his world.

Billy thought of Louisa and the girls, how the girls were growing tall as weeds and how him and Louisa's love for each other had faded till it wasn't hardly love at all but more akin to the feelings of a brother and sister who didn't care for each other very much. He thought too about how Texas Jack had abandoned him. And he thought about Wild Bill and Georgie

Custer, now gone for all eternity. Never again would those old boys ride into the teeth of a blizzard, nor have to face the prospect of death. One thing about being dead was you didn't have to worry about it any longer.

He made a point of checking the others over his shoulder every few minutes, knowing from experience how easy it was to lose men and beasts in a storm. He tried to read the map in his head, even while everything in front of him looked like a white sheet somebody was waving.

After a mile or so, Teddy could only sense the others were still in front of him. He worried about Anne and the others back at camp, knew that there wasn't much even John could do for them against such fury.

The wind's force became a roar that deafened as well as blinded. His moustaches grew thick with ice and he had to swipe his eyes and keep his head tucked. There was little they could do but forge ahead.

They rode maybe an hour, maybe two, it was hard to tell. Teddy thought he heard something through the shriek of wind, couldn't be sure, then came upon the lump in the snow, his mount almost stumbling

over the struggling form of Edgar Rivers.

"Whoa!" Teddy barely managed to side-step his horse around the man who was struggling to gain his feet.

"What happened?"

Edgar Rivers looked at him, his face caked with ice and snow, his skin bluish.

"My horse threw me . . . He . . . he ran off."

It was a bad piece of news. Teddy kicked a foot free of one stirrup and reached a hand forth, telling the man to climb aboard behind him. Edgar struggled but finally got purchase and Teddy hauled him up.

"I think he ran off that way," Rivers said.

"It doesn't matter, we can't chase after him in this."

Edgar shouted in his ear that he was genuinely apologetic for being a burden, saying he owed Teddy his very life.

Teddy could only guess the others were still ahead of him, that he was still headed in the right direction.

They rode on for maybe another half hour, then Teddy said, "We'll have to dismount and walk for a spell to give the horse a blow." He knew that they would fall farther behind and were now completely separated from Cody and Banks.

"Grab a handful of tail," Teddy shouted. "Yell out if you stumble." Teddy took the reins and led the horse while Rivers grabbed its tail. The snow was now nearly to their knees in some places.

"How long?" Edgar Rivers shouted.

"How long what?"

"How long will we have to walk?"

"Twenty minutes, maybe; we can't break the horse down. Walk twenty, ride twenty."

Their feet began to grow numb, their hands, as well. Teddy's face stung like it had been burned. The realization that they might die became a real possibility with every step. If the storm didn't give up its fury sooner rather than later — and he'd heard of storms that lasted for days — they were in some nasty trouble.

After what he guessed was the allotted time to walk, Teddy could see that Rivers was having a hard time of it. He stopped and went back to him and said, "Climb aboard," then helped him into the saddle.

"What about you?" Rivers said when he saw that Teddy was still going to walk.

"I'm good for now. One of us riding is better than two. I'll go as long as I can."

Oddly, he felt a reserve of strength flooding into his blood that he hadn't counted on. It was as though the storm

had become an adversary, a thing that wanted to beat him down, defeat him, possibly kill him. The threat was as real as the gunfighter, Hank Rain, who'd tried to kill him in Cheyenne — the first man he had ever shot. And like that situation, he felt a calm resolve take over.

John had told him once long before that fateful day that every gunfighter had a certain cool reserve when faced with a foe. "It's something you can see in their eyes, in the way they moved with deliberation. You can't scare 'em when they get like that. They're like rattlesnakes," John said. "They get coiled because they know what they need to do and they get zeroed in on their target and then you better kill them or they're sure as hell going to kill you."

Teddy understood it that day in Cheyenne when he was faced down by Hank Rain. He felt the rattlesnake in him. He felt it again now. The storm might kill him, but it didn't scare him, and if it was going to kill him, the killing wasn't going to be easy.

They went on and he wasn't sure how long he walked, but he heard Edgar shout, "Should I get down and walk now too?"

Teddy turned his back to the wind to look at the rider.

"You feel like you can walk some more?"

Edgar shrugged.

"Maybe."

But Teddy could see the man had no resolve, that asking too much of him would be the same as putting a bullet in him. He thought of Anne and Edgar together. He thought how easy it would be to just keep going and let Edgar flounder — survival of the fittest. No one would blame him for saving himself. Edgar stumbled and fell and stumbled again. He seemed a pathetic figure. Teddy turned to face the wind, stood there for a long few moments, considering whether to just go on without Edgar. But at last he turned back and trudged toward the man. He figured he owed it to Anne to bring her fiancé back alive. She had a right to make her choice, not him, not an easy death. He grabbed Edgar up and helped him into the saddle. They went on, the storm battling and battering them every step of the way.

Come on, Teddy thought. *Come on, you son of a bitch.*

It only got worse and both men knew it.

The horse began to falter. Teddy stopped and told Edgar he'd have to get down.

"I can't feel my feet or hands," he said as

323

he dismounted, fell, and Teddy helped him up again. "We're done for, aren't we, Mr. Blue?"

"No. Hang on to its tail," he said.

They stumbled on.

Then something appeared out of the blizzard. It was Billy.

"Jesus!" Billy called above the storm. "We thought we lost you boys."

"Colonel," Teddy said.

"Come on, they's an old shack up ahead. It ain't much but it will give us some shelter."

And when they made it to the shack they stumbled inside, glad for the relief from wind and snow. Rudolph Banks was there waiting for them.

"Edgar," he said worriedly when he saw his assistant's condition.

They helped him to sit, trembling as he was. He was barely able to speak.

Billy pulled a silver flask from an inside coat pocket and said, "Have some of this firewater."

The whiskey helped warm the blood and they sat in a circle Indian-style, passing the flask back and forth, and Billy said, "The one time I should have carried more liquor on my person, I didn't. There's a half case of it back at camp if White Eye

and Yankee ain't drank it all up."

The wind rattled the loose boards and blew in through the small open windows and sifted in through the multitude of holes in the roof. But for the most part they were protected.

"I wonder how the others are making out at camp?" Banks said.

"Yankee and them have been through tough winters before," Billy said. "They'll make out."

"This must be a dreadful trip for the women," Banks replied, taking another sip from the whiskey flask.

Teddy took out his makings and said, "Anyone else want a shuck?"

Edgar Rivers waved a shaky hand, said, "I never developed the habit."

"Take my advice," Teddy said. "It'll warm you some."

Banks said, "I'll have one, if you don't mind."

Teddy rolled one and handed it to Banks, then rolled himself one. He found a match and struck it and lit the ends of both cigarettes.

"Too bad there aren't extra boards in this old shack," Billy said, "or we'd build us a fire."

Teddy saw that one wall had been lined

with old newspapers, yellowed and curled and as fragile now as butterfly wings. There wasn't a chair or a single stick of furniture to burn. He wondered about the person who had built the place and what sort of man he was and did he have a wife and kids or was he a loner, a trapper maybe, and what had happened to him to cause him to abandon the place?

"Too bad we ain't got us a deck of playing cards," Billy said. "Something to pass the time by."

"I think we'll cut the trip short," Banks said abruptly. "I think soon as we return to camp we should head back to town and catch the first train east."

"The contract states seven full days of hunting," Billy said.

"Oh, not to worry, Colonel. You'll get the amount agreed upon."

"The bonus too?"

Banks hesitated a moment and said, "If you get us all back safely, the bonus too."

Billy seemed satisfied and about drank the last of the liquor, then thought better of it and said, "They's one swally left, who wants it?"

Banks extended his hand for the flask, took it and handed it to Edgar Rivers, saying, "He needs it more than any of us."

It earned him some points in Billy's eyes and it did in Teddy's too.

The storm raged on without letup as Teddy studied Edgar, thought to himself his decision could have just as easily gone the other way out there before Billy showed up. And he wondered what sort of man he was turning into.

Chapter 29

White Eye and Jane had been wrapped in each other's arms and faded dreams when the storm struck. Yankee had been off in the toolies, squatting with his pants down. John had been trying to get a fire going to heat coffee before the red dawn. He was the one who felt the first winds of fury cutting down through one of the canyons. Then it began to snow. And John knew it wasn't an ordinary snow, the on-and-off kind they'd dealt with the last several days, but a true snow, the kind he'd seen only once or twice before — the last being in Montana when he worked for the Lazy Hat Cattle Company. He swore after that winter he'd never let himself get caught in another bad snowstorm if he could help it and promptly went off to south Texas, where all a man had to deal with were cyclones, stampedes, and murdering drunks with guns.

Yankee came trotting back to camp, buttoning his drawers.

"It's a bad one coming," he said.

"I know it," John said. "Better get every-

328

one rousted and figure out what we're going to do."

"You go wake the women, I go get White Eye and Jane."

John called into the tent opening of Emma Banks.

"What is it, Mr. Sears?" Emma asked.

"Bad storm, ma'am. We're going to have to find better shelter."

John saw no panic in the woman's eyes when she emerged from the tent.

"I'll get my sister," she said calmly.

Yankee ducked his head into Jane's tent. She was sitting up and White Eye was trying to put on his drawers.

"You all better hurry and get dressed," Yankee said. "It's coming a bad blow."

Jane said, "Oh, Yankee, that's such a brave thing for you to do — to come and warn us."

Jane's gushing did not escape White Eye's notice. "Okay, you was real brave to warn us, now you better run off and warn the others," White Eye said sarcastically.

Yankee said, "I could have just let the storm blow you away, if that's what you want," and then ducked back out again, angry he'd even tried to save White Eye's jealous old hide.

They all joined John and he told them

they'd better go on up in the canyon and try to find a lee from the storm and nobody disagreed with him.

"What about the horses?" Yankee said.

"You and White Eye rope 'em together and lead 'em along; don't bother taking time to saddle 'em, just tie 'em together." Then John and the women began to gather up blankets and what food they could carry.

The wind blew Yankee's hat off his head and he started to chase it but saw that he'd be chasing it for eternity and said, "Hell," and went with White Eye to rope up the horses.

John told the women to hold hands as he took Emma's, leading them up into the nearby canyon, the wind shrieking down through it, but they had no choice — it was either the canyon or staying out in the open. Yankee and White Eye brought along the horses that were beginning to balk. In minutes the full brunt of the storm was on them all.

"They want to run," Yankee shouted. "They want to run ahead of the storm, stay out in front of it."

"Hell, they got more sense then us."

"We should have blindfolded 'em."

"It's too late for that now."

"We can't lose 'em."

"I know it."

But they did lose them. The horses broke in a mad dash and tore the ropes out of Yankee's hands and White Eye's too.

"Hell!" they shouted in unison.

"Let 'em go, let's stay with the others!" White Eye yelled.

"First my goddamn hat, now my horse," Yankee said.

They stumbled on, up the canyon in pursuit of John and the women.

The storm stung their faces like sharp teeth as they fought their way along. They finally found a hollow cut under the brow of a sand hill, a cut, no doubt, made by an ancient river and used on and off by animals for shelter. The gathered into it and huddled together while the storm's fury raged around them.

John didn't want to say anything, but Emma Banks said what he had been thinking: "I wonder if the storm caught the men?"

White Eye said, "Billy knows this country, he grew up in it. Anyone knows where to get out of a storm, it's him. You don't have to worry, ma'am, Billy will bring your feller home safe, and yours too, miss." He looked at Anne.

Anne thought about Edgar and about Teddy. One she'd promised her hand in marriage to, the other she'd promised nothing, but knew that what they'd shared together was a promise of its own kind. It was ludicrous, she told herself, to expect anything from Teddy, to even consider something like a future with him. She said his name to her secret self: *Teddy Blue* and wondered what it was about him that had captured her imagination so.

"It's a good thing you ladies didn't go with them," Yankee said, then realized immediately what that sounded like. "I mean, they'll make it back just fine, but they'll have their hands full as it is. Least this way they don't have to worry about you fine ladies."

Jane liked the way that Yankee made a mistake and then fixed it. The more she considered him as a potential suitor, possible husband, the more she became convinced she'd taken up with the wrong man in the form of one White Eye Anderson.

John was worried about them all, Teddy most especially. This country was full of things that could kill you — snakes, rivers, bad men, bad women, and storms of all kinds. He'd seen lightning kill cowboys, and cyclones that blew away whole houses

with women and kids in 'em. He'd seen winters that froze men to death. And this could be just such a storm. They could get blinded and walk their horses into a river or ride off a bluff and break their necks. There was a lot bad that could happen to 'em and little good the way he saw it. But he didn't say anything, for he didn't want to bring bad luck down on them.

Instead, he rolled a shuck and passed the makings 'round to Yankee and White Eye and Jane spoke up and said, "I'd like me a shuck too," hoping Yankee would roll one for her. The other two women thought it was quite something to see a woman smoking a cigarette and admired Jane for her boldness.

And for a little while, at least, they were out of the worst of it and could find within themselves a sense of hope yet.

Chapter 30

Mysterious Dave felt lost in a world that suddenly turned white and wind-whipped. One minute he'd been riding along, simply cold and exceptionally unhappy, and the next he was caught in the bowels of a blizzard.

"Christ Almighty," he said. He saw little in the way of shelter, half thought about turning back to the cabin where he'd come across the Irish crone, but he wasn't sure which direction it lay, now that the snow had obliterated everything.

The one-eared horse was skittish and Dave took off his bandanna and tied it around the animal's eyes to calm it. It was a trick an old cowboy taught him when Dave was a deputy town marshal either in Abilene, Hays, or Creede, Colorado. He and the cowboy had become chums until they got in a fight over a woman, a whore most likely to Dave's flawed recollection. That tying a bandanna over the eyes of a horse trick was about the only good thing to come out of the friendship. Dave might

have even shot the cowboy, he couldn't be a hundred percent certain, now that he thought about it.

"Now we're both blind," Dave said to the horse. "But at least you ain't gon' buck me off."

Dave tried to keep a close watch through slit eyes for the river. He wanted no further adventures of falling into rivers. He knew the river lay mostly off to his right. He jammed his hat down hard over his head so it wouldn't blow away.

"This must be a nightmare I'm having," he said as the storm grew worse by the minute.

Dave wasn't sure how far he rode but suddenly racing out of the storm were several horses, some of which nearly crashed into him.

"Now I know it's a damn nightmare. Ain't none of this happening. I'm going to wake up and find it is all a dream." The thought that it was a dream and that he'd wake up from it made Dave feel somewhat better. Maybe the whole deal with Dora throwing him over for a dead rich man's money was just a dream too. Why, any minute he could just wake up and find himself in Dora's bed again, warm and happy.

But another half hour of riding into the belly of the storm made Mysterious Dave realize it wasn't a dream, not even a bad dream. His subtle joy turned to anger. He pulled his pistol and shot the storm, but it didn't seem to even slow the storm down or make one bit of difference.

"Goddamn, it don't seem like I can kill anything but human beings," he said.

"I don't even know how I got to this country," he said.

He wished the horse could talk so he'd have somebody to gripe to.

"Look at me, riding a one-eared horse in a blizzard!"

He momentarily saw the mouth of a canyon off to his left and rightly figured if he rode up into it, the sand hills might afford him some small measure of protection from the driving wind.

It did some, but then the canyon eventually opened up into broad flat stretch and the wind and snow attacked him again and stung his face and hands and bit at his ears something terrible, which caused him to curse and grow angrier by the minute.

"I'm going to find that Buffalo Bill and kill him dead, dead, dead!"

The snow increased and the wind increased making it colder. Dave's toes grew

numb and his hair filled with ice.

"I know you're trying to rub me out," he shouted. "But it's me who's going to do the rubbing out." He shook his fist and dared God to send ten more storms down on him.

"I ain't afraid. I ain't afraid."

The wind snatched Dave's crazy words from his mouth and flung them away.

Chapter 31

The storm raged throughout the night, but by morning it was over.

"Listen," Billy said, lifting his head from his knees.

"What is it?" Rudolph Banks said.

"The wind, it's not there anymore."

Teddy pushed open the door and the weight of snow that had drifted against it. The horses stood as if asleep, tied securely all three. The land looked scrubbed clean with the fresh snow on it.

"It's over," Teddy said as the others emerged. The world had fallen as silent as death.

Their boots crunched in the snow when they went to get their horses.

"We'll take turns riding double with Mr. Rivers," Billy said. "Come on, old son, you can ride up behind me for a spell." Billy helped Edgar Rivers up onto the back of his horse and the riders headed out through deep drifts and in the direction of the camp.

Teddy had had a fitful dream during the

night, one in which he dreamt that he had attended Kathleen Bonney's funeral. In the dream he stood beside her casket and gazed upon her thin beautiful face and touched her silken hair. He awakened in that cold dark night, the snores of the other men around him, the howl of the wind steady as wolves outside the cabin. And in his wakefulness he thought about her and he thought about Anne, then looked over to see the shadow of Edgar Rivers huddled and shivering.

He was grateful it was only a dream.

It would be a long ride still back to camp, he only prayed that the others were safe and unharmed by the storm. He had every confidence in John's ability to keep them that way. He recalled what Rudolph Banks said to Billy the evening before about cutting the hunt short. It would mean that they would return East and that would be the end of it between he and Anne — that she would go with them and he would never see her again.

They crossed one broad plain and headed up the slope at the other end of it, topped the ridge and down the other side before heading into the first of two canyons. They traded off riding double every half hour, and when they stopped to rest in the

second canyon they thought they were only an hour or two from camp and it felt good to them that they were near the end of this unpleasant journey.

Billy and Teddy unloosed the cinches to give the horses a blow while Banks and Edgar Rivers stood by.

"I need to go off into the bushes," Edgar said.

"Don't wander off too far," Billy said.

They watched him go off.

Teddy rolled a shuck, said to Cody, "It's about over. We'll get back, you'll get paid, and that will be it."

"I'm glad you were along on this ride," Billy said. "We'd most likely have lost him in the storm."

Banks came over and said, "I was beginning to believe we'd never make it back."

"This country can be tricky," Billy said.

They heard a scream from off in the same direction Rivers had gone. Billy jerked his rifle from its scabbard, but Teddy was already running in that direction.

They saw a flurry of brown fur almost at the same moment they heard the bear's roar. It had Edgar beneath it, raking him with its claws and trying to bite down on his skull.

"It's a damn griz!" Billy shouted.

Teddy jerked the Colt from its holster, knowing he'd have to get up close in order not to hit Rivers when he fired. Billy could see the same thing and held his rifle while trying to take careful aim.

"Careful, he'll turn on you," Billy warned.

Teddy shouted, trying to distract the bear. He could see that Edgar Rivers's face was bleeding badly; the blood was flecked out over the snow, turning it a bright crimson.

The bear paused momentarily, then renewed its attack, all fury and muscle.

Teddy saw no choice. He stepped in close enough to plant the barrel of the pistol into the bear's thick fur and was set to empty his pistol when a shot rang out, causing the bear to roar and lurch up on its hind legs.

Teddy saw Rudolph Banks holding the Krag a dozen yards away, smoke curling out of its barrel. It was a dangerous and unnecessary risk. The bear turned suddenly toward Teddy, its small eyes fixed on him, its head twisting this way and that as it roared and came forward.

Teddy felt the calm come over him, the rattlesnake in him coil, as he jammed the

341

pistol's barrel into the bear's mouth, even as one large paw came sweeping down. He pulled the trigger and kept pulling it until the blow from the paw knocked him aside.

Both went down together.

He heard Cody say, "Jesus Christ!"

The weight of the bear was atop Teddy but unmoving. It took a few moments for the pain to set in and when they pulled the dead bear from him, he could see a good portion of its skull had been shot away.

He tried to sit up and that's when the pain in his left shoulder ripped through him like a hot brand.

"You okay?" Billy said.

"I think my shoulder's broke."

Cody looked at it.

"Could be for sure, he tore you up some."

"What about him?" Teddy said, looking at the unmoving Edgar.

Cody looked over, said, "I think he's gone."

When they looked closer they could see where the bear had torn open Edgar Rivers's throat.

Rudolph Banks kept saying over and over again, "No, no, no . . ."

Billy got between Banks and the dead man, said, "I'm sorry about this, but

there's nothing we can do for him except get him back."

"Oh, this goddamn terrible place," Banks moaned.

"I'll go get the horses," Billy said and went and got them and brought them back, but before he brought them back he cut loose the bundle of buffalo hide and took out the skull and tossed it into a snowdrift.

He got Banks to help him wrap Edgar's body in the buffalo hide. Then they found a pair of small saplings and cut them down with their knives and made a crude travois and lashed the body to it.

"It's the only way," Billy said to Banks. "The ground's too hard to bury him, even if we had shovels."

"Oh God, we can't just drag him along like an animal," Banks protested.

"We've got no choice," Billy said. "We've got three riders and three horses."

Billy turned to Teddy and, cutting another length of rope, he bound Teddy's shoulder as best he could, trying to immobilize it for the journey.

"That arm will be useless to you, but at least you'll be able to ride, even if it hurts like somebody throwing rocks at you every step of the way. You ready?"

"Let's go," Teddy said.

Neither he nor Billy said anything about the risky shot Banks had taken that could just as easily have killed Edgar Rivers or Teddy. There was no point in furthering the man's misery, or their own either.

"Let's get back to camp and get out of this goddamn country," Banks said. "I hate it!"

Billy rigged the travois poles to his saddle, then looked at Teddy. They nodded to each other, then spurred their horses forward, the body of Edgar Rivers trailing behind. It was a sight that told Teddy he'd been right not to let Edgar die in the storm, that to see him now, as he was thus, was not something he could have lived with if it had been he who had been responsible for the man's death.

He turned his eyes away and wished the man's fate had been otherwise.

Chapter 32

Louisa stoked the fire. Wind rattled the windows. Outside the snow became lost in darkness. She wished Bill were home with her. She'd always been afraid of storms ever since she was a child. But now, with children of her own, she couldn't show any fear, not with her husband gone, their father gone, and just all of them there alone.

One of the girls, Arta, said, "Mama, I hear wolves howling."

"Oh, don't be foolish," Louisa said. "There's no wolves around these parts; your father has shot and killed them all."

"I hear the crazy woman, Mama," Orra said.

"Mama, I hear ghouls," Irma said.

"Oh, ghouls and crazy women, tsk, tsk, you girls better get on to your beds."

She'd tucked them in and stayed with them until they finished their prayers to God to bring home safe their papa and to let the storm pass quickly. And afterward Louisa went and stood before the fire and thought that if she went to the windows

and looked out into the black and snowy night she might well see wolves and ghouls and maybe even a crazy woman lurking about, waiting to get in to carry them all away.

Oh, how she wished Bill was there with them.

She poured herself a rare glass of brandy and sipped it and felt how nicely it warmed her blood. And when her nerves became calm again she thought of that afternoon there on the porch sitting with Mr. John Sears, the two of them drinking tea and how lovely the weather had been and how nice the conversation.

Oh, she told herself, she shouldn't dwell on such things, for such thoughts were not for a woman married, and especially not a woman married to Buffalo Bill. She thought about the young actresses who practically flung themselves at him and how he seemed not at all inclined to discourage their behavior.

She loved him, but she wasn't sure how much longer she could stand his roguish ways, his wanderlust. He was forever searching for the pot of gold at the end of the rainbow. She prayed that he would either stay forever with her or go forever from her.

Odd, she thought, *how it is that the very things that attract us to someone are the very things that in the long run repel us?*

She poured herself a second brandy, hoping that it would dull her senses and make her sleepy as an old cat and not care about the storm or her always-gone husband.

As soon as the weather turned better, she told herself that she would take the girls and return to St. Louis for a visit with her mother. Perhaps the time away would give her a chance to think through everything: whether to remain Bill's wife or to divorce him. He dallied when he was away, of that she was sure. What robust man of such natural attraction could resist adoring young women?

Oh, she hated him.

The windows rattled.

Oh, she wished he were here with her.

She had gone about the house earlier, lighting every lamp until the house was filled with warm light that put her more at ease. She did not like the darkness, and when Bill was gone and she'd go up to her room at night to bed, she'd leave several of the downstairs lamps burning and also the one by her bed and would fall asleep watching the flame dancing in its sooty glass chimney.

She thought of the last time Bill had come to her bed, had insisted she give herself to him. She had not denied him; it was her duty to meet his needs. But she had not enjoyed it either — at least not to the extent she made him believe that she did. *Were all men like her Buffalo Bill?*

She caught a movement out of the corner of her eye, something that passed by one of the windows. She nearly dropped her glass. She held her breath, afraid almost to the point of screaming. She listened. Fire crackled in the hearth. The rooms were warm with light but outside all was blackness and wind. Pellets of snow pecked the windows.

Her imagination? Still, she held her breath, listening. There was nothing but the wind, it seemed. She went and checked on the girls. They were asleep in their beds. She felt suddenly tired, the brandy having turned her blood sluggish, making her limbs heavy.

She checked the bolt on the door to make sure it was secure, even though the doors were rarely locked. She went then into Bill's study, where the hideous mounted heads of animals he'd slain looked down from the walls at her with glass eyes, and she took a pistol from a

case — one that General Custer had presented him — a long-barreled pistol with ivory grips. She didn't know what sort of pistol it was, but Bill had shown her once how it should be used — "Make sure you got shells in it is most important," he teased. And he showed her how to cock the hammer back, explaining that it was a "single-action" — that the hammer had to be thumbed back in order to pull the trigger.

"Now, you be mighty careful, Lulu, you don't shoot yourself or one of the girls."

It was heavy.

She carried it upstairs with her. It was, in a way, a comfort to her and, in a way, it frightened her all the more that she might need to use it.

She undressed and used the chamber pot and climbed into bed, unsure of just where she should place the pistol to keep it handy. Then a terrible thought occurred to her: What if in the night one of the girls got up and came into her room and she mistakenly shot the child as an intruder?

Oh God.

She rose and took the pistol and put it into a drawer in the bureau on the other side of the room. Far enough away not to make such a fatal mistake, she told herself,

and yet not so far away that she couldn't get it if need be.

Once in bed, she turned onto her side and lay there staring at the dancing little flame inside the lamp's chimney. As always, it mesmerized her. And in spite of her fears, she soon fell into a weary sleep.

But then, sometime during the night, she awakened without reason and lay there staring into the dark, the lamp without oil and thus without flame. She lay there barely breathing, certain that someone was there in the room with her.

"Bill," she said softly. "Is that you, Bill?"

Silence.

She could sense someone there but the room was completely dark and the storm still raged and the windows still rattled and the wind still moaned along the eves.

Her whole being began to tremble and she thought what a terrible mistake it was to have put the gun in the drawer across the room.

"Orra," she said. "Irma, Arta? Is that you, darlings?"

The house creaked.

She tried desperately not to scream.

She thought that surely her heart would stop.

It did not.

She made a desperate lunge from the bed, scrambled blindly to the door and, flinging it open, went running down the hall to her daughters' bedroom. Her motherly instinct was to protect them first.

She found the lamp in their room, the box of matches, and lit the wick. The room glowed with buttery light and her daughters were as she'd left them, sleeping little angels. She felt such great relief. She'd been foolish, a frightened child herself. She quickly left before she awoke any of them and, carrying the lamp, went cautiously back to her room, turning the flame up higher.

She looked around and saw no one there.

It was just some silly old dream I'd been having. This storm has ruined my nerves.

She moved toward the bed. She guessed by the level of the oil yet left in the lamp that there would be enough to burn until dawn. No matter. She told herself she probably wouldn't sleep any more this night. Perhaps she would go downstairs and bake cookies for the girls and biscuits for breakfast. Yes, that is exactly what she would do. It would take her mind off things and if she needed to sleep eventually, she could do it during the day.

Still telling herself how foolish she'd been and feeling better, she started out of the room, then remembered the pistol and turned and opened the bureau drawer where she'd put it.

It was not there.

Oh, dear. My nerves have truly betrayed me. Had it been a dream that she'd brought the pistol up to the room with her and placed it in the bureau drawer? Oh, she was so confused.

Well, if someone were in the house, they surely would have killed her in her bed by now, for that was the nature of monsters who broke into other people's houses — to kill them in their beds and rob them blind.

Oh, you're just being a foolish old ninny.

Steeling herself with the absurdness of her wild imagination, she went downstairs and into the kitchen to bake cookies and biscuits and otherwise spend away the last hours of night and wait for the dawn to come, and with it, she was sure, would be a nice sun and crystalline sky. A new day where no wolves or ghouls or crazy women or murderous house-breakers would be found.

He was sitting there in the kitchen at the table and he had a gun and was a very young man with black hair and dark fea-

tures and he said, "Ma'am. Are you Mrs. Buffalo Bill?"

She thought she might scream but something in his manner warned her it was better if she did not.

"Have you come to murder us all?" she said, surprised at how calmly she'd asked him the question.

"No. I've come to kill your husband, is all."

She swallowed, trying to relieve the dryness in her throat.

"My husband is not here," she said.

"I know," the young man said. "I already looked around." And she realized that he had been in her room when she'd awakened and she saw now that the gun he was holding was the ivory-handled pistol she'd placed earlier in the bureau drawer.

"I'd like a cup of coffee and I'm very hungry," the young man said.

She stood frozen, not quite sure what to do. Perhaps he did not know about her sleeping children and, like a mother hen, she thought it best if she distracted him from her little brood by being cooperative, and if he was going to murder someone, let it be her and not her daughters.

"It will take me a few moments to make coffee," she said.

"I've got all the time in the world," he said.

She went about preparing him coffee and fixing him something to eat — some slices of salted beef and he sat there, calmly watching her. She felt brazen and vulnerable being watched by a complete stranger while she was dressed only in her nightgown and robe. But he surely was too young to have such lascivious thoughts and she surely was too old.

Finally when she poured him a cup of coffee and handed him the plate of salted beef, he said, "Please sit down. There." He waggled the pistol's barrel to an empty chair across from him and she sat immediately.

She watched him eat and could see sorrow in his eyes.

Why, he can't be more than sixteen or seventeen, she told herself.

"If you've come to rob us, we have so little but take what you want."

He shook his head as he chewed.

"No. I haven't come to rob you," he said. "I've come here for only one reason and that is to kill your husband."

"May I ask why you want to kill my husband?"

"Because he killed my father. Blood for

blood. That seems fair, doesn't it? Don't white people believe in that sort of justice — an eye for an eye?"

She shrugged.

"Who was your father?" she said. She really didn't want to know any of these things, of course. She didn't wish to be having this conversation or to be sitting here in her own house with a stranger holding a pistol. This was the sort of madness that men like her husband and his friends attracted — men of violence, men with guns and crazy ideas.

He told her his father's name was Yellow Hand and that he was once a great Cheyenne chief and that his killing must be revenged. He then told her that after he killed Buffalo Bill he was going to the land of his people and reclaim his heritage.

"You speak awfully well for an . . ."

"Indian," he said, completing her sentence. "You've got pretty children," he said.

She gasped.

"Don't worry," he said.

"How can I not when you're sitting there holding a gun and have broken into our house?"

"It's cold outside, that's why I broke in. That, and I wanted to find that husband of yours."

"Please," she said. "Don't hurt the children."

He looked at her then with a certain disdain.

"I don't kill people if I don't have to."

She didn't say anything.

He said, "Can I have some more coffee, please?"

She thought him an awfully strange and frightening young man but went and got him more coffee nonetheless and prayed that Buffalo Bill's uncanny luck would hold for a time longer and spare her and the girls a horrible fate.

Chapter 33

A blue dusk settled over the land as they rode into camp. White Eye and Jane had started fires while the women had helped Yankee and John re-pitch the tents that had blown down in the storm. They all stopped and looked up at the approach of the riders.

John saw that there were three, not four. He saw what they were hauling on a travois. The women saw it too. John stepped in front of them and said, "Easy."

Rudolph Banks spurred his horse ahead and rode into camp first, rode up to where his wife stood with Anne and said, without dismounting, "Something's happened to Edgar."

They looked at him, then back toward the mounted riders — Billy and Teddy — who stopped just shy of the camp, not wanting to bring the corpse all the way in.

"Best we drop him here for the time," Billy suggested.

Teddy looked back 'round and saw that the body was still bundled tightly inside the buffalo robe, then dismounted and

Billy did too, both of them weary from the long eventful ride.

Emma stood with her hand on her husband's knee, not fully comprehending what had happened to Edgar, disbelieving that anything could have happened to him. Anne stood next to her, her gaze going from the object on the travois to Teddy Blue walking toward the fire.

"He's dead," Rudolph said to the women. "He was killed in a horrible accident."

Yankee and White Eye and Jane came over from the camp and stood among the others.

"It was a bear," Billy said, then dropped his gaze.

Then for a moment there was just the stillness of the falling night.

"Oh, Edgar," Emma said, almost as a whisper, a prayer, but one that wouldn't get answered.

"We thought it best to bring him back," her husband said. "It just didn't seem right to leave him out there," and he turned halfway in his saddle and looked back into the direction they'd just come, into the pale darkness that would soon be pitch night.

Emma began to cry but not loudly.

Anne's face turned to a frozen mask of disbelief. For while she wasn't sure at all that she'd loved Edgar, this seemed like an unbelievable fate.

John said, "There's hot coffee and supper will be ready soon. I imagine you boys had it pretty hard."

Nobody said if they'd had it hard or not.

"I'm truly sorry," Billy said to the women. "I truly am."

Rudolph Banks dismounted at last, his motion like that of a hundred-year-old man. And when his wife put her arms around him, he began to cry and nobody thought any less of him because he did.

Everyone began to ease back to the camp, toward the fires, toward light and life, such as it was and away from the cold encroaching darkness. Everyone but Teddy and Anne.

He didn't know what to say to her, nor she to him.

"I want to see his face one last time," she said finally.

"You sure?"

Their eyes met and he walked out with her to the body and took out his knife and cut one of the upper ropes and with his good hand pulled back the hide enough so she could look at Edgar's face. His flesh

was bloodless now but for where the bear had raked and bit him. The dry frozen blood was the color of rust. Teddy had not lowered the hide enough for her to see the throat.

Anne knelt there in the snow next to the body and kissed the tips of her fingers and pressed them to Edgar's lips, noting as she did how like ice they felt. Teddy eased the flap back over the face, said, "Enough, don't torture yourself with this."

Something broke in her and he thought she would cry, but she did not and he helped her to her feet.

"It is payment for my sin," she said. "I was unfaithful to him and now this is God's punishment."

"You don't believe that," Teddy said.

"Then tell me what it is I'm supposed to believe, Mr. Blue? Tell me why he had to pay for my sin with his life and now I must live with that fact?"

"I don't have any answers to questions like that. I just don't think it's what you think it is. This is hard country, Anne; there are a hundred ways to die out in this country. It could just as easily have happened to any one of us. Sin hasn't got anything to do with it — yours or mine."

He looked down at the robe.

"And whatever sins he may have com-

mitted had nothing to do with it either."

She turned away and walked back to camp and he followed her.

There was silence around the fire and Teddy came and stood close because he'd never been so goddamned cold in his life as he was that very minute. John came over and stood next to him and looked at the binding around him and said, "What happened to you?"

"I think I broke my shoulder."

Billy spoke up and said, "He was shooting that bear off Mr. Rice and it swiped him and broke his shoulder."

He saw the way Anne looked at him when Billy said that.

"Come on in my tent and let me doctor you," Jane said. "Go grab a bottle of liquor, Yankee."

White Eye looked at her, looked at Yankee, looked back at her.

"I can get it," he said.

But Yankee already had gone off to the supply wagon and was pulling a bottle out of it.

Inside the tent Jane and Yankee helped him off with his coat, then his shirt, and he almost bit his tongue off when they did. Yankee thrust the bottle at him and said, "Start working on this, old son."

Teddy drank while Jane washed the parts of his flesh the bear's claws had raked. She pulled out fragments of his shirt from the blood-crusted places and washed it with some of the whiskey, then handed him back the bottle as she applied fresh bandages, saying, "You'll need a real doctor to fix that shoulder."

They eased him back to a reclining position on the blankets and then covered him with more blankets and Jane rubbed warmth into his feet while Yankee squatted on his heels and watched and drank some of the liquor too.

"You feel like eating?" Jane said.

He shook his head.

"Maybe come morning you will," she said. "You just rest here tonight. I'll sleep in your tent."

He was amazed at how utterly exhausted he felt.

One moment, he could hear them all outside talking and see the flickering lights of the campfires through the canvas walls of the tent, and the next he found himself falling in and out of sleep.

Rudolph announced to the women that because of what had happened they would be starting back for North Platte at

first light and once arrived would catch the first flier east. And also that he would have Edgar's remains shipped home with them to be buried back in New York.

He said all this with a steady sonorous voice as though he was making a business decision and no one disputed his plans.

"We owe a great debt to Mr. Blue for risking his own life to save that of Edgar's," Banks said. "Colonel, I want to make sure that he is rewarded financially for his efforts, something we'll discuss in more detail later."

Then Banks looked at his wife and said, "I'm all in. I can't go another step tonight. Will you help me to our bed, dear?"

They stood together and walked off to their tent, the eyes of the others watching them.

Billy was still trying to warm his feet and had asked White Eye to retrieve them each a bottle of liquor from the wagon, and White Eye gladly did. The lot of them sat around with their eyes full of firelight, passing the bottles back and forth between them. Nobody said much. The mood was somber and black as the night itself.

And when at last Billy stood and walked to his tent and climbed in it, John stood and said, "Mr. White Eye, since Teddy's

not up to standing night watch, I wonder if you'd split it with me?"

White Eye wasn't in much position to turn down such a request, seeing as how things had gone so far on this sorrowful evening.

"Yes, sir. You want me to stand first watch or second?"

"I'm best when I've slept a few winks first," John said. "I'll take second watch."

Then John stood and went to his own tent, taking what was left of one bottle with him, leaving the other three there at the fire.

White Eye looked at Jane and he looked at Yankee and he could see there was something transpiring between them, and even unsaid, it was plain enough what it was that he didn't want to see any more of it. He got up and walked over and took a rifle and an extra blanket and off from the camp to stand watch.

He climbed up the sand hill and settled into the snowy notch with the blanket pulled over his shoulders and sat there watching down on the camp where the fires burned and he watched until he saw Jane stand up and walk over to the empty tent and crawl inside. Then he saw Yankee stand up and walk over there and crawl inside too.

He thought he ought to feel a lot worse about it than he did. But somehow he didn't and it troubled him that he didn't, for he was until that moment sure that he was in love with Jane about as bad as a man can be in love with a woman.

He still had love all over his mind when Mysterious Dave shot him.

Chapter 34

The shot rolled like thunder and Teddy Blue sat bolt upright, the pain in his shoulder like someone had hit him with a sledge.

He grabbed the Birdseye on the way out of the tent. Others were scrambling out as well and he saw Yankee scurrying out of Jane's tent, Yankee with a mouthful of words he never got out before a second shot rang down and knocked him flat against the tent, caving it in as he fell.

Teddy saw the flame of the rifle there on the rise up above the notch he and John had used to stand watch and he couldn't make any sense of it, John shooting down into the camp. Then he saw John come out of his tent, hat jammed down on his head, galluses hanging, gun in hand.

"What the hell's going on up there, John?"

"I sent White Eye up to stand watch. What the hell's he done, gone mad?"

Jane was screaming from inside the tent Yankee had collapsed on.

"Well, I don't know, but shoot the son of a bitch," Teddy said, and fired toward the notch where he'd seen the rifle spit fire. John fired too, and when Billy emerged, he opened fire up at the ridge, saying as he did, "He must have got into the whiskey bad to have gone crazy!"

Bullets punched holes in the tents and kicked up spits of snow around their feet and some shot into the fires, sending sparks flying.

"Stay clear of the firelight," Teddy shouted. "Don't let him get a good look at you."

Teddy was already running for the ridge, sticking close into the shadows, and John was running too. They kept their distance from each other, knowing that the shooter wouldn't be able to concentrate on both of them at once.

Behind them they could hear the distinct crack of the Krag and knew that Rudolph Banks had joined the fight.

"I hope that son of a bitch doesn't shoot one of us in the back," John yelled.

Teddy said, "He's up higher than that notch, John," indicating the shooter on the hill.

They held their fire as they climbed, not wanting to give away their location to the

shooter. They could see the burst of fire from his rifle every time he fired into the camp and they could hear bullets ricocheting off the rocks and below they could hear the rush of the river swollen with snow runoff.

Then they came to the notch and they found White Eye lying there, slumped over on his side, his breathing like the sound of coffee percolating, and John turned him over and when he did, White Eye groaned and said, "Goddamn, but don't shoot me again."

"It's us," John said. "Teddy and me."

White Eye squinted up through the pain.

"Why'd you fellers shoot me?"

"We didn't," Teddy said.

"Oh. I thought you did."

John said, "Why the hell would we shoot you?"

"I don't know. I thought maybe you was Yankee and shot me over Jane or something crazy. It hurts like somebody's stuck a hot iron up in me."

"Just lay still," Teddy said.

Teddy saw a movement against the skyline when he looked up and said to John, "Keep him busy, I'm going to swing around and come up behind."

"I can't hardly see nothing to shoot at," John said.

Teddy pointed. "Just up in there," he said. Then John saw the shadow of a man and the flame spit of his rifle when he fired again and began to lay in some shots of his own, keeping himself low to the ground as Teddy skirted the hill.

"You shot in a bad place?" John said to White Eye in between shots.

"I don't know of any good place to get shot in, do you?"

"No, sir, I sure don't."

"Then I'm shot in a bad place."

John fired, said, "Bad don't mean fatal, just so you know."

"I guess if it was fatal, we wouldn't be holding this conversation, would we?"

"No, sir, we sure as hell wouldn't."

John fired again.

Teddy came 'round and started up along the south spine of the hill, came close enough to hear the ejected shells of the shooter's rifle clinking off the rocks. He saw the shadow kneeling on one knee firing, levering, firing.

He worked his way in close, the rattlesnake in him coiling. Stealthy he eased up to within a few yards of the man. He could hear the shooter snorting, talking to himself.

"Why, you sons a bitches. I'm gonna get

that big old hat and that high-stepping horse and ever thing else you got and them others got and —"

"Hey," Teddy said.

And when the fellow turned his head to see who spoke, Teddy shot him. The muzzle flash from the Colt lit the man's features for the mere second of a heartbeat, enough so Teddy could see the look on the man's face: that surprised look a man will get when he realizes what's happened and knows it's way too late to do anything about it.

The man fell back, the rifle dropping onto the snow-covered rocks, clattering as it slid down the hill.

Teddy eased up on him, his pistol cocked and aimed, knowing sometimes a man isn't as dead as he should be. Teddy still felt coiled, ready to strike again.

The man breathed hard through his nose, a soft wet sound that bubbled up from his throat.

"Who are you, mister?"

The man blinked as Teddy struck a match and held it close to the man's face.

"I said, who are you?"

"What the hell is it to you who I am?"

"Nothing," Teddy said. "Unless you want me to send notice to your next of kin

that you've been killed. Of course, it's no skin off my teeth if you die out here and nobody knows . . ."

The hard features of Mysterious Dave grew soft as he thought about the only creature he ever had any true feelings for.

"They is somebody I'd like you to get word to . . ."

"Who?"

"Send word to Dora Hand that her loving Dave Mather has been killed by a no-good son of a bitch assassin . . ."

"Consider it done."

"Thank you kindly, you dirty son of a bitch."

Dave's grin leaked blood as Teddy's match burned down and he snapped it out, letting the blackness of night become a shroud for Mysterious Dave.

"Buffalo Bill, Buffalo Bill, Buffalo Bil . . ." were Dave's last uttered words. He died with Billy's name still trying to escape his lips. In that final moment he saw himself riding off into a lot of light upon Billy's high-stepper. Goddamn, but it felt about right . . .

Teddy shouted down to the others it was over and the gunfire stopped and later Bill came up the hill, carrying a lantern, and looked at the man very close.

371

"You know him?" Teddy asked.

"Never seen him before in my life."

"He kept repeating your name. I'm guessing he's the same one that tried to take you down before."

"Well, it's a mystery to me who this feller is."

"Sometimes it doesn't take much reason for someone to want to kill you," Teddy said. "Maybe he just wanted the reputation of killing Buffalo Bill."

"Probably about like that feller that shot Wild Bill. It's the price fellers like us pay for fame," Billy said. "I almost wish half the time I wasn't nothing but a cattle breeder."

"How's White Eye?"

"John says he might live, but if he does he'll be a lot slower than he used to be." Billy held the lamp away from the death mask.

"You did good here, son," Billy said.

"He's only the second man I ever killed."

"Let's hope for your sake and mine he's the last on this trip."

Teddy looked at the face of the dead man once more before they started back down to camp.

"You think we should bury him?"

Billy shook his head, said, "The ground's

froze hard as rock, we'd have to wait until spring to bury him. And we ain't got enough horses even to drag him back to North Platte — not that I'd favor doing that anyway."

"What do you suggest we do with him?"

"Well, we could let the critters have him, but that'd seem un-Christian, even for fellers like us and him."

Billy looked down the hill and they could see here and there in the rising moon's light the white riffles of the Dismal River.

"We could take time to gather rocks and bury him like we did Buck," Billy said.

"To hell with that," Teddy said.

"Yeah, to hell with that," Billy said.

"Sailors bury their dead at sea," Teddy said.

"It ain't hardly the sea, the Dismal River ain't," Billy said.

"There must be a reason it was named that in the first place."

"I reckon there was."

The ceremony was brief and without fanfare. Nobody knew the dead man, nor did they have a great deal of empathy for someone who tried to massacre them in their beds. Most especially White Eye and

Yankee Judd, who was shot through the hip. Jane nursed them both while the little ceremony was held.

Billy said as they prepared the final act, "Anyone wish to say a prayer or something over this poor soul?"

John spoke up and said, "It's too god-damn cold to stand out here," then looked down at the corpse and said: "Good-bye. That prayer enough for everyone?" No one said it wasn't.

And so it was that Mysterious Dave came to find himself once more in the Dismal River. This time he'd ride it to its end. The one-eared horse watched its rider float out of sight. Then something unknown spooked it and it ran off into the night — probably with wolves prowling in its head.

Chapter 35

They arrived in North Platte, wounded and not the same as they were when they left. Rudolph Banks and the two women went directly to the hotel. After delivering the body of Edgar Rivers to the mortuary, Billy and Teddy stopped at Doc Tillison's for the care and treatment of White Eye and Yankee Judd. It was Doc who told them about the murder of Henry Egg.

"It must have been the same feller we sent floating down the River Styx that killed old Henry," Billy said. "That mysterious feller . . . What'd you say his name was?"

"Dave Mather," Teddy said.

"Looks like he shot the shit out of you boys," Doc said, looking over the wounds of White Eye and Yankee.

"He didn't do any of us any good," White Eye said. "I'm leaking like a rusty bucket."

"My dancing days are over," Yankee said, holding the silk bandanna Jane used to plug the hole in his hip with.

"Well, good God, but let's hope the

killing is over too," Doc said. "We gone almost three months without a shooting or a stabbing and now it's like an epidemic has befell us. Must be the bad weather is bringing out the worst in folks."

Billy said, "Patch these boys up and send me the bill," then he shook hands with White Eye and Yankee and said he'd check in on them later.

"What about you, young feller?" Doc said looking at Teddy, the binding holding his shoulder in place.

"I'll come back later when you've finished these two; I'm not bleeding out."

"It was a hell of a hunt," White Eye said, then coughed up blood. "I hope it wasn't my last."

Yankee lay quiet, Jane holding his hand. White Eye could see where love had gone.

Billy and Teddy left out of Doc's office and walked over to Tobe Cicero's Funeral Parlor. Tobe had the corpse of Edgar Rivers laid out on a metal table for embalming, a sheet pulled up under his chin.

"Need to fix him good for the trip back to New York," Billy said.

"I know it," Tobe said. "I got a zinc-lined coffin I'll pack him in with ice, seal it good and tight."

Billy started to say something, but then

turned and went outside again and Teddy could see Billy was stricken by the sight of the dead man.

"He had life by the horns," Billy said, "didn't he? But tell me what good it done him?"

"Let me buy you a drink over at the tavern," Teddy said.

"Hell, I won't fight you on that offer."

They walked over and stood there at the bar and drank a whiskey, then drank a second one.

"What now, Colonel?"

"My plans haven't changed any. I'll collect my fee from Banks and put together a Wild West combination to take on tour back East. I'd like you to join me, old son."

"I'm no actor."

"My guess is you wasn't a mankiller either before you did it the first time."

"Big difference."

"I know it is. Hell, you think I like making a fool of myself?"

"Then why do you do it?"

"Because the ways men like me used to have for making a living are just about all gone now. They ain't no more buffalo to shoot, no more Pony Expresses to ride, no more real wars against the Indians to fight. I ain't like old Wild Bill was, someone with

a knack for being a hired gun — no offense, Mr. Blue."

"None taken."

"Being famous is about all I got to play on, the only thing left I can make any real money at."

"Well, sir, a man has to do what needs doing if he's got a family like yours to think about."

"Speaking of which, I want you and John to come out to the house and have a home-cooked meal and drink a little of my whiskey as a way of showing my appreciation before you go."

"You firing me?"

"I am, unless you want to hire on for the combination and come East with me. I think the threat to my person is over with now that mysterious feller is riding the wet trail, don't you?"

Teddy looked around the room. Men sat playing poker and dominoes and smoking and talking cordially to one another.

"I suppose it is, for now at least."

"Speaking of John, where you reckon he got off to?"

"He's his own man," Teddy said. "Hard telling."

"Well, let's have another snort or two. It ain't hardly suppertime yet."

And when they finished their drinking Billy walked with Teddy back over to Doc Tillison's and sat watching curiously as Doc cleaned and dressed Teddy's wounds where the bear had raked him, then bound up his shoulder proper, Doc saying, "You'll have to wear that holster rig some other way for now."

"I hope I won't be needing to wear it at all for a while."

"Just in case," Billy said, taking the Birdseye Colt out of the holster and slipping it into Teddy's coat pocket. "You might need to shoot a snake or something."

"Snakes go to ground when it gets cold like this," Doc said.

Billy winked and said, "Hell, they's all kinds of snakes, Doc."

They mounted their horses and rode over to the hotel and Billy went inside and left a note for John with the desk clerk telling him to come out to the house for supper, then he and Teddy rode on out together.

Two hounds lay in the yard, both shot dead.

"What the hell . . ." Billy said.

Then the front door opened and Louisa stepped out and stepping out with her was

379

a dark-skinned young man holding a pistol on her. He looked at them and said, "Which one of you is Buffalo Bill?"

Bill didn't hesitate and said, "That would by God be me, and kindly taking your son of a bitching hands off my wife."

The boy glared at him.

"Get off that horse, Mr. Buffalo Bill. I've come to kill you."

"He's not Buffalo Bill," Teddy said, "I am."

The boy looked from one to the other. He said to the woman, "Which one is he?"

Louisa had not suffered the celebrity of being the wife of Buffalo Bill without learning how to protect him along the way.

"I forget," she said.

Teddy and Billy dismounted and stood away from their horses and each other so the boy would have difficulty concentrating on both at once.

"Well," Bob said, "I guess I'm just going to shoot you both, then."

"Before you go to taking lives, why is it you want to shoot us, son?" Billy said.

Teddy knew if the Colonel could keep the kid talking, they might stand a chance.

"Revenge," Bob said. "You ever heard of it, mister?"

"Revenge on who and for what reason?" Teddy said.

"Whichever one of you is Cody, the Indian Slayer, is the one who killed my father, Yellow Hand."

Billy said, "Shit, I always knew that accident was going to come back to haunt me someday."

The boy swung his pistol at Billy, knowing now which one of the two men was Cody.

"My wife has nothing to do with this," Billy said. "Let her go. You've got the drop on us."

Bob said, "Vengeance comes at a dear price."

"Not that dear," Billy said. "Old Yellow Hand was too good a warrior to go about killing women. You're no sort of kin to him if you take up the practice now."

Teddy could see a certain doubt creep into the boy's eyes.

"Go on, then," Bob said to Louisa, shoving her aside as he fired at Billy. The bullet snatched Billy's big sombrero and sent it flying.

Bob had a look of surprise and disappointment that his bullet missed the mark. Billy was trying to draw his own

piece, a big Navy Colt, from his belt as Bob re-cocked his pistol.

Teddy's bullet took him through the collarbone and flung him back along the porch. Billy's shot went wild and knocked the head off the brass cock atop the weather-vane. Teddy rushed up onto the porch, even as Bob struggled to regain his feet.

"Stay down," Teddy said.

Bob looked at him.

"Stay down, goddamn it!"

"White men," Bob said, and aimed his pistol and fired.

Billy heard two reports simultaneously.

He saw the boy on the porch slump back and lay still, Teddy standing almost di-rectly over him, both enveloped in a cloud of blue smoke. Billy held his breath, waiting for Teddy to fall dead.

Louisa was next to Billy, trembling now.

"He hurt you?" Billy said.

"No," she said.

Teddy knelt next to the boy, searched his pockets for identification, found a wallet with a card on it that read: *Robert Parsnip #1187 — Lawson Private School for Boys.* There was a spot of blood on it. Teddy slipped the card back into the wallet and returned it to the boy's pocket. Teddy guessed the boy couldn't have been more

than seventeen or eighteen years old. Too damn young to die.

Billy walked Louisa into the house and came back out with a blanket and covered the body of Bob Parsnip. His girls stood at the window, trying to see what the commotion was, now that their mother had freed them from a locked closet.

"Jesus," Billy said as he drew the blanket over the boy's face. "Just a damn kid."

Teddy went out into the yard and looked off toward a line of trees in the distance, but instead of seeing trees, he kept seeing the face of Bob Parsnip — that youthful innocent-looking face and how it grew slack when death took him.

Billy came out into the yard and said, "I'm sorry as hell it was you who had to kill him and not me."

"I don't guess it made any difference to him who killed him," Teddy said.

"No, I don't reckon it did. I think if he was anything like his daddy, though, he was ready to die."

"I don't see how any man is ready to die," Teddy said.

"Indians, the ones I know personally at least, the fighting Indians, are born ready to die. He died brave, if foolishly."

"I feel bad about it, Colonel."

"I know you do, old son."

A murder of crows flew overhead, their black wings oily against the emerging sun, their caws echoing over the land.

"Might be them crows is carrying off that boy's spirit," Billy said.

"You believe in that sort of thing?"

"I do, yes, sir. I sure do."

Then the sky was quiet again.

"I'll get the wagon," Billy said. "So we can take that boy in to town for a proper funeral."

"You hold no animosity toward him then?"

"No, sir. He was just doing what he thought he needed to do to honor his daddy. Can't blame him for that. I lost my boy this last spring. I'd been proud of him if he had done the same thing for me that boy yonder did for his daddy."

Teddy thought of his own father and of his late brother. What Billy was talking about was family, and what family blood meant.

"Too bad he didn't find another way to defend the honor of his father than to have to die for it," Teddy said.

"Maybe he just didn't have no choice in the matter," Billy said. "Indians believe their fate is writ in the stars for 'em, even before they're born."

Teddy and Bill stood silent for a moment, letting the wind speak a prayer for them and for the dead boy. Then they went and got the wagon and loaded Bob Parsnip into the back of it and rode into town with him.

Chapter 36

Louisa had just finished washing the blood from the porch when she saw him riding up the lane — John Sears. She splashed the bucket of rinse water over the stain she'd scrubbed as best she could and set the bucket down, wiping her hands upon her apron.

John reined in and said, "Ma'am."

Louisa didn't know quite what to say.

"This is for you," John said, handing her a small package wrapped in butcher's paper.

"Thank you," she said.

"For the kindness," John said, and she knew that he meant for that afternoon they'd sat on the porch together drinking tea and talking.

"It is very thoughtful of you," she said. "But not at all necessary."

He sat his horse as though waiting for an invite to dismount. She did not offer him one.

"We had a real rough time of it out there on that hunt," he said. "I reckon you may have heard by now."

"Yes," she said.

He looked toward the house.

"The Colonel home?"

"He was here, but he and Mr. Blue have returned to town."

"I see."

John saw the girls standing in the window watching him, their bright young faces pretty and curious.

"I just wanted to say something," John said.

"Perhaps it would be better if you didn't," she said.

"I got to thinking when we was out there on that hunt and things were at their worst how nice it would be to know somebody was home waiting for me, caring about me and whether I was safe or not, caring to have me return home to them again."

"Is that not something you've had before?" Louisa asked.

"Once, I did. A long time ago."

"I'm very sorry you don't have that now, Mr. Sears."

"Ma'am. I am very sorry too. The Colonel's a mighty lucky man. That's all I wanted to say, I guess."

"It's not wrong to want such things, Mr. Sears."

"Ma'am. Could you call me John, just this once?"

"John," she said. "It's not wrong to want someone to care about you and want you with them, someone who worries about you when you're gone and loves you when you're not."

"It just needs to be right," he said.

"Yes," she said. "It just needs to be the right one."

"Well, I best be getting into town. I suppose . . ."

"I wish it were different for you, John."

He smiled.

"Someday, maybe," he said. "It was kindly of you to be so nice to me. You've got a nice family."

She watched him turn his horse back toward the lane. And she kept watching him until he'd ridden out of sight.

Then she opened the package John had given her and saw that it was a music box. And when she turned its key the music made her cry.

Chapter 37

Teddy was in his room waiting for John when there was a knock at his door. Thinking it was John, he didn't bother to put on a shirt.

"May I come in?" Anne said.

He stepped aside and she came into the room and he closed the door behind her.

He could see her eyes were red from crying, no doubt.

"I'm sorry about Edgar," Teddy said.

"You don't have to apologize; it wasn't your fault."

"I feel responsible."

"Don't be," she said. "Does your shoulder hurt terribly?"

"It will heal."

"What will you do now?"

"John sort of wants to go down to Mexico."

A silence fell between them. Time itself seemed to stop.

"It's too early for me to know what my true feelings are," Anne said. "I must have a period of mourning for Edgar, as much

for myself as out of respect for him."

Teddy nodded.

"But afterward . . . after time has passed and I reach a point where I know my life must go on, that's when it will be the hardest for me — not having you in my life."

"I could always come to visit you," he said. "If that's something you think you'd want."

"I think it is something I'd want."

"Then that's what I'll do."

"I don't want you to feel you have to wait for me to make up my mind. I mean, I know you have to live your life as well . . ."

"You don't have to tell me," Teddy said. "I'm my own man and you're your own woman. Take the time you need, and if and when you're ready to see me again, let me know."

She stepped close to him, her hand reaching to touch the bandages on his shoulder so tenderly they felt like feathers brushing across his skin.

"Teddy . . ." she said.

He lowered his head until their lips touched.

It was a good kiss. A nice warm kiss that would seal their feelings for each other within their hearts for whatever time it

took to work through everything they were each facing.

"Here's my address," she said, slipping a piece of paper into his hand.

"I'll write you," he said.

"No promises, remember."

"No promises," he said. "But I'll write you anyway."

She smiled. They kissed again. She left. He felt alone, but not completely, for her spirit was still there in the room with him.

And the next morning he walked down to the station with the trio — Anne and Emma and Rudolph Banks — and waited with them until the train came. And before it arrived, Billy rode up on his high-stepper and dismounted and said, "I've come to see you off," and Rudolph Banks discreetly handed him a bank draft for the full amount plus a bonus, saying, "I'm sure you'll see that the others are taken care of, Colonel." The two shook hands. Then the flier arrived and Billy and Teddy and John stood on the platform until the others boarded. Farther down, workers loaded Edgar Rivers's coffin into a baggage car.

The three of them stood there listening to the hiss of steam from the locomotive and were still standing there until the train shuddered and set into motion, slow at

first, then soon enough picking up some speed.

Teddy saw her face there in one of the windows and their eyes met and held for as long as was possible before the train carried her and the others away toward the East.

"Well, boys," Billy said. "It has been one hell of a week, to say the least. I know it's early, but I could use me some breakfast, preferably one that included an eye-opener, couldn't you?"

And John said, "Hell, yes, I could."

So all three of them started up the street and got close to the hotel, where they saw Yankee Judd and Jane Nebraska coming out holding hands and practically moon-eyed over each other. White Eye Anderson was tagging along behind them, not sure at all how he felt about life these days, but not unhappy entirely because he was still part of it in the main — a living, breathing human soul who'd seen much tragedy and known a little love and wouldn't mind knowing a little more someday.

They all went to the restaurant together and ate and drank cocktails and Billy said afterward they'd traipse over to the bank and he'd pay them all plus a bonus.

And once out of the bank with the others

paid off, Billy offered Teddy and John his hand and they shook it.

"Boys, I owe you my bacon," Billy said. "I wish you'd join my new combination and come East with me."

"Maybe in the future," Teddy said, remembering that he and John were still wanted men.

"Well, anytime, anywhere is fine with me," Billy said. "You'll always have a job with me if you want one."

"Much appreciated, Colonel," John said.

They stood there for a moment, then Billy waved adios and he and the others went off down the street to whatever their own particular future held for them while Teddy and John went to get their things from the hotel.

"I wouldn't mind being one of those show people," John said, "the more I think about it."

"You wouldn't like it much after you'd done it awhile," Teddy said.

"I don't know, I'm sort of changing in my ways," John said, allowing himself to think about Louisa Cody, what it would be to have himself a steady wife and children.

"What's that supposed to mean?"

"Means a feller can change his ways if he wants to, is all it means."

"We're still wanted men."

"I ain't forgot."

"How long do you think we'll have to lay low?"

John looked at him.

"You think I'm some sort of expert on such matters?"

"I reckon, more than me."

John grinned then.

"Three, four months, maybe. I guess Hoodoo Brown ain't caught us by then, he'll find something else to occupy his time."

"I need to send George Bangs a telegram before we leave town."

They walked a little farther.

"You get that thing worked out with her?" John said.

"I could ask the same thing of you, couldn't I?"

"Shit," John said.

And they walked on.

About the Author

Bill Brooks is the author of eleven novels of historical and frontier fiction. He lives in North Carolina.